RENDEZVOUS WITH DISASTER!

Faster and faster he drove, until his foot was against the floorboard. The speedometer leaped to seventy, to eighty. The wind whipped through Bette Carey's hair.

"Bill!" she screamed. "Slow down. You're coming to the bend!"

As her terrified cry died in her throat the bend in the road rushed at them. She didn't know whether Bill tried to make the turn or if he just let go.

The car rose into the air. It seemed to Bette they stayed up there forever, suspended between earth and sky. Then the car struck the ground with a terrific crash and swerved sharply.

Bette was thrown free. *So this is the way it ends for me,* she thought before blackness overcame her.

We will send you a free catalog on request. Any titles not in your local book store can be purchased by mail. Send the price of the book plus 503 shipping charge to Tower Books, P.O. Box 270, Norwalk, Connecticut 06852.

Titles currently in print are available for industrial and sales promotion at reduced rates. Address inquiries to Tower Publications, Inc., Two Park Avenue, New York, New York 10016, Attention: Premium Sales Department.

FOUR WOMEN

Marie Butler Coffey

TOWER BOOKS NEW YORK CITY

A TOWER BOOK

Published by

Tower Publications, Inc.
Two Park Avenue
New York, N.Y. 10016

CHAPTER 1

Anne Elsnar usually awoke with dreammists trailing across her mind, like the rosy fog streamers of returning consciousness after anesthesia. But this morning when she opened her eyes, the rosy glow was crowded out by the sounds and scents of her awakening household. The rattle of dishes and silver and the tantalizing aroma of coffee and sizzling bacon came spiraling up the stairs, accompanied by Mandy's stentorian tones calling, "Mistah Elsnah! Mistah Bill!"

Somewhere outside a mocking bird sang. A patch of blue Florida sky was visible from her window, and a soft little breeze stirred the curtains, bringing a whiff of ripening oranges from the grove.

Bart moved in his bed. He stretched and yawned and heaved his big body upright. Briskly rubbing his hands through thinning dark hair, he barked happily, "Mornin', Mother. How's my girl?" and headed for the shower.

Anne closed her eyes and cringed as from a physical

blow. Bart's energy and sparkling good health seemed to emphasize her own frailty. She listened to him sputtering and snorting and puffing under the shower, like a big black bear she had once seen under a waterfall in the mountains of Vermont.

"What's on the agenda today, Annie?" he called, as his electric razor began to buzz.

She moved her slender body impatiently. A pain shot through her and she groaned. "I'm have a bridge party to raise money for Dr. Emmett's hospital. *Sweet* charity. The way I feel—"

"Oh, come now, Anne," Bart put in soothingly. "Just make up your mind to have a good time at your party. Let Mandy take care of everything. You be a good girl and stay right there in bed till noon."

He bustled back into the bedroom, and she ached with weariness just watching him slip on his shirt, knot his tie with a couple of deft manipulations of his big hands, and shrug into his coat. There wasn't a gray hair in his head, and this morning his face looked as smooth as a teen-ager's, yet he was—incredibly—fifty-five. But all Bart's burdens were light.

"Off to the salt mines," he boomed. "Got to show the Rogers house to a couple of newlyweds this mornin'. S'long, Annie. Take it easy now."

He bent over her, smelling of delicately scented shaving lotion. His lips brushed her cheek and he was gone. The room seemed to quiver as though recently shaken by an earthquake.

Bart's kiss, which had once warmed her down to the cockles of her heart, sent a little chill down her spine this morning. She turned over and lay with her face to the wall, but she could hear hurrying feet and high young voices and doors banging downstairs as Bill and his friend Marty left for college.

"Take it easy, you kids," Bart roared. "Your mother's sleeping."

In spite of her annoyance, Anne had to laugh. Never a dull moment in this house. There had been a time, eons ago it seemed, when her own vitality had matched that of her effervescent family. For this was not the life Anne Elsnar had planned for herself in the morning of her days, when her senses were unworn and tender.

At an early age she decided she wanted to study medicine. Having been brought up in the rugged environment of a Vermont farm might have had something to do with her decision, for doctors were rare in that neck of the woods. She was literally "shaking in her boots" the day she broached the subject, but she stood tall and faced up to her parents.

She recalled now how Jesse Tallman's black eyes narrowed as he pulled at his graying beard. "A doctor. Land o'goshen, Anne, you come up with the weirdest notions."

"This is no notion, Pa," she declared. "I've been thinking about it for a coon's age."

"Well, I never held you young 'uns back from any sensible notion. And takin' care of the sick is sensible, I s'pose. Are you sure that's what you want?"

Reed-slim and tough-fibered, but bright-eyed as a kitten, she tossed back her answer. "I'm sure, Pa. Ever since I was twelve and set old Rusty's leg, I've been sure. I always took care of you and Ma and the boys when any of you were sick."

He nodded. "And real good, too."

Her mother was appalled. "A *woman* doctor? Never heard of such a thing. It's a bewilderin' thing for a girl to want."

"I don't know why, Ma. There's plenty of women doctors in the big cities."

"Big cities. That's the rub. Scares me half to death to think of sending you off to a big city."

Her father settled the argument in his blunt way. "I'll put ye through the school and I'll keep track of every penny I lend ye. You can pay me back when you get doctorin'. Just don't get the idee you can waste money on clothes and football games and all such fancy doodlin' around."

"Don't you worry, Pa. I won't waste your money or my time on frivolous things," Anne promised.

She kept her word. A big, strong girl, magnetic and with vitality, she swept aside all obstacles and was making a name for herself in medical circles when they brought Bart into the hospital with a broken leg.

He told her later that, when he saw her striding long-limbed and graceful down a corridor one morning, he clutched at the little blond nurse who was arranging his breakfast tray.

"Who's that nurse?" he demanded excitedly.

"That's Doctor Tallman," the nurse said.

"*Doctor* Tallman!" he gasped. "Impossible!"

The nurse laughed. "That's what everybody says."

"Is there any way—?" Bart clenched and unclenched his big hands excitedly. "I've got to meet that girl."

The nurse giggled. "Well, just relax, Mister. I'll see what I can do."

The next morning she hailed Anne. "Dr. Tallman, can you help me here a minute, please?"

"This big fellow giving you trouble?" Anne twinkled, as she came into Bart's room.

When her eyes met Bart's that first time, she was captivated by his lazy southern charm, his gaiety and good nature. It seemed to her he possessed the same

8

vital spark that electrified her. It was love at first sight for both of them.

Their castle of dreams was an amazing structure. "I haven't settled on a career," he told her, "but there's plenty of time. I'm not thirty yet." He'd seemed so confident, speaking in glowing terms of business ventures "by which a man could make a little money." How many times over the years was she to hear that phrase!

"Some day, we'll have a house in the suburbs, a couple of maids, a nurse for the children, and an office downtown for you, Anne."

Oh, it had been delightful, dreaming with Bart!

After they were married, he said one day, "Honey, don't you think you could forget your career for a bit?" When he saw the consternation on her face, he went on quickly, "What I mean is, we ought to start raising a family. Isn't that what you want?"

She had laughed at him. "I'm young and strong, Bart. I can be Dr. Tallman and Mrs. Elsnar, too. Raise a family with one hand and heal the sick with the other. And I'll be a whiz at both. You wait and see."

Bart, glowing with pride in her, seemed satisfied with that.

They hadn't counted on the accident.

It happened that first summer while they were vacationing on the Tallman farm in Vermont. Anne, who often boasted that she had been born on a horse, suggested a ride up the mountain trail.

"I can't wait to show it to you, Bart. There's the most beautiful view from up there."

Anne's mother seemed apprehensive about the trip. "That trail is awful narrow in places, Bart," she warned. "You be careful. Anne's such a tomboy."

9

"Sure, sure, Mother Tallman. Don't you worry about me," Bart laughed. "I'm pretty good on a horse myself."

Hand in hand, they went out to the hay-scented barn to select the horses.

"You take Starling," Anne said. "He knows the trail, and he's as sure-footed as a mountain goat. Young Pericles here is a bit skittish, but I can manage him."

She was as deft as he about saddling her horse and mounting. They set off through the fields at a brisk trot, the soft summer breeze blowing through their hair, the sun warm on their faces, as their lungs filled with the clear, fresh mountain air. The horses slowed their gait as they began to climb, and Anne's heart was light as she looked down into her green valley, where doll-like farmers on toy tractors were at work in the fields.

"It's like looking down from heaven, isn't it, Bart?" she called back gaily. "Keep a light hand on the reins now, we're coming to a narrow ledge. Don't worry, Starling will make it."

Afterward, Bart said he hadn't heard her. He'd stopped to admire the view, and when he looked up she was out of sight around a bend in the trail. He took off after her. His big organlike voice, booming at full timbre, frightened Anne's horse.

Pericles reared up unexpectedly. The reins slipped from Anne's relaxed hands and she fell backward. Crashing through a flimsy fence. She screamed as she felt herself hurtling down the steep bank. She landed on a bed of rocks far below, her breath cut off suddenly and her body crying out in agony. Before she lost consciousness, she looked up and saw Bart's white face staring down at her from the trail.

When she awoke in a hospital bed, everything seemed strange an unnatural. Surrounding her were the familiar odors of anesthesia and sterile solutions, but she was lying in bed, still and helpless, instead of standing over it, talking to a patient. She had lucid moments, waking up now and then, everything spinning around and blurring, and then back to drugged sleep.

It was many weeks before she was able to get up and walk about, and then kindly old Dr. Phelps explained as gently as possible the prospective pattern her life must follow—due to the state of her health.

"A good marriage is a career in itself, Anne," he said. "If you take care of yourself, you can still have a rewarding life."

She stared at him, unbelieving. Then, for a few minutes, she seemed to go mad. "I will not give up my career. I've worked and slaved and studied. I gave up everything for it. I'm *Doctor* Tallman, do you hear? Take care of *myself*? I'm as strong as an ox. I always have been. I'll take care of my *patients*!"

She stood up and flung herself across the room to an open window, gulping in great breaths of fresh air. "I will not give up," she stormed. "I'm young. I'll soon have my strength back. I love my profession. Can't you understand that?"

Dr. Phelps came to her and laid a gentle hand on her arm. "My dear child, there's one more thing you need. And if you don't have it, pray for it. It's courage to accept what you can't change."

He went out and closed the door softly after him.

The tears came then, great racking floods of them. Deep down inside, she knew Dr. Phelps was right.

Weeks later, Bart said, "You know how sorry I am, dear. I wish I could undo what happened. Why don't I take you home—back to my home in Florida? The sunshine and sea air will be good for you. Maybe some day we can start planning for some little Elsnars."

The first fear she had ever known quivered through Anne at the thought. She realized by that time that she'd lost the ruggedness that had once given her such confidence. "Do you think it's safe, Bart?" she asked anxiously.

"Sure it is. But if you have any qualms, we'll consult a doctor first."

They did consult a doctor, a specialist who knew and admired Anne. He shook his head. "No!" he said.

Out on the street, Bart laughed his big, booming laugh. "Nonsense," he scoffed. "I don't believe him. Specialist, my eye. Even Dr. Phelps said you were wise to marry. Remember that? Sometimes, women are stronger after they've had children."

"You're talking about normal women, Bart. Not one who tumbled down the side of a mountain and got crushed on a rock pile," she reminded him.

He winced as though he felt the lash of a whip. "Anne, are you never going to stop throwing that up to me?"

She was instantly repentent. "I'm sorry, Bart. I'm not blaming you. All right, we'll go to Florida, if that's what you want."

They moved to Oceana Beach, and in the course of time, Rita, a bewitching pixie, was born on a torturing night, during which the attending doctor alternately cursed and prayed.

Anne knew it was worth all the pain and discomfort when she saw the baby. Almost from the day she was born, Rita was a Southern Belle.

"We're spoiling her, Bart," Anne declared one day a couple of years later, when the tyke cried for an expensive doll buggy. It was much too big for her, but they bought it.

Bart grinned guiltily. "I've been thinking the same thing. Rita should have a little sister to grow up with."

"If I only had the courage." Anne cringed at the memory of the bedridden invalid she had been for weeks after Rita's birth.

During those years, Bart had a dozen different jobs. He went blithely through his own money and lost Anne's carefully hoarded savings, too. And he was not averse to an amorous interval with somebody's "little stenographer" or a waitress with a flirtatious eye. Anne never knew for certain when he was seeing these creatures, but she knew instinctively when his interest in them waned.

Following one such "crush", as she elected to call them, he came to her one night and knelt beside her bed, abject and repentent.

"Anne, you're an angel. You're much too good for me. I know I've been a fool. I don't know what possesses me when a pretty woman gives me the eye. But I'm through with all that, honey. I promise. All I ever want is you."

Because she was still very much in love with him, she took his face in her hands and looked deeply into his eyes. "All right, Bart. As long as you *love* only me."

His reaction was quick and overpowering. She tried to retreat through fear of the consequences, but she found herself responding wholeheartedly.

That was the night Bill was conceived. When they knew for sure, Anne became frightened and Bart

13

haunted by guilt. He acted as though he was afraid, that she would break if he touched her, like a piece of delicate china. He was selling automobile tires that year, so he was on the road most of the time. But he was at the hospital the night Bill was born—prematurely.

Bart walked the floor for hours, cursing his selfishness and stupidity, while the doctors fought for Anne's life.

"I never put in such a night, Annie," he said later, looking white and stricken. "Don't ever let me do that to you again."

"I won't," she whispered. "You can count on that."

The letter had come only a few weeks before—from a woman named Celia. That letter had shattered Anne's world completely. Her love and respect for Bart flew out the window, and she settled down to a life of bitterness toward Bart, but with a consuming love for her two children, plus the conviction that, for the rest of her life, she would be a semi-invalid. She felt like a mouse in a maze. No matter which way she turned, there was no way out. She was trapped.

Anne sat up in bed and slipped her feet to the floor. She had no intention of sleeping till noon. There was too much to do. The bridge party was scheduled for two o'clock. Already, the van with the tables and chairs from the club downtown had arrived. She could hear it puffing away in the driveway, the voices of men blending with Mandy's excited whine down on the patio.

Anne winced at the sound of confusion. Mandy was efficient enough for the daily routine but extra guests for dinner or a party like today's for bridge sent her

14

into nervous spasms. She needed constant supervision. Anne hurried through her shower and dressed hastily.

Downstairs, she moved quietly about the house, which had an instant calming effect on Mandy. An orderly person herself, Anne had a way of inspiring confidence in others.

"It's good you're here, Miz Elsnar," Mandy said, crossing her hands over her ample middle. "What I do next?"

"Let's set up these chairs and tables, Mandy," Anne said with a twinkle. She knew she wouldn't have to lift a finger once her "girl" was captained into action. "Leave room for people to walk between the tables, and set some of them up in the breezeway."

While Mandy finished, Anne set out the score cards and pencils before going out to the garden. It was a beautiful morning, and she breathed in great gulps of the sea air as she gathered bouquets of zinnias and marigolds to arrange in vases on the mantle and cabinets. She smiled to herself as she listened to Mandy's contented humming. Mandy was herself again, setting out the china and silver on the dining-room table, as she had been taught.

Back in the kitchen, Anne blended her special recipe for spiced tea to be brewed in silver pots at the last minute.

Finally, all was ready. The day was off and running—the day that was to turn the tide of events in the lives of four women.

CHAPTER 2

On the other side of town, Anne's daughter, Rita Wybron, awoke in a rosy glow. She had been dreaming about Ron again. The glory disappeared like fog in a brisk breeze when her hand touched the empty pillow beside her.

She sat up abruptly. The dreams she had shared with Ron were over. Only months ago, here in this room, with the blond mahogany furniture they had selected together and his clothes hanging beside hers in the closet, those dreams had been sweet and within the bounds of possibility. But, at twenty-six, she couldn't go on forever feeding on memories. There were two little children depending on her, and the continued success of the Wybron Lumber Company, of which she was sole proprietor now, rested on her shoulders.

The house was so quiet she could hear Cindy in the kitchen greeting the day with one of her spirituals; not a song, but something between a hiss and a hum.

Cindy had stopped singing the day Ron Wybron died.

Rita covered her eyes, remembering the virile voice chanting a childhood poem that ended, " 'God's in His heaven, all's right with the world.' Right, Cindy?" And Cindy's delighted laughter. "Right, Mistah Wyb'on."

Slipping out of bed, Rita deliberately drew a curtain over her memories while she showered and dressed. She brushed her thick brown curls until they shone with bronze highlights and outlined her mouth in a clear red color. Her peachblossom skin needed no enhancement. She spent a little time looking in the mirror these days. The beauty that had enchanted Ron didn't matter anymore.

She opened her son's door and went to kneel beside his bed. As she ran her hand over his bright hair, six-year-old Bobby awoke with a start, his big blue eyes still hazy with sleep. "Time to get ready for school, son," she said.

He yawned and smiled at her. "Okay, Mom."

The childish "Mommy" had disappeared six months ago, after Ron's brother, Jack Wybron, had told Bobby he was the man of the house now. Rita resented that, as she resented her brother-in-law's interference in every facet of her life and the children's. *I don't want this little boy to feel such a responsibility*, she thought. So often she could see in this child the light-heartedness that had characterized his father. She would allow nothing and nobody to change that. It frightened her sometimes to think of the difficulty of raising her son alone. But she would manage. One day at a time.

She kissed him lightly on the cheek. "Don't be long, dear."

Three-year-old Babs was asleep, curled into a pink

17

ball, when Rita looked in on her.

Downstairs in the sunny dining room, she greeted Cindy with a cheerfulness she didn't feel. The love and concern in the black girl's eyes was comforting. Together, they plodded through the motions that had once held a touch of lightness and gaiety.

"Babs will wear the blue dress today, Cindy."

"Yas'm."

"I won't be home for lunch."

"Miz Wyb'on, you oughta eat somethin'. You'll be sick."

I am sick, Cindy, sick to my very soul. She didn't say the words aloud but busied herself fixing Bobby's cereal, the way he liked it, with brown sugar and a sprinkling of raisins. She spread raspberry jam on his toast and was smiling when he came down. It was a pleasure to observe his hearty appetite while she sipped her orange juice and coffee.

After Bobby left for the school bus, she went to Ron's study. She went there every morning before leaving for business. It was a man's room, with heavy dark furniture, red drapes, a world globe on a standard, and hunting pictures on the walls.

She sat down in the chair across from Ron's desk, where they used to discuss the lumber business they had built up together. Just looking at his chair seemed to bring him closer. She had loved him from the moment they met. They had been students at Oatfield College—Ronald Wybron in Business Ad and Rita Elsnar an art student. She had a habit of sliding down the banister in Crandall Hall when nobody was around. That morning the lobby was empty, so she took the quick way down and ended up in the arms of a laughing

18

young man with blond hair and brown eyes, who said, "I've been waiting for this twenty-one years."

She chuckled now at the memory. He was always surprising her, sending her flowers to commemorate the silliest occasions—like their "ups and downs," when they fell at the roller-skating rink; and when she broke a nail helping him tie up a package; and when she *didn't* win first prize at the art exhibit. Or he might suggest a hike through the woods to gather pecans in an old abandoned grove, or an invitation to a Knights of Columbus ball in St. Augustine. Life had been a delightful adventure with Ron.

A tiny voice at the door piped, "Mommy? Daddy?"

Rita turned to see her little girl in rumpled pink pajamas looking at her with *his* eyes and his sunny smile. She stood up and took the child in her arms. *Poor baby. She misses him, too.*

She kissed Babs and set her down. With a little pat she said pleasantly, "Go let Cindy dress you now, dear."

She glanced at her watch. It was time she was on her way. It was a blessing to have the business to wrestle with during the long, dreary days. At least that was what everybody told her. Keep busy, Rita. Time is the great healer. If only she could believe that.

Calling goodbye to Babs and Cindy, she opened the front door to a glorious October day. The trees in the grove at the side of the pink brick house hung heavy with golden oranges and tangerines. There was a scarlet flutter of cardinals and the high, sweet notes of mockingbirds among the green and gold. Backing her car out of the carport, she drove swiftly down the street to the business section of Oceana Beach. Two cars

19

were parked beside the office of the lumber yard. Her glance lifted to the sign in bold red letters above the office door: Wybron Lumber Company. How proud she and Ron had been the day that sign was erected. She was grateful now that she had the business to keep her occupied, grateful for the experience of seven successful years.

Edith Edwards, her plump, middle-aged secretary, was already at her desk, sorting the mail.

"Good morning, Miss Rita," she said brightly. "Lovely day, isn't it? Nothing much here. Couple of checks. I'll take them to the bank on my lunch hour."

"Fine, Edith." Rita sat down at her desk and took out the account books. "I'll enter the checks in accounts paid. Our customers are really coming through, aren't they?"

Everybody is bending backward to help poor little Mrs. Wybron, she thought wryly.

"You look so pretty this morning," Edith said as she laid the checks on Rita's desk, her eyes crinkling into a warm smile. "You never lost that soft, little-girl look."

"Why, Edith!" Rita sat back and stared. "What a nice compliment. Thank you."

If it was just Edith's way of giving her young employer a lift, Rita accepted it gratefully, straightened her shoulders, and went to work.

The pace of business became brisk as the morning progressed with the telephone jangling constantly. The Rupert Company lacked some of its order and asked to have it sent right away. A slow-paying customer called with another excuse. There were orders from contractors working on two new projects in nearby towns. Customers came and went.

20

After a restless, dream-filled night, Rita's nerves were like twisted wires as she tried to cope with the rush.

At the busiest moment, Joe Lally came strolling in. "I'm goin' over to Rupert's now, Miz Wybron. Want I should take those two-by-fours to Clements on the way?"

The twisted wires snapped. "For heaven sake, Joe, can't you make one little decision yourself? Of course, deliver the Clements order."

Joe Lally looked at her with patient tenderness on his lined face. It had the effect of being like a whip curling around Rita's conscience. Joe had been with them from the beginning. Ron once said they owed half their success to Joe Lally.

Rita stood up and called to the man on his way to the door. "Joe, I'm sorry. I didn't mean to growl at you. I don't know what came over me. I'm not myself sometimes lately."

"I know," he said gently. "It's all right, Miz Wybron. You'll work it out."

"Thank you, Joe." Tears threatened, but she winked them back. "I'm trying very hard to—work it out."

When Joe left, she went back to her desk and began to doodle on a memo pad. *I'm not handling myself very well*, she thought. *When I begin stabbing my faithful employees with the thorns of my own heartache, it's time I took stock of myself. Perhaps Mother is right. I need to come out of my shell; to relax among friends. It's been over a year.*

"You know what I think I'll do, Edith?" she said. "Mother is having a bridge party for the hospital this afternoon. I think I'll go home and get dressed and go to Mom's party. A little socializing might help untie the knots.''

"Oh, yes, Miss Rita," Edith said at once. "I think you should get out with your friends. You've tied yourself down too long. Joe and I can look after things here.''

"If you really don't mind," Rita picked up her papers and account books and slipped them in the desk drawer. "I noticed a cute dress in the window of the Vogue Dress Shop this morning. Maybe I'll stop and try it on.''

"The rose one with the little butterfly jacket? I know the one you mean. I thought of you the minute I saw it." There was a chuckle of hope in Edith's tone. "Nothing bolsters a woman's ego like a new dress.''

Rita sat for a moment staring at Ron's picture on her desk. For over a year she had been on a treadmill: the children, the house, the business. If she were to move back into the social whirl, it meant being a loner, a rudderless ship. It was rather frightening, but she knew it was what Ron would want for her, and she stood up resolutely.

"You're in charge, Edith. Wish me luck," she said and hurried away before she could change her mind.

It was the first time in two years she had entered a dress shop. It surprised her that she could be looking forward so eagerly to buying something new. The saleswoman seemed reluctant to remove the dress from the window. Close up, it was even prettier.

As she tried it on, Rita could almost feel Ron looking over her shoulder, his dark eyes shining. He had always been pleased to see her looking well and in the latest fashion. The dress, a soft shade of primrose pink, was tight waisted with a swingy skirt and a short jacket.

She had to agree with the saleswoman that it could have been designed just for her. She twisted and turned before the mirror, examining the material and looking at the price tag again. While the saleswoman waited, a smile of approval came over her pleasant face.

At last Rita said, "It's really my dress. You won't need to wrap it. I'll wear it. Going to a party this afternoon."

"You'll be the prettiest one there," the other woman agreed.

As she settled the skirt over slim hips, Rita knew she was taking her first step back into the social world—alone.

CHAPTER 3

It was unseasonably warm for October, but a little breeze whispered through the open casement windows of Anne Elsnar's living room. Groups of smartly dressed women sat at small tables and spilled over into the breezeway, as intent on cards and bridge scores as astronauts over their charts, planning a trip to the moon.

At the moment, Anne was dummy, so she relaxed her tired body as comfortably as the hard little chair would permit. Her mind was not on the bridge game but on how lovely her daughter, Rita, looked today. Wasn't that a new dress? It was vastly becoming, and Rita was a lily that needed little gilding.

Anne winced as a sharp pain stabbed her. She was faced with a new worry. And ever since seventeen-year-old Bill had been born, this seemed to happen whenever worry lifted its Hydra head. At lunch today, Bart had declared he was tired of his real-estate and insurance business and threatened to "look into something by which a man could make a little money." Bart was always chasing rainbows.

Anne's thoughts were suddenly interrupted by two talkative, elderly women on a small red sofa who were busy with teacups. They had bright beady eyes and chattering tongues. Neither of them played bridge. But as buxom Mrs. Devitt boasted to her guest, Mrs. Crook, she had bought tickets to help Mrs. Elsnar's pet charity, so they had a right to be here.

"See those four women at this here table?" Mrs. Devitt asked, raising her teacup so she could talk behind its fragile china screen. "Miz Elsnar, the tall dark one, is our hostess. Used to be a doctor. The pretty little redhead is her daughter, Rita Wybron, a widow left with two small children."

Mrs. Crook clucked sympathetically. "A widow! So young. What happened to her mister?"

"A fine young man. Successful, too. Came down with a virus. It was summer vacation time. His office force was away and he overdone, they said. Time they got him to the hospital, he had double pneumonia. Went out like a light."

Their voices were rising. Anne looked at them sharply, but they didn't appear to notice.

"Who's the plain young woman?" Mrs. Crook asked.

"Lawyer Tony King's wife. Tony's been in love with Rita Wybron since they were in high school, I guess." Mrs. Devitt wet her lips as though oiling her clattering little tongue. "Seems Rita turned him down for Terry Wybron, a boy she met in college. Tony was furious, they said. Told her he'd never trust another fickle beauty like her. He'd go out and marry the homeliest girl he could find. So he married Margaret, a teacher here in Oceana.''

"And the blonde in red?''

"Dwight Carey's wife. The Careys are the richest family in Oceana. She's some kind of actress. Not the important Broadway kind, I guess. More burlesquey. Seems Dwight was wild a while back, and he picked up the girl and married her. How she gets her hair up in that ridiculous fashion, I'll never know. And the stuff on her eyes!''

Anne became increasingly uneasy. She looked around her table, but her three companions, absorbed in their game, didn't appear to be listening. When Mrs. Devitt's whiney voice sharpened, Anne stood up and approached the two little gossips. "Well, ladies, did you have a pleasant afternoon?'' she asked. "Can Mandy bring you more tea?''

They declined politely, making cooing remarks about the lovely party and fluttered away.

"Look at that gorgeous hibiscus hedge of Anne's,'' a voice seeped through the buzz of talk.

Anne's eyes switched to the hedge with its flaming red blooms and swept it into her thoughts. She had once possessed a youthful beauty as dark and vivid as the speaker's. But now, at fifty-five, she felt old and used up. *Deceitful Nature*, she thought, *endows a woman with strength and beauty, utilizes it for her own purposes, then flings the empty shell on the scrap heap. Of course, it takes something called love to accomplish it.* That element had come into her life the day they brought Bart into the Vermont hospital where she was a doctor. Sunny Jim, the nurses called him. He was always laughing, joking, scattering flattery

26

around like rose petals in his enchanting southern drawl. The first time he saw Anne, he told her he was taking her home with him when he left. All the nurses envied her. Sunny Jim was taking Dr. Tallman to Florida to live!

Bette Carey's sharp exclamation scattered Anne's thoughts. "You should have played that queen on Rita's tenspot and we'd have had that last trick, Margaret!"

Anne began to gather up the cards. "Never mind, Margaret. It isn't a matter of life or death," she said soothingly.

"It's so warm today." Margaret King brushed a thin hand through her limp brown hair, making it look even more disordered than usual.

Anne knew Margaret's listlessness was not due to the weather. She had been staring at Rita as though she couldn't tear her eyes away. The two young women were as unlike as two people could be. Rita was small and pert, with lustrous bronze hair and laughing blue eyes. Margaret was tall, angular, all plain brown, with sad eyes like dark wounds in her face. One would expect Rita to be the more helpless and unhappy of the two, with the fresh grave in her heart. But Rita, like her father, faced the world with a blithe spirit. Only her mother, who knew her so well, sensed the heartbreak beneath her sunny demeanor.

Pain grabbed at Anne again, and she jerked foward in her chair.

Rita noticed instantly. "Mother, you're not feeling well."

"Perhaps we'd better add our scores and call it a day," Bette Carey said, as though she had endured all she could of the listless playing. "I'm a dunce at figures. Would you mind, Rita?'' she asked, tossing her scorecard across the table.

Arrogant and studiously graceful, Bette took a cigarette from her red beaded bag, tapped it lightly on the back of a slim hand, and slipped it between her lips, where it hung slackly while she poked around in her bag. She made quite a production of displaying a gold lighter, monogrammed in what looked like diamond chips. After a snap and a flash, she sat back, lazily blowing smoke in the faces of the other women.

Anne raised her eyes and gave Bette a long look. She disliked the idea of women smoking.

"Do you object to smoking, Mrs. Elsnar?" Bette asked. "I seem to be the only one."

"Yes, I do. My friends all know I consider smoking a hazard to everyone's health," Anne said bluntly.

Rita laid a restraining hand on her mother's arm.

Bette slowly unwound her slim body from the hard little chair. Her smile was almost a grimace. "I've had a *lovely* time Mrs. Elsnar," she said. "But I have to run now. I promised Dwight I'd pick him up at the Riomar Club at four."

She glided away, her slinky red gown revealing graceful thighs and long legs. As she waved a condescending hand, the smoldering cigarette scattered ashes in her wake.

"Poor Bette," Margaret King said. "I feel sorry for her."

"Sorry for her!" Anne laughed.

"Well, yes," Margaret rushed on breathlessly. "Oceana can be hard on a newcomer, especially if she's—different. Some people just wilt under it. Bette seems to be trying to brazen it out. I guess she has the right idea."

In order not to have to look at her, Anne busied herself collecting cards and pencils.

"I must be running along, too," Margaret said. "I really did enjoy your party, Mrs. Elsnar. Glad it was such a success. Goodbye, Rita."

She stood up and walked jerkily away between the tables, a set smile on her face. Eyes stabbed her in the back and little whispers, like light breezes, stirred in the warm room.

The other bridge players finally ended their games, added their scores, and collected their prizes.

As her departing guests straggled off, Anne waved them down the shell driveway to their cars. The late-afternoon sunshine was still hot, but there was a breeze from the ocean. She dropped down on the wide stone coping of the entrance and thought longingly of lying relaxed on the beach, the waves dashing against the shore at her feet with a musical beat, the sun beating down healingly on her tired body. What heaven!

But Mandy's plaintive wail was already coming toward her through the foyer. "You want me to fold up these chains and tables, Miz Elsnah?"

"Yes, Mandy," Anne said pateintly. "You finish up here while I have a look at the dinner."

Rita followed her inside. "I'll help Mandy, Mother. Dad and Bill will be here any minute."

On the wings of her words, seventeen-year-old Bill clattered in, slamming the screen door. Anne winced at the noise, but her heart lifted at the sight of her son.

"Your bash over, Mom?" he asked.

"Yes, and I'm practically dead. How was college today?"

Bill sidestepped her question with an eager one of his own. "Did Bette Carey come?"

Bette Carey's name falling so glibly from her son's lips caught Anne like an unexpected blow. "Yes," she said calmly. "Why?"

Out of the corner of her eye she witnessed his sudden confusion. "Oh, nothing," he replied casually.

She gave him a long, speculative look. He was a head taller than she, with her own quick, dark eyes and black hair. Almost a man. In her heart, she had been thinking of him as a little boy. Youthfully graceful, he sprawled in a deep chair, one long leg draped over the arm, his rosy face hidden behind the evening paper.

Anne sighed. So now he was interested in women. A woman, rather. And such a woman! Another phase to see him through.

"Where did you meet Mrs. Carey?" she asked.

"Dwight's brother, Jody, brought Bette—Mrs. Carey—to the beach party we kids had a few weeks ago. She's heaps of fun. You know, keeps things going. She was an actress on Broadway! Can you imagine? Real friendly and easy. She asked us kids to drop in on her any time."

"Just make sure there's a crowd along when you drop in," Anne said dryly.

"For Pete's sake, Mom. Can't you cut the apron strings? I'm sick of being treated like a baby. I'm old enough to make my own decisions."

Anne's eyes snapped. "Don't use that tone to me, young man."

He subsided, holding the newspaper before his face, but it rattled in his shaking hands.

"What's all this about Bette Carey?" Rita asked at the door. "I take it you don't like her much, Mother.

30

She *is* quite a character. Something new for Bill and his birdwatchers.''

Blessed little Rita, Anne thought. How often her coolness and amiability acted as a buffer in the intense encounters between the other members of her high-strung family.

Anne relaxed. Her eyes crinkled with sly humor. "This Carey bird's feathers were fire-engine red, Bill. She had at least sixty-two yaller curls piled on top of her head, and her skirt was so tight she had to hitch along like a snake upended. She seemed to enjoy her cigarettes—it was such fun blowing smoke in our faces. Eti-cat personified.''

Laughing, Rita dropped down among the pillows on the sofa. "You make her seem a rare bird, indeed.''

"Permit me to demonstrate the Bette Carey shuffle.'' Anné began to parade before them, hand on hip, in an exaggerated slouch, remindful of Bette's walk.

Bill chuckled. "Mom, you're a dope.''

At moments like this, when she was able to cast aside the cloak of stern discipline and clown with her children, Anne felt close to them. They seemed to speak the same language.

A car rattled into the driveway and screeched to a stop, leaving every movable part chattering in protest for a full minute. Anne's smile narrowed and her body became taut. There was a commotion on the front steps. The banging of the door shook the walls, and Bart Elsnar stood in the door, rubbing his big hands together gleefully.

"Well, well, well, how is everybody? Hello, Rita. Kiss for Dad? How are ya, son? Hello, Mother.''

Bill and Rita pounced on the big man, dragging him

31

to the sofa.

Rita plumped herself down on his knees. "Just time for one smack, Daddy. Then I've got to run."

Bill began pommeling his father playfully, and Bart's deep laughter boomed.

Anne sighed and put her hands to her throbbing head. She walked wearily to the kitchen and directed Mandy to take up the roast so she could thicken the gravy in the pan; Mandy's lumpy gravy always brought groans from the family. As Anne stirred the brown liquid, she was conscious of a jealous twinge. The children were so different with Bart. She had to do all the scolding and guiding. Bart just humored and indulged them, and they adored him.

"Dinnah is raddy," Mandy shrilled. "Evenin', Mistah Elsnah." Even Mandy was more cheerful when Bart was around.

Anne was beginning to feel like the skeleton at the feast every time they sat down to a meal. Bart and his son were forever clowning while she tried to insist on decent table manners.

"Hit me with the bread, Dad," Bill said.

Bart picked up a slice in his fingers and flung it at his son's son's chest.

Anne laid down her fork, frustrated tears filling her eyes. "Bart, when I try so hard—"

"Oh, now, Mother, we were just having a little fun," Bart said, with a smiling patience that enraged her. "This kid knows better than to do a thing like that when he's out in society."

"Bart, this is my table," she said stonily. "I have a right to expect you—both of you—to treat me with common courtesy."

As usual, they quieted down, stole surreptitious

glances at each other, and began to stoke themselves like the healthy, vital people they were. Only Anne was unable to eat. Her nerves were quivering. She even felt a little guilty about spoiling their "fun."

Bill broke the uncomfortable silence. "How about some shekels for the movies tonight, Dad?"

"Taking a girl?"

"Who wants to know?"

"Sorry, son. If you want to entertain girls, you'll have to do it on your allowance."

The ensueing argument lacked logic, in Anne's opinion, but the volume of Bill's rhetoric was awe inspiring. Presently a note crackled and coins clattered on the table. Her son had won again.

After he left, Anne marshaled her forces. "Bart, why can't you cooperate with me in guiding the children?"

"Cooperate? In what way, dear?"

"Like giving in to Bill just now. I know you sensed my objection. Another thing. That young man could do with a little fatherly counsel. Right now he's interested in, of all people, Bette Carey."

Bart grinned. "Well, Bette is quite a dish."

"Your indulgence just makes weaklings of the children. Look at Rita."

"I don't see anything wrong with Rita," said her father. "She's the town beauty, a fine little mother, and as brave a kid as I ever hope to see. Look at the way she's taken hold since Ron died."

"I admit all that. But what about Tony King?"

"What about him?"

"He's been seeing Rita altogether too much. A married man. I feel sorry for Margaret. She knows, of course, and she tries to be dignified about it."

"Have you asked Rita's side of it? Maybe the tramp's been bothering her."

"I spoke to Rita, and she said everybody knows Tony is her lawyer as well as an old friend of hers and Ron's. So what harm if he drops by now and then? I said, 'Rita, before people start talking, you'd better tell Tony to take care of your business at the office and not come to the house anymore.' And what do you think she said?"

"What?"

"She didn't want to hurt his feelings. She's exactly like you, Bart."

"That's a compliment I cherish, Annie."

Unable to contain her anger, she flared, "Bart, you're impossible. Wait till your daughter gets mixed up in a scandal. Then see what you can do about it. Don't exert yourself to speak to her now. Just give her an indulgent pat on the head."

Bart's face darkened. "I think I'll go see Bill's movie," he said and left the table.

The door slammed after him. Anne's shaking hand went to her throat. She had driven her family out of the house again. She knew they resented her nagging, but there seemed no other way to get anything across to them. When she was casual, they dodged the issue. If she tried to be amusing, they were entertained, which accomplished nothing. It was maddening that both children should turn out to be as easygoing and flippant as Bart.

"You want anythin' else, Miz Elsnah?" Mandy said, at the dining-room door.

"No, thank you." She knew Mandy was in a hurry to get her work done and be on her way, so she left

34

her cooling coffee and went to the living room to spend another lonely evening stretched out on the sofa.

If only, she thought desperately, she and Bart could see eye to eye and solve their problems quietly and sensibly. But they were poles apart. As Rita once reminded her, she probably was biased by her life on the rugged, rock-bound Vermont farm on which she had grown up, while Bart was a human counterpart of his buoyant, lazy, sunny Florida.

"And, apparently, never the twain shall meet," Anne muttered with a sigh of defeat.

CHAPTER 4

On her way home from her mother's Rita drove down Milburn Avenue and across the railroad tracks into the lumber yard. Her heart plummeted when she saw the brown car parked in front of the office. Jack Wybron, her brother-in-law, would be inside examining her books, ordering Edith and Joe Lally about, and otherwise making himself obnoxious.

Ever since Ron's death, Jack had been a constant threat to her peace of mind. His interest seemed to be more in meddling in the lumber business than in the welfare of his brother's family. Rita resented his constant intereference. Poor Ron! If he could have forseen how she was being badgered, he would never have appointed his brother executor. But Jack was practical and shrewd, and Ron had trusted him.

Although the day outside was warm, the atmosphere of the office was chilly when she walked in. Joe Lally's lined face, with the thinning gray thatch above it, was dark as a thundercloud. Edith pounded the keys of her typewriter, her face beet red. Jack Wybron sat at Rita's desk, boldly going through her books.

There wasn't the slightest resemblance between Ron and his officious brother. Jack was big, dark, blustering, inclined to stoutness, with a clipped black moustache that twitched across his upper lip like two little battling caterpillars.

"Hello, Rita," he said. "Hear you were out partyin' today. The business cain't run itself, you know. But that's all right. Little ladies are more at home in the social whirl than in the business world."

"Really? I hadn't noticed," Rita said pertly. "I'm able to be at home, as you put it, in both worlds."

He grinned and shook his head. "I don't agree. I was just tellin' Edith and Joe I'm puttin' a competent man in here to run your business for you. Name's Roberts. Comes well recommended. Got to beef up sales somehow."

Rita's face burned. "I'll trouble you for my chair, Jack," she snapped.

He lumbered awkwardly to his feet.

"Why wasn't I consulted about this?" she asked as she took her place at the desk.

He pursed his lips and his moustache twitched. "I didn't see the necessity of botherin' you."

"Bothering me! Aren't you forgetting this is *my* business?"

He sat down on a corner of the desk and began jabbing at the blotter with a paper knife. "In my opinion, women know very little about business," he said. "I'm tryin' to help you."

"When I need your help, I'll call on you," she retorted. "And when any changes are made, *I'll* make them."

He stood up and flung the paper knife down on the desk. "Just remember I'm executor of Ron's will. He'd want me to do whatever I consider right for the best interests of his family—*and* the business."

Rita began to quiver inwardly. She felt suddenly young and helpless, but she dug her nails into her palms. When she spoke, her voice was steady. "Our books show a fair profit this past year. There's plenty of building going on around here. And with Joe's help I've corralled all the big orders, just as Ron and I always have."

"I guess. But it took a lot out of you," Jack drawled, watching her closely. "Most importantly, a mother's place is at home, taking care of her children."

She drew in her breath slowly. "That notion is a little outdated."

"I wouldn't say so. If Ron were here," he paused delicately, "I'm sure he would insist that you put the kids first and let him run the business. At least, while the children are small."

"You're wrong. Ron was modern in his thinking and we both agreed—"

"If it can be proved a woman is neglectin' her children, they can be taken from her," he broke in.

Rita jumped to her feet. "Jack Wybron, you wouldn't dare!"

He looked down at her from what seemed a great height. "I think you'd better stay home and look after those kids of yours, Rita. That little black girl cain't take the place of their mother. I'll put Roberts in charge here the first of the week."

It seemed as if she would never catch her breath. She watched him pick up the big white sombrero he affected as he walked calmly out the door. It was so quiet she could hear the breeze whispering through the palm trees outside the windows. She didn't realize she was crying until she felt Edith's arms around her.

"Don't, Miss Rita. Please, honey. You'll make yourself sick," Edith pleaded.

Rita turned her head against the plump shoulder and felt comforted. One of her hands was suddenly pressed between two calloused palms. She looked up into Joe Lally's kindly face.

"I don't know what I'd do without you two," Rita said. "If my charming brother-in-law tries anything funny with either of you, I'll fight for you with my last breath."

"We know that, Miss Rita," Joe said.

She went out to her car and climbed listlessly behind the wheel. For a long moment, she sat looking at the big square building with the bright suite of offices in front. Her glance lifted to the red-lettered sign, "Wybron Lumber Company," and she recalled once again how proud she and Ron had been of that sign and what it stood for. It was more than just a matter of pride. It spelled security for them and their children. Ron had been an excellent salesman. He could charm surprisingly large orders out of tight-fisted customers. Rita had soon proved she could run the office like a veteran. It had been a perfect combination, and they had been well on their way to success.

We had a good life, she thought. *It wasn't all business. There were picnics on the beach, dancing at the club, planning the children's future.*

She started the car and backed it into the street. Memories of Ron always brought on an icy, hollow feeling that shook her to the depths. Her absorption in the business helped conquer that feeling sometimes. Now, even that was to be taken from her. She'd have only the children to think about. And Jack was holding them, like a sword of Damocles, over her head to force her to submit to his preposterous demands.

Her thoughts turned to Tony King. She didn't know what to do about Tony. Because he disliked Jack, Tony avoided coming to the lumber yard office. He came to the house when she had to consult him. She was fond of Tony. Always had been. Sometimes, the thought of him was comforting in her loneliness. She could see the hunger in his eyes when he looked at her, but she hadn't the heart to tell him not to come anymore. For one thing, Bobby was fond of him. Perhaps to the small boy, Tony was a father image. Besides, he was her lawyer. Ron had trusted him. She was planning to call him about this last outrageous move of Jack's as soon as she got home.

Still, she was worried. Anne had warned her that people were beginning to talk about her and Tony. But Anne was always borrowing trouble. She demanded nothing short of perfection in other people, while she was far from perfect herself. It was inspiriting to have a parent like Bart Elsnar. The light touch. Ready laughter. Her father bore his burdens lightly, his daughter thought fondly.

Driving her long blue car straight into the glory of the setting sun, Rita tried to shake the burdens from her own shoulders. Tony would be coming in tonight to play with the children a while before their early bedtime. Then they would have their talk. He would know what to do about Jack.

The children fell upon her with shouts of joy when she opened the door.

"Where've you been, Mom?" Bobby demanded.

Rita dropped down on the floor and tumbled them into her arms. "Gram had a party."

"Oh, Mom, a party!" The small boy's eyes filled. "And you didn't take me and Babs."

"But, honey, there weren't any little boys and girls there. Just grown-up ladies, like Mommy and Gram and Mrs. King. Tell you what we'll do. We will have a party next Saturday and invite all your friends. Cindy and I will make pink ice cream."

They both hugged her, shrieking their delight.

"Prettiest picture I ever saw," said a deep masculine voice at the door.

Rita looked up, startled. "Tony! I didn't hear your ring. I was about to call you. Jack's giving me trouble again. Why don't you have dinner with us so we can talk?"

"I might be induced to have a cup of tea and a crumpet." He dropped down on the floor beside her, and Bobby went to him to sprawl in Tony's arms.

The quick tropical night had already descended. The moon, round and golden and unbelievably large and low in the eastern sky, peeped at them from behind the scraggly fronds of a banana palm in the yard outside. The good smells of Cindy's steak and the spicy fragrance of baking gingerbread came enticingly from the kitchen.

Tony phoned Margaret and told her not to wait for him; he was having dinner with a client.

Rita felt a little odd about his referring to her as a client. Even though it was true, it seemed a bit misleading. In spite of her misgivings, she felt at peace with the world again.

When Cindy announced dinner, Tony was on his

feet instantly, reaching for Rita. She put her hands in his, and he pulled her up, trying to hold her close.

She shook her head and glanced at the children, who were watching them wide eyed. Suddenly remembering those two old ladies, Mrs. Devitt and her friend, whispering behind their teacups today, she pushed him away.

Holding out a hand to each of her children, she said, "Come, darlings." They danced along beside her, and she clung to them, thanking God for them. They had saved her from Tony. Saved her, she thought wonderingly, from herself.

The dinner table seemed quite festive tonight. Even Cindy seemed more like her old self as she served them. It pleased Rita to see how happy Bobby and Babs were, having a favorite of theirs as their guest.

They were laughing over something Babs said when Rita looked up from her coffee cup, the smile froze on her face.

Anne Elsnar was standing in the doorway.

"Mother!" Rita exclaimed.

Anne said nothing. She just stood there, looking at the little group, disapproval written all over her stern white face.

"Have dinner with us, Mother?" Rita asked lightly.

"I had dinner long ago." Anne's tone was crisp. "How do you do, Tony?" she added coldly.

Tony seemed to wither under her cool scrutiny. He didn't stay long. With hasty excuses, he kissed Babs and promised Bobby he would come again. His glance touched Rita caressingly, then he was gone. They hadn't discussed business or Jack's latest presumptuous dictum, which was the reason she had invited him to dinner.

"Rita, I don't like this," Anne said, seating herself at the table and breaking Bobby's roll into small pieces for him.

Rita became absorbed with Babs, but the hand that held the child's glass of milk trembled. As usual, Anne made her feel guilty.

"I'm sorry for Margaret," Anne said more gently. "She must have heard some gossip. She kept looking at you today."

"Staring at me? She gives me the creeps with those big eyes of hers."

"Poor girl!" Anne sighed.

Rita regarded her mother speculatively. Sometimes, in her lighthearted moments, Anne looked pretty and young, but tonight her face was pale and drawn, and her shoulders drooped dispiritedly.

"Aren't you feeling well, Mother?"

"Wretched. It's a hopeless thing, I guess. Dr. Kirby seems to think so. He can't understand why I can't relax, let things go, lie on the beach in the sunshine. I wish I could."

"I don't see why you can't. Mandy takes beautiful care of the house. Daddy and Bill can take care of themselves. Where are they tonight, by the way?"

"Gone to the movies," Anne said. "I couldn't stand it there in the house facing my problems alone."

"What problems, Mother?" Rita said as she stood up and lifted Babs down from her highchair.

"I'm worried about Bill. That hussy, Bette Carey, is his latest crush. You heard him."

"Kid crushes," Rita laughed it off. "We all had them. Bette is colorful and amusing. Different from anyone Bill knows. Is that all?"

"No. Your father is getting restless again. I expect

43

any day he'll come barging in with crazy plans for a new job. Upsetting routine. Changed hours and everything. If he'd just stay put.''

"Well, Mother, nobody stays put very long. As Mandy would say, the world do move. Come, Mother, we'll go out on the patio. Cindy will see to the children. I'll make you a nest of pillows, and you can lie on the chaise and be comfy.''

Anne let her daughter fuss over her. She lay back among the soft cushions with the moonlight on her face. Characteristically, she took up the conversation where she had left off. "Don't you expect your children to live good lives, Rita?''

"Of course. But I also want them to enjoy every minute. Life should be fun for youngsters.'' Rita looked very young herself, curled up in a rocker, her lovely face raised to the moon.

"Fun," Anne said softly. "That seems to be the byword of young people these days. Duty was the byword of my youth. You never knew your grandmother. She was a thin, harassed woman, absorbed by her house and four children. Father was stern and hidebound, the direct opposite of Bart. I suppose it's no wonder you and I don't speak the same language.'' The little imp of mischief that sometimes peeped from Anne's eyes danced in them now. "I wonder if a woman could begin to have fun in her fifties?''

"Of course she could," Rita said. "Just picture yourself in a long, slinky gown dancing at the Riomar Club. Or whacking a golf ball down a carpet of green velvet. Lunching with a group of women on the country club veranda. Or bicycling across the county causeway down to the ocean.''

"Oh, Rita, stop!" Anne laughed. But such lilting

thoughts seemed to draw her heart out of her cumbersome body. She was not one to prolong her stay on Mt. Olympus, however. "Like your father, you seem to think pleasure is the end and aim of existence."

"No, Mother, I realize how serious Life is. I admire Daddy's attitude, though. Maybe his light touch made a deeper impression on Bill and me than your—preachments."

"You mean I haven't been a good mother?"

"I didn't say that. Of course, you are a good mother. Some of your dictums seemed unreasonable, though. I remember soon after Ron and I were married, we all had a picnic on the beach one Sunday. On the way home, Daddy and Bill were planning to make some crazy sandwiches for supper, like the fellow in the funnies. You said, 'Dagwood. Those infernal comics are making you all foolish.' You promptly canceled the daily papaers and subscribed to a religious paper. Daddy and Bill came over here every day to read our papers. You see, Mother? You can't keep life away from youngsters. I plan to give mine all the help I can to cope. I'll love them and let them enjoy life."

Anne lay still. "I suppose you're right, honey. Sometimes you surprise me. You seem to have a keener insight then most young people."

Her mother would be even more surprised, Rita thought, if she knew that her daughter, in spite of her serene demeanor, was crushed by burdens that were tearing her apart.

After Anne left, Rita sat on alone in the moonlight, going over the events of her day. It had been pleasant meeting old friends and being welcomed so heartily. For a little while that afternoon, she had been able to forget herself and her problems. But it seemed to her she had come home to face an even greater one. Jack and his officiousness. She sidn't quite know how to deal with it. The fact that he had already hired a man from somewhere up north to manage the business posed a problem. She had been too angry to ask who the man was, what his qualifications were, what salary he had been offered, and when he was expected in Oceana.

Now, in a saner moment, she wondered if Jack didn't have a point. Perhaps she should be free to give more time to the children. That had bothered her for months. Now that she was the sole owner of the business, she had to spend more time in the office. Occasionally, she had the feeling she was neglecting Bobby and Babs.

"Oh, Ron, darling, I wish I knew what is best for all of us," she whispered into the night.

And Tony. What about Tony? Her mother was probably right about him, too. She shouldn't encourage Tony to come around so often. Just tonight, she had been frightened by his ardent impetuousness—and even more concerned by her own reaction.

Cindy's voice broke into her thoughts. "You goin' stay out here all night, Miz Wyb'on? It's gettin' on to midnight. I open up your baid."

Rita sprang up, contrite. "Oh. Cindy, I'm sorry. You didn't have to do that. You really spoil me."

"Yas'm," Cindy agreed. "Somebuddy have to look after you."

Rita sighed as she followed Cindy inside. There had always been somebody looking after her.

CHAPTER 5

The sun was setting as Margaret King walked home from Anne Elsnar's bridge party. Thick clusters of palmettos in a vacant lot rustled softly in the slight breeze, and a giant cypress hung a veil of Spanish moss across the sidewalk. It looked, Margaret thought, as though the tree were weeping gray tears; tears that found an echo in her heart.

She felt tied up in little knots inside. She left Anne's party early because she couldn't bear the thought of the cheerful talk she knew would follow the games.

As she hurried toward the little Spanish bungalow Tony had built for her on Osceola Avenue, she recalled the day he carried her across the threshold, when she thought he loved her. That had been a little more than three years ago. Today, she had found out, quite by accident, what a fool she had been.

Though she had seen Tony hovering over Rita Wybron at parties, after she and Tony were married, it had never occurred to her to be jealous or suspicious.

All men admired beautiful women, she thought. That was only natural, and she had always accepted the fact philosophically. Margaret had no illusions about her own lack of physical charms, but she tried to make up for it in other ways. She worked over her little house with all the fervor of her artistic soul. Its bright, airy rooms, with the painted furniture and happy chintzes, had been photographed for a national magazine as a Florida bride's Spanish bungalow. Tony had shown the article to everyone who called at the house for weeks. The kitchen was her favorite room, and Margaret had acquired a reputation as a good cook. She played golf with Tony, talked over his law cases with him, waited on him, entertained him, adored him. But it wasn't enough.

This afternoon at the bridge table, bedazzled by Rita Wybron's beauty, she wondered if her own nose were shiny. It usually was. And her hair! Rita's naturally curly hair had such a vibrant sheen. Why should one woman be blessed with both beauty and charm?

The moment she became dummy, Margaret had gone quietly to Anne's bedroom mirror to see if there really was as much contrast as she imagined between Rita's beauty and her own plainness. On the way, she passed behind a small red sofa on which two old ladies were chatting and drinking tea. On hearing Tony's name mentioned, she had stopped involuntarily.

"It seems Rita turned Tony King down for Ronald Wybron, and Tony was furious," cackled one of the old ladies. "He told Rita he was fed up with her fickle beauty, and that he'd go out and marry the homeliest girl he could find. So he married this schoolteacher, Margaret Calvin. But since Wybron's death, they say—"

48

Somehow, Margaret had managed to get to the bed-room and close the door. Her cheeks were burning and her hands shaking. "I don't believe it! I *won't* believe it! It's not true."

Yet, why fool herself? So many things were clear to her now. The nights Tony had spent away from home since Ron Wybron's death. His unpredictable moods after an evening at the "office." She knew Tony and Rita had once been in love—"We were kids in high school," as Tony explained it, "but Rita went to a different college and met Ron. And I met you."

In Anne's guest room, Margaret leaned toward the mirror and carefully scrutinized her reflection. Her brown eyes looked too large for her thin face, but they were warm and sweet. Her one mark of beauty. For the rest, she was all sallow brown angularity, with hair that was flat and limp. It was only this morning that the hairdresser had put such a pretty wave in it. *But that's the sort of person I am,* she thought. Her hair lost its curl an hour afterward, ten minutes after pow-dering her face it was shiny again. Her clothes hung peculiarly on her thin figure; there didn't seem to be anything she could do about it. She hadn't minded—much—until now.

All afternoon she had been enjoying Rita's beauty, just as she enjoyed a sunset or the moon shining on the ocean or a Bach concerto. But after hearing the old ladies' gossip, it was torture to go out there again and watch each lovely change of expression, each graceful gesture of the enchanting young widow who was captivating Tony to the point where he was getting talked about.

Margaret ran up the steps of the little Spanish house, still smarting over the afternoon's disclosures. She was grateful for her own four walls that closed her in from the world outside. She walked slowly into the bedroom—hers and Tony's room. She touched his brushes on the dresser and put away a blue tie he had left on the back of a chair. Dropping down on the maple bench, she picked up his photograph from her dressing table, staring at Tony's eyes with their little laugh wrinkles at the corners. At his hair, dark and thick. At his amusing little moustache, above his smiling lips.

"Oh, Tony!" she whispered, biting back tears.

She thought of the first time she had seen him. He had come to visit the school with some of the other board members. They had left visiting the kindergarten until last—"Like sherbet and coffee, Miss Calvin," old Judge Reynolds had said gallantly.

Margaret had her small charges sing for them, and she proudly displayed the children's drawings. At least, she looked up into the eyes of a tall, dark young man holding one of the children in his arms. She had never seen such a look of tenderness in a father's eyes before. The man was Tony. The child was a merry little red-haired boy with twinkling blue eyes.

Her son, Margaret thought now. *And I didn't know. All I could think of was that I was weak and hollow inside, and my heart was jumping crazily. And when Tony spoke to me, I could hardly get my breath to answer him.*

He'd said, "This is my boy, Miss Calvin. Aren't you, Bobby?"

Bobby Wybron hugged him and said, "Yeth."

"Oh, you're Mr. Wybron," Margaret said.

She recalled the shadow that had passed over his face. "No," he replied soberly. "I'm Tony King. But Bobby and I are good friends."

50

Poor Tony! He probably loves Rita as much as I love him, she thought. *Now, I suppose he wishes he had waited. Only three short years and he might have married Rita, after all.*

But he hadn't waited. Perhaps that winter day in the school room he was touched by the breathless change in the slim little teacher when she looked up at him.

"How long have you been in Oceana?" he had asked.

"Just this term. I came down from Orlando in September."

"Thought I hadn't seen you before. Have you met many of the Oceana people?"

She shook her head. "Not many. Just the school people."

"We'll have to remedy that," he had said with his warm smile. "What do you like to do—dance, swim, play golf?"

"I couldn't say which I enjoy most."

"How about nine holes of golf Saturday morning? Say, around seven-thirty, before the sun gets too hot? Good. On the Royal Park course. Have you tried it? It's the best we have. I'll call for you."

Thus, casually, had begun for Margaret Calvin the most joyous years of her life. She was so happy that she glowed. She must have made Tony forget, for whole days at a time, that he was in love with someone else. She could have sworn Tony was happy then, too. But now, looking back, she could see, as she hadn't been able to see then, that there were signs all was not as it seemed.

The night Tony proposed, for instance. The Tennants, who wintered in Oceana Beach and summered on Cape Cod, had given a party at that Riomar Club

51

in April, just before leaving for the north. Tony and Margaret had been invited.

She had been Rita Wybron for the first time that night. Rita had had another baby, a girl, early in the winter, and this was her first social appearance since. Margaret had never seen anyone as lovely as Rita looked that night. She wore a gown of chiffon, the color of peachblossoms, and she had the radiant Madonna look seen so often on the faces of young mothers.

Margaret had been dancing with Tony when the young Wybron couple came in. Tony stiffened and missed a step. When Margaret looked up at him, he tried to cover up. "My fault. I slipped. Having a good time?"

She laid her head against his shoulder for an instant. "A marvelous time," she said.

Ron Wybron had been very handsome, she remembered. Smaller and slimmer than Tony but just right for little Rita. Ron's eyes were dark. Somehow, you never forgot their expression when he looked at his wife. While they were dancing, he would suddenly hold Rita away from him and look at her as though wondering if she really were as lovely as he thought; then, convinced, he would pull her close again.

Later that evening, Tony danced with Rita. Margaret watched them with the first jealous twinge she had ever felt about him. The little pink figure held itself close to him as Tony's tormented eyes stared over Rita's head. There was tension in both of them. When they suddenly disappeared, Margaret just sat by herself, clasping and unclasping her hands, screaming inside, "Tony, where are you? Where *are* you?"

A long time afterward, when he came back to Margaret looking pale and unhappy, her heart raced to meet him.

"Had enough of this?" he asked abruptly.

"Why, yes, if you have."

"Then let's get out of here." He swept her to her feet and danced her toward the check room.

He was morose and thoughtful as his car flew along the narrow sand road on the way to the apartment Margaret shared with two other teachers. His driving was so erratic, it frightened her.

"Ever think of getting married?" he asked.

Her heart almost jumped into her throat. "Why, yes. I—I guess every girl thinks about it sometimes," she stammered.

"I mean you and me," he said, stopping the car so abruptly she was almost thrown into the windshield. He cuaght her hands in a tight grip. His lips were shaking.

She went limp and quivery inside. "Oh, Tony," she said, "I've thought of nothing else for weeks."

"When will you marry me?"

Her throat was dry, but she managed to get the words out. "Whenever you say."

"Let's make it as soon as the school term is over."

The suddenness left her breathless; she could only nod in agreement.

Only then did he seem to remember to kiss her. It wasn't the kind of kiss she expected. It was a fierce and possessive one, a little angry. It frightened her. But she needn't have been alarmed. He never kissed her like that again. When he thought to kiss her at all, it was always a bit listless. Tony, she had thought fondly, wasn't much of a lover.

Now she wondered as she stared at her unhappy

53

face in her bedroom mirror. If only there was something she could do, some act of magic that would transform her face into one with piquance, with enchantment.

She snatched the pins from her hair and brushed her tresses angrily, attempting to copy Rita's hairdo with its pert waves in front and rows of shining ringlests across the back. But Margaret's hair separated, drooped, and hung limply about her head in sad caricature. She stared at herself helplessly. There was nothing, *nothing* she could do, and she threw the brush down in disgust.

She had just started to prepare dinner when the telephone rang. Tony was dining with a client, he said. She thought instantaneously of Rita. But Rita wasn't Tony's only client. The incident of the afternoon was still fresh in her mind. It was affecting her thinking.

It was after eight when Tony came home. He pecked at her cheek as he passed. "Have a good time at the hen party?" he asked casually.

"Yes. Your Rita was there." She caught herself up quickly. What had possessed her to say that?

Tony looked at her sharply.

Forcing animation into her voice, she began to tell him about the little tiff between Anne Elsnar and Bette Carey.

"Mrs. E had better watch her step with Bette Carey," Tony commented. "I understand Bette has added young Bill Elsnar to her string of admirers. She's displaying him like a new pup on a leash."

"Not really," Margaret said. "A married woman and a little boy? She wouldn't do that."

Tony laughed. "I guess you don't know her kind. If I were Dwight, I know what I'd do."

"What would you do if you were Dwight?" she asked softly.

"I'd take that kid by the scruff of the neck and throw him out of my house. And I think I'd blacken one of Bette's pretty wandering eyes."

"Yes, of course," Margaret snapped, picking up the evening paper, "that's what a man would do. Beat up his wife and throw her lover out. But what does a woman do under those circumstances?"

"What are you talking about?" His face turned red and his eyes looked startled.

"Oh, nothing," she sighed. What would she gain by antagonizing him?

"Look, Meg," he said, blinking nervously, "I hope you didn't mind about dinner. This was an important client."

"I understand," she said. "Tony, I've been giving some thought to an idea that has occurred to me several times lately. Wouldn't it be wise to move away now, while we're still young? Branch out? Business might be better for you in a large city. Don't you feel sort of cramped here?"

"Leave Oceana?" He was pacing the floor and turned sharply. "Leave a place where I'm well established? I just had my office done over the way I want it. Where would I find the exceptional clientele I have here? Surely not if I was buried in a big city, competing with dozens of other lawyers. This is my home, Margaret."

"I know," she agreed, surprised at his stormy reaction. "It was just a thought."

"Aren't you happy here? "You have a nice home, friends, your clubs. Maybe you'd like to return to teaching?"

"No, of course not. I was merely thinking about you. Let's forget it. It was just an idea."

What would really make me happy, she thought, *is*

to remove you as far from temptation as possible, my love.

"I think I'll go for a walk," he said. "Blow away the cobwebs. Want to come along?"

"No, dear. I walked home from Anne Elsnar's this afternoon, which was quite a hike. So I'll just stay here and catch up with the news."

The closing of the door as he went out was like the thud of a fist against her heart. She forced herself to be calm as she picked up the newspaper and held it before her unseeing eyes. Life must go on, she told herself stoutly. If only those two gossiping old ladies hadn't upset her so!

CHAPTER 6

Bette Carey was in an unpleasant frame of mind as
she drove her smart little car down Osceola Avenue.
She knew that all those women had been watching her
every move this afternoon. The cats! She hoped she'd
given them something to keep their silly tongues wag-
ging. Those two old crones, staring and whispering,
were the ones who had upset her in the first place.

Perhaps her hair and dress *were* a bit extreme, but
they were becoming. She was fond of extremes in
clothes, cars, jewels. She liked to attract attention, to
see heads turn and eyes goggle. It had been amusing
to bait those three women at her table. Anne Elsnar
had probably put Bette at her own table out of "consideration" for her other guests. Bette might prove to
be embarrassing to some of the elite: the charming
Mrs. Elsnar wouldn't want to embarrass anyone.

They can't patronize me, Bette thought angrily. *I'm
as good as they are. I'm Mrs. Dwight Carey.*

Somehow, down deep, she realized that wasn't good

enough. She was one of the wrong-side-of-the-track people, and it probably showed through her glitter. She wasn't a Carey and never would be. She was a Molenenski. No matter how hard she tried, she couldn't conform.

Born in a city tenement, she had fought her way up the hard way. After a meager schooling, she went to work in a five and dime, learning to put over a song and dance by watching movie stars. Back in those days, she was always warbling and practicing dance steps every time she had a spare minute.

"Look at that kid, will you?" her Ma used to chuckle proudly over her can of beer. "Ain't she a caution?"

Bette, christened Elizabeth Hortense, learned at an early age to make the most of herself and her opportunities. She had set her restless feet on the bottom rung of the theatrical ladder the night she met Carky Vann in a cheap dance hall. Carky was an old vaudeville song-and-dance man, years older than she, but smitten with the little blonde with the amusing line.

"You and me ought to team up, baby," Carky had said. "You dance like a dream."

"Team up for what?" she asked pertly.

"I got an act in a joint down the street. Old vaudeville act that always wows 'em. They say vaudeville's dead—"

"Yeah? I bet I know who killed it,"

"Oh, come now, baby! It'll come back some day, and you oughta be ready. How about it?"

"What would I do? Dance, sing, maybe?"

"Yeah, and chatter a bit. You're good at that. You got good timing."

"Um." She strangled her aversion to this balding

58

little man with the thin lips and stained teeth. "All right, Carky. Beggars can't be choosers. Besides, you old fraud, you know I'm crazy about you."

Because Carky believed his passion for the "little filly" was reciprocated, he wangled a spot for her in the rowdy little bistro he was performing in. But he was promptly jilted for his pains. An alert manager, looking for a special type of girl for a small part in a new play, spotted Bette one night. After a tryout, she got the part.

For a while after that, her ascent was rapid. Her goal was Broadway, but she never made it. She managed to land one or two good parts in road shows, but she didn't possess that certain spark necessary to lift her out of mediocrity. Not that she would ever admit it to herself. She was certain she would have landed on Broadway eventually—if a juicier plum hadn't dropped into her lap. That plum was Dwight Carey, son of an Oceana citrus and real estate tycoon, who happened to see her in a second-rate version of *Rain*. Dwight was slumming, of course, when later that night he turned up at a party at Charlotte Hedden's.

Bette knew Dwight was Somebody the minute he walked in that night. Ten minutes later, when he was standing beside her, tall, gangling, and not particularly handsome but with the easy air of the born aristocrat, she said to herself, "This is for me."

He didn't say, "Hello, baby. How's tricks?" Instead, he said, "I saw your play tonight, Miss Vincent. Your Sadie was excellent."

She choked back the saucy words that wanted to leap to her lips. "Thank you," she said simply and smiled at him with a shy smile that made her eyes look big and round and baby blue. It was a look never

59

failed to knock a guy off his pins. "I've never met anyone like—like you," she said breathlessly.

The goof blushed to the roots of his curly blond hair. "I was just thinking the same about you. Did you come with anyone? I'd like to drive you home."

She knew he was one of the elite when she saw his car. She was such a dope, she fell in love with him just because he didn't try to force his way into her apartment but instead shook hands at the door. At least, she *thought* she was in love. She couldn't be sure at first. It might be because he was Dwight Carey—with all that money.

Perhaps Dwight was infatuated with her because she was pert and witty, different from the girls in his set at home. He became Bette's shadow. When, at the end of four exciting weeks of what she called "the high life," he was suddenly called home, he begged her to go with him.

"In what capacity, Dwight? Valet? Clown?"

"As my wife," he replied matter of factly.

Her eyes softened and she surprised herself, saying, "You'd better think it over. I'd only make trouble for you."

"Why?"

"Dwight, honey, what would your family and friends think if you brought home a third-rate actress?"

He frowned at her across the table in a posh bistro. "You're not third rate. You're beautiful. You could be a Broadway star. You could make me awfully happy, too," he added with the wistful, one-sided smile that turned her heart to water.

Bette shook her head. For the first time in her life she was giving first consideration to someone else. This *must* be love if she didn't want to hurt Dwight.

She looked around the quiet dining room at the smart-looking people talking in low tones. She was aware of the scent of flowers and expensive perfume and deft, quiet service. A string trio was playing chamber music. It made her feel like a lady. With Dwight, she was sure she'd always feel like this. The rest of the troupe were probably holding forth in some roadhouse, where the management was indulgent and the food cheap, where the girls would be screaming to one another across the room, blowing smoke rings and listening to obscene stories—or telling them—with relish and gusto. Noise. Cheapness. Tawdriness. That had been her life all the years she could remember. She shivered in the warm room.

Dwight smiled at her. "How about it?"

"All right, Dwight." Realizing, even then, that she might have to face coolness and snubs from his family and friends, she repeated firmly, "All right, darling."

Busy days followed. She bought a whole new wardrobe of the plainest clothes she had ever owned in a shop Dwight had recommended, though she couldn't quite agree with the saleswoman and her emphasis on the smartness of simplicity. *A sequin or two won't make me a whore,* she thought. She also bought a book on etiquette and studied it diligently. She would be ready for society with a capital S.

They were married quietly before coming south. Bette's first real misgivings came when she and Dwight drove into beautiful Oceana Beach. It was so new and strange. The picture-postcard hotels. The streets like parks. The colorful houses, beautifully shrubbed and surrounded by gardens of tropical flowers. She saw glimpses of imposing mansions bulwarked by high walls and rows of trees hung with the ragged gray lace of Spanish moss. Dwight's house was one of the mansions, hidden from the road by tall hibiscus hedges.

Having to face Dwight's family was harder than any first night she had ever experienced. Dwight's mother looked like a Lady, with her white pompadour and expensively corseted figure. His father was a smudged carbon copy of Dwight. Bette saw their faces tighten when they looked at her. She might have fooled their son, but she wasn't fooling them. They were polite, even haughtily kind, and as coldly and solidly against her as twin icebergs in the way of a drifting ship.

Dinner that night was about as cheerful as an inquest. Afterward, Dwight's father took him off to another part of the house, leaving Bette alone with the "dowager."

Dwight's mother led the way to an airy balcony that commanded a magnificent view of the sea. "I'm afraid you won't find Oceana as lively as New York, Elizabeth," she said.

Bette was startled for a minute. She hadn't heard that name since leaving the eighth grade where she had had a particularly obnoxious teacher.

"Oh, I don't mind," she replied agreeably. "Dwight and I are planning to tour around. I've never been in Florida before. We'll spend a lot of time on the beach."

"Mrs. Carey's tone dripped icicles. "I'm afraid Dwight won't have time for much of that sort of thing now. A married man has certain responsibilities."

"Yes, I know."

"And so has a married woman. I shall see that you meet the right people. By the way, what was your school?"

62

Bette's eyes twinkled in the early dusk. She was tempted to say Hard Knocks University, but it wouldn't do to be that impertinent. "Twinklecliff Manor," she fabricated on impulse.

"Oh?" said Mrs. Carey uncertainly.

"It's a very exclusive school on the Hudson," Bette explained without a qualm.

"Oh, I see. How—very nice."

The ice was melting, it seemed to Bette, and she winked to herself in the darkness.

A moment later, Dwight strode out on the balcony and snapped on a light. His mouth looked tight and angry. "Want to go up now, honey?" he said.

"Elizabeth has been telling me about her school, dear," his mother said.

"School?"

"Twinklecliff Manor," Bette explained sweetly.

"Oh." The grimness left his mouth and he grinned. "Oh, yes. Are you ready?"

She stood up and reached for his hand. Together, in silence, they started upstairs to their suite.

"Sky fall, darling?" she asked anxiously when they were out of ear shot.

"Um," he said glumly. "We'll get a place of our own tomorrow."

She turned to look at him as he closed the bedroom door. "I tried to tell you, Dwight."

"Tell me what?"

She walked over to the dressing table and took off the matched string of pearls he had given her as a wedding present. Her eyes softened as she looked at him. "I've had you turned out of your beautiful home, Dwight. I tried to tell you."

He had her in his arms instantly. "My home is

wherever you are," he told her firmly.

Now, as she drove down Osceola Avenue with the sunset in her face, Bette recalled that precious moment and held it close to her heart. There hadn't been many such moments since. Almost at once, the wolves had gone to work, tearing her and Dwight to pieces. They said Dwight had added another oddity to his collection of snake hides and seashells.

Because she loved Dwight, Bette had made an effort to conform to Oceana's social standards, but it was uphill work. When people spoke of her as an actress, the word carried the tang of an eipthet rather than a tribute to artistry. Everything she did or attempted to do was misinterpreted. All of Dwight's friends seemed to assume she had married him for his money and family prestige. She particularly relished telling them she had never heard of the Careys or Oceana Beach until she had met Dwight.

She and Dwight each reacted differently to her poor reception: Dwight became hunted looking, while Bette turned defiant and brazen.

Not being able to get along with either the older generation or those her own age, Bette was quick to realize that younger people found her to their taste. They flocked around her, copied her, and admired her. So she took up with them. Admiration and applause were the breath of life to her. The young crowd of Oceana admired and applauded unstintedly.

Of all the youngsters, she liked Bill Elsnar best. A handsome, big, dark creature, he oozed charm. He was terribly young and naive, of course, but his admiration was heady. Bette flattered him, taught him the latest dances, and basked in his youthful esteem. . . .

She turned her car into the long, circular driveway leading to the Riomar Club. *Another of their snooty institutions hidden from the eyes of the common herd,* she thought grimly.

Dwight was standing on the veranda, talking to Tony King and two or three other men. He waved to her, picked up his golf bag, and ran down the steps.

"Party over already?" he asked, slipping into the seat beside her.

She smiled and waved at the men on the clubhouse veranda. "I came away early," she explained, swinging the car in a wide circle.

"Oh?" he looked at her uneasily. "Have a good time?"

"Yes, very." She couldn't keep the sarcasm out of her voice. "Two gossipy old dames sat and stared at me all afternoon, and the charming Mrs. Elsnar showed her claws over a small remark I made."

"Probably has it in for you because you're making a fool of her precious son." Bette's face flamed. If Dwight had been the least bit sympathetic; if he had said, "Don't let them get you down—"

Perversely, she asked, "Jealous?"

"Jealous!" he echoed scornfully. "Of that little twirp? Well, hardly. It is a bit cheap, though, Bette."

Cheap! The word was like a blow between the eyes. Angry tears burned against her lids. "What can you expect of someone you picked out of the gutter?"

"Oh, good heavens!" Dwight barked, settling further down in the seat in grumpy, masculine silence.

Another pleasant evening ahead, she thought. *Another night of cold, refined politeness. No tears. No scenes. No hot words. People like the Careys don't go in for that sort of thing. Why can't he, just this*

*once, fight it out to a finish? Clear the air. Why can't
he give me a chance to melt in his arms? Putty? If
he'd just give me a chance. I'd do
anything—anything—to please him, the damned aristocrat!*

"I'm having dinner at the Imperial Coach House
with some of the fellows," he said as she turned into
their driveway.

"How nice for you," she replied coldly. "While
I spend the evening alone in Honeymoon Lane, I suppose?"

"I'm sorry. This is something that came up this
afternoon. You weren't home, so I couldn't call you.
It isn't as though I leave you alone five or six nights
a week."

"Oh, forget it." she snapped as she leaped out of
the car and ran ahead of him into the house.

She went directly to their bedroom and closed the
door. Slipping hastily out of her dress and into a baby-
blue chiffon peignoir, she tied a blue ribbon around
her hair and waited.

He didn't come in. Presently, she heard the car door
slam and its motor purr to life.

"Honeymoon Lane," she whispered. She wished
she had never heard of the Careys or Oceana Beach.

CHAPTER 7

Everyone seemed surprised when the news got around that Rita Wybron had hired a man from up north to run the lumber business. She answered the telephone a dozen times a day to tell the same story about deciding to stay home and look after her children.

At Rita's suggestion, Tony stopped at the lumber yard office to take a look at Mark Roberts. His report was rather vague. "Nice-looking chap. Young. Full of business. A bachelor. Nothing like Jack, but that doesn't mean he isn't a tool of your brother-in-law's. To tell the truth, Rita, the fellow puzzles me."

Tony's report didn't satisfy her completely. On an afternoon when she knew Jack was playing golf with some of his cronies, Rita decided to drive down to the office to see for herself what was going on.

The cream-colored car standing closest to the office door caused the first pang. That had always been her parking space—and Ron's. The car looked fairly new and still bore New York license plates.

Rita opened the office door and stood quietly for a moment, studying the man at her desk. An old-fashioned expression, "clean cut," came to her mind. The deep wave in Mark Roberts's dark hair and the fresh, untanned look of his skin gave him a boyish appearance as he bent over his papers.

As she closed the door he stood up, his face beaming with surprise and pleasure.

Edith stopped typing, and Joe Lally shouted from somewhere in the shadows, not too pleasantly, "Here's your boss, Roberts."

"I'm Rita Wybron, Mr. Roberts," she said.

He looked embarrassed. "Oh! Mrs. Wybron. I didn't expect you to be so—so young," he finished lamely. His handshake was firm, not clinging. "Won't you sit down?" He waved her to her own high-backed chair at the desk as he sat down nearby. He was studying her with his earnest brown eyes.

Rita liked the tweedy smell of his after-shave lotion and the crispness of his white shirt. "I thought it was time we became acquainted," she said.

"Yes, of course. First of all, you'll want to know something about me. I'm twenty-nine. Busniess administration, Syracuse University. After college, I worked for Sterns and Wilmot, manufacturers of air conditioning equipment."

This sounded too pat. Like something he had memorized.

"How long have you known Jack?" she broke in.

"Quite a while—casually. He's a friend of my Uncle Jim's. I owe Jack a lot for giving me this opportunity. I've always wanted to live in the South." His voice dropped intriguingly to a deeper note *tone* at the end of each sentence. "I hope you find my work here satisfactory."

If Jack had searched the country over, he couldn't have found a chap more appealing—and perhaps more devious? That remained to be seen.

"How are things going?" she asked.

A shadow crossed his face. "Not too well. Everybody I contact wants to know when Mrs. Wybron is coming back. Old customers of yours don't seem to want to do business with me."

She sat back in the chair and thought for a minute. Her first reaction was that here was a chance to prove to Jack the business might founder without her at the helm. On the other hand, if that happened, she could lose everything she and Ron had worked so hard for. It might be safer just to play along, at least for a while.

"If you'll give me the names of customers who seem reluctant to deal with you, I'll put in a good word."

He looked relieved. "Thank you, Mrs. Wybron. I really appreciate that."

She stood up and walked over to pat Edith on the shoulder. "Mr. Roberts, this lady and Mr. Lally are the backbone of this business. Don't ever forget that."

"I won't," he said. "I depend on them a lot. I hope you will drop in often, too."

The door opened and closed briskly. Jack Wybron was standing there, his eyes snapping, the two little worms on his upper lip wriggling agitatedly. "What are you doing here, Rita?" he asked.

"I own the place," she said. "Or have you forgotten?"

He looked grim for a moment. Then, apparently

remembering they had an audience, he asked, "How are the bairns? Which reminds me, I'll have some papers for you to sign in a day or two. The certificates for the kids' bank account."

"I'll take care of it," she promised.

Before having banished her from her business, Jack had discussed with Rita a savings plan for the children's education. He had suggested that a percentage of the lumber business' profits go into savings certificates that would bring in high interest. The bank of Jack's choice was located in Ohio. After Tony King approved of the institution, Rita agreed to Jack's plan. He purchased a thousand dollars worth of the certificates in October, and now, in November, he was planning on doubling that amount.

Driving home, Rita's thoughts were centered on Mark Roberts. Tony had said, "The fellow puzzles me." Roberts was a bit of an enigma to her, too. He was polite and appeared honest and open, but that might be a pose. He could be, as Tony suggested, a tool of Jack's and would thus bear watching.

One morning, a few days later, Jack telephoned Rita for her to stop by the office as soon as possible to sign the papers of transfer to the education fund in the Ohio bank. Before she had a chance to comply, Mark Roberts phoned to ask if he might bring the forms to her home.

"It really won't be necessary," she said. "I'm driving downtown tomorrow. I can stop at the office and—"

"Please, Mrs. Wybron, let me bring you the papers," he broke in. "I'd like to explain something. It's very important. Otherwise, I wouldn't bother you at your home."

"Well," she hesitated. This was irregular. What

did the man have up his sleeve? She still wasn't sure she could trust him. However, she felt fully able to deal with him in case he had any idea of trying to ingratiate himself into anything more than a business association. "All right," she agreed. "Say, one o'clock this afternoon."

She was dressed in a simple beige suit and was sitting in Ron's chair at the desk in the study when Cindy ushered in her caller. Rita smiled inwardly when he appeared at the door. In his conservative suit, white shirt, and striped tie, he was the image of a northerner. He had not yet learned that he could relax and be more casual in his business attire.

"Sit down. Mr. Roberts," Rita said, indicating a chair across the desk. "You wish to explain something concerning the trust fund for my children, I believe you said."

He took a typed sheet out of his brief case. "Read that."

"It's a simple statement that I'm transferring two thousand dollars from the Oceana account to the Ohio bank," she said.

"Don't sign it," he said as she picked up her pen.

She sat back and regarded him coolly. "Mr. Roberts, aren't you interfering in something that's none of your business? When it concerns transactions at the office, I'm willing to listen to your suggestions. This matter is strictly a family affair."

"Your children's trust fund," he said.

"Exactly."

"Does it say anything on that paper about a trust fund for your children?"

"No. It doesn't have to. My lawyer approved of the plan, and Jack agreed to handle it."

"I hope you won't consider me officious, but I think

71

you should examine this.'' He pushed a bank passbook across the desk.

''This passbook belongs to Jack and is none of my business—or yours.''

''Will you please examine the account number? It's the same as on the form you were about to sign. Does it mention anywhere that it is a trust fund for Robert and Barbara Wybron?''

She examined the passbook again. There was just one entry of a thousand dollars, made on October third, payable to John H. Wybron.

''Where did you get this?'' she asked.

''It was in an envelope addressed to the bank, waiting for the document requiring your signature. I found it buried under some orders on my desk. I thought you should see it.''

She felt a little weak as she considered the situation. It would be foolish at this point to show her ture feelings to this stranger. ''Well, thank you for coming,'' she said quietly. ''I'll take this up with Jack. Your name and your visit here today will not be mentioned. You may just tell Jack I refused to sign.''

''Thank you,'' he said and left, quickly and quietly.

Rita sat on at the desk in the gathering dusk. After this afternoon's session, Mark Roberts was more of a puzzle than ever. She had supposed he was hand-in-glove with Jack, yet his actions today upset that notion. Why, exactly, had he come to her? She tried not to like him, but there was something disarming about him. He seemed to be acting in her interest, but she was still not quite sure about that. As for Jack, she was grateful that his little scheme had been nipped in the bud. What a hypocrite—stealing from children! Month after month, her money would have been siphoned off into that account in the Ohio bank, until Jack had enough to take control of the business. She decided not to sign anything more until Tony investigated it thoroughly.

She called to Cindy, who was passing through the foyer, "If Mr. Wybron calls me on the phone, tell him I'm not to be disturbed at any time."

"Yas Ma'm," Cindy agreed. "I sure will tell him."

Jack would demand an explanation for her refusal to sign over the two thousand dollars. She would keep her promise not to involve Mark Roberts. He had saved her from what might have been a disaster for her and her children. She wondered why he had done it. If Jack could fool her so easily, so could Roberts. She would have to be extra-vigilant from now on. Her life seemed to getting more complicated every day. Her dependence on Tony for everything that came up was a habit she would have to break. It was time she stood on her own two feet. That was probably the way it would have to be the rest of her life.

She was so concerned about her new business manager, Rita decided to take Edith to lunch to get her opinion.

It was a warm October day, perfect to enjoy an outdoor table at the Hidden Garden Restaurant.

Edith was delighted with Rita's invitation. Her graying hair was salon fresh, and she wore a becoming new gray fall suit. Too seldomly was she able to get out like this, she said. It was a real treat. Rita knew Edith's aging ailing mother kept her from enjoying much social life. Today, she was full of bright talk about what was going on, both in town and in the world of business.

"How do you like Mark Roberts?" Rita asked,

when she was finally able to bring up the subject casually.

"Well, I like the boy," Edith said. "There was a period there at first when we were feeling each other out and I wasn't quite sure about him. But, you know, it's surprising how quickly he took hold. He's got a real good business head. And the customers seem to like him, now that they've gotten acquainted. I guess he surprised Jack, too. He just doesn't go for any of Jack's interference. He really put him in his place a couple of times. He said he would check with his boss—meaning you—if things got tied up."

It was obvious Edith approved of Mark wholeheartedly.

"How does he get along with Joe?" Rita broke in.

"Well, for a while there, Joe was kind of short with the boy, but he's coming around. I think Joe likes him now. You know Joe. He's easygoing, gets along with most people."

Evidently, Roberts had charmed his way into the hearts of her employees. In a way, it was encouraging. At least there was no feuding or disputes in the office, but Rita couldn't bring herself to feel completely confident about the man. He would still bear watching in her opinion.

CHAPTER 8

Anne couldn't recall a pleasanter first of November in years. Taking Rita's advice, she left everything in Mandy's capable hands that morning and drove down to the beach.

The sun was warm and bright, the sea gray-green, and the sky an unbelievable shade of blue, tossed with feathery white clouds. She spread her blanket down with a little sigh of delight. At nine in the morning, the beach was deserted; even the lifeguard's seat loomed loftily empty, like King Neptune's throne.

Anne lay on her side, dreamily aware of the fascinating sweep and thunder and wash of the breakers. Gulls swooped and screamed above the old hulk of a ship that many years ago had been wrecked not far off shore. Tiny gray-and-white sandpipers tripped primly down the beach, deftly escaping even the longest wash of the waves on shore. Funny little things. There was something instinctive about their hopping back just the right distance to keep their feet dry every time. A sand crab crawled lazily past Anne's feet on a mysterious quest of its own.

The sun burned through her blue swimsuit, warming her through and through, crowding out pain and discomfort. She put on her dark glasses and lay back, burrowing luxuriously. Almost at once the sweet, soothing, harmonious sounds of nature lulled her to sleep.

She awoke to find the sun high in the sky, the lifeguard big and brown and alert in his box. People were pouring across the sand to the fenced-off bathing area. Northern tourists, most of them. Nobody else would be silly enough to go swimming in the ocean in winter, Bart always said.

She sat up and took an orange from her wicker lunch basket. With a sharp knife she cut out a square of the outer skin from the top of the orange and plunged the knife into the heart of it to loosen the sections. She sucked the sweet juice through the opening as she had seen the natives do, turning the fruit expertly until only the empty shell was left. Two more oranges comprised her lunch.

It was amusing to watch the bathers. Little family groups setting up beach umbrellas, spreading blankets, opening books or lunch baskets, or walking barefoot through the sand in search of seashells. There was a camaraderie among most of them that Annie envied. That stout woman with five small children gathered around her and a beaming husband beside her. What sorcery did she possess to surround her with an aura of deep affection? The woman's laughter tinkled, high and melodic, and Anne smiled sympathetically. Somehow, it reminded her of sleigh bells jingling on frosty air. She closed her eyes and thought of her own youth. How differently she had planned her life. That bright-eyed girl would never recognize the harassed, unhappy woman she had become. Perhaps, if she tried harder. . . .

Right now, as she lay in blissful comfort and peace, Bart and the children seemed close and endearing. She wouldn't give a fig for a family of dry-as-dust puppets. She should learn to enjoy her family, like that woman with the carefree laughter. This opportunity for clear thinking and planning fortified her. While she lolled in the warm sand, many things seemed possible. If she chose, she might even change the pattern of her life.

As she felt a stirring beside her, Anne sat up abruptly. A little freckle-faced girl sat there, studying Anne with big brown eyes. "Are you a mother?" she asked.

Anne smiled. "Yes. I have two children, but they are grown up now."

"I'm Karen. I haven't got a mother," the child said.

Instinctively, Anne reached for her and pulled her close. "I'm sorry," she said. "Do you live in Oceana?"

Karen shook her head. "Daddy and I live in New York. With El'nor."

A blond young woman came racing down the beach, calling, "Karen!"

The child stiffened against Anne, but the woman saw her and puffed up beside them.

"Karen, you naughty girl. You ran away again!" she said. "I don't know what possesses her," she added to Anne.

"Are you her mother?" Anne asked.

"Stepmother." The woman dropped down on the

77

sand. Her hands fluttered nervously as she tried to explain. "I'm Eleanor Trent. I married Karen's father last summer. I've tried so hard, but she won't do a thing I tell her. I'm at my wit's end."

"May I offer a word of advice?" Anne asked.

"Please do," the woman said.

"I'd say what Karen needs right now is patience and understanding. And lots of love. She isn't a naughty girl. She's frightened and resentful. She's probably used to being everything to her father and considers you an intrusion. Am I coming across at all?"

"Loud and clear." The woman smiled, but there were tears in her eyes. "You see, I've never had a child before, and I don't know how to cope with one. I love her father very much, and I've tried so hard."

Anne nodded. "Too hard, maybe. Why don't you just love her and let her know it? It will pay off in the long run."

"Thank you," Eleanor Trent said and held out her hand to the little girl. "Come, honey, Daddy is waiting for us," she said.

The child's body relaxed against Anne as she reached for her stepmother's hand. Small as she was, she seemed to sense the change in the woman's attitude and went with her willingly.

Anne watched them till they were out of sight, the woman smiling and talking animatedly and the little girl trotting alonb beside her, her small freckled face beaming.

"I guess I was in the right place at the right time, Lord," Anne whispered.

It was four in the afternoon when she picked up her gear and started home, her nerves smooth and quiet.

Her body felt warm and vital.

Palm leaves rustled lazily in the breeze as Anne drove through the park. Someone was clearing a spot for a new home in a tangle of palmettos. Men and women, black and white, lined either side of the bridge across the causeway, their fishing poles dangling hopefully in the Indian River. Life at the end of this peaceful day was good.

She saw the Johnson boys playing catch in the vacant lot next to the house as she drove down the street. Carl Roise was mowing his lawn. Bart's car was in the driveway. Anne waved to the neighbors and went humming into the house.

Bart lay on the living-room sofa, his hands behind his head, a familiar dreamy look in his eyes. Anne's heart stumbled as she looked at him. She dropped down in a chair nearby.

"Hello, Mother," he said.

"Aren't you home early?" she asked, a feeling of apprehension gathering inside her.

He ran long fingers through his thinning thatch and sat up. "You know, Annie, I've had about all I can take of the real-estate business. Nobody's buying. Nobody's selling."

"They must be selling! Someone must have sold one of those choice lots over on the Island recently. They're clearing it off, getting ready to build."

"One lot." He waved it off scornfully.

"One of those lots is worth plenty of money. The main thing is, you're tired of your job again, aren't you?"

His face flushed as he spoke quietly. "There ought to be some business by which a man could make a little money. Real money."

79

"Not without work," she flung back, her gorge rising in spite of all her resolutions. "If I could get back my strength, I'd go in with Dr. Emmett over at the hospital and put an end to this constant worry about finances—once and for all!"

"A couple of women doctors running a hospital!" Bart scoffed.

Anne jumped up—too quickly—and her side twinged with pain again. "You didn't think so lightly of women doctors twenty years ago," she reminded him crisply. "If I'd kept on with my work, I'd be a successful physician by this time, instead of a slave to your whims."

"Oh, for God's sake!" he roared. "Might have been better for all of us if you had kept on with your precious profession."

He got up and strode out of the room. She heard him clumping down the back steps to the cluttered workshop behind the garage, where he spent most of his leisure time. Another of his extravagences. The money he spent for tools and equipment for that silly hobby would have paid for Rita's and Bill's education, without having to scrimp eternally. Anne hated that workshop.

She went upstairs to bathe and dress for dinner, her nerves jumping again, the pain marshaling its forces for a fresh onslaught. As she passed Bill's bedroom, something crashed behind the door. She stopped and turned the knob.

Bill was on his knees on the floor, picking up his alarm clock and military brushes.

"What on earth are you doing?" she asked.

"Practicing the samba," Bill explained breathlessly.

"Where did you learn it?"

"Bette—Mrs. Carey—taught me. I swung my hips a little too far, I guess."

Bette Carey again! Anne sat very still.

Bill stood up and began to brush his thick, dark hair, frowning in the mirror.

"Getting ready to go out?" she asked.

"Well, yes," he admitted hesitantly. "That is, after dinner. Bette—Mrs. Carey, is teaching me to play contract."

"How nice," Anne said quietly. "Who else is going?"

"Well," Bill became absorbed in an eyebrow, leaning close to the mirror. "My eyebrows are so thick, they makes makes me look like a pirate."

Anne's eyes didn't leave his face. When he could no longer avoid her gaze through the mirror, he turned a flushed face to her. "Nobody else is going," he said defiantly.

"I thought it took four to play contract," Anne said.

"Yes, but—you have to learn the—the fundamentals of the game first."

Anne sighed. "Bill, I have always been proud of you," she said. "I hope I always will be. Your father and I are making sacrifices to send you to college. Suppose, for a change, you show a little interest and gratitude by applying yourself to your studies tonight."

His glance fell. "Okay, Mom," he agreed.

After leaving him, opening her own bedroom door, she thought, *The minute I come into this house there is no longer peace. Why? Why can't my family be like other families?*

She tried to be leisurely as she showered and

81

dressed, but her thoughts continued to be chaotic. Bart out of a job again . . . Bill and Bette Carey . . . Rita and Tony . . . the same circle, over and over.

She focused her attention back to dinner. It must be nearly ready. She stood listlessly at her bedroom window, looking at the tall, straight royal palm tree that always reminded her of her own youthful self. Abruptly, the years fell away and she was back at St. Mary's Hospital. It was six in the evening. With dinner over, patients were getting ready for visitors. Young nurses' admiring eyes followed her down a corridor. "Good night, Dr. Tallman. "Good night, Doctor." There had been another young doctor in those days. Dr. John Painter, a handsome, dedicated young man with a gift for laughter. He was a famous surgeon now.

One night, in a corridor of the hospital, he had greeted her warmly. "Hello, Anne. Out stepping tonight? Wish it was with me. There's an appendectomy tomorrow at eight. I want you with me." *I want you with me*. Working at something together, something we both loved. Perhaps falling in love and marrying. Oh, John, John. . . .

Anne looked down at her hands that, for over twenty years, had been moving rebelliously among saucepans and needlework, playing cards and doing children's laundry. Her eyes filled with tears. Life might have been so different. Of course, she couldn't have hoped for finer children. She had known how to make their bodies strong and beautiful, but she had never been able to reach their minds and hearts the way she wanted to. How glibly she had advised the young stepmother on the beach today. Why couldn't she take her own advice? Love, yes. She had given her children plenty of that. But understanding and patience?

She turned away from the window and went downstairs, trying to retain the warmth of that day's sun, the peace of sea and sky, wanting them to sustain her through the coming hours.

In the kitchen, Mandy was singing of the golden slippers she was gwine to wear to reach the golden shore. Any moment now, she would send out a lusty call that would gather three grumpy people around the dinner table.

Anne thought of the pleasant atmosphere around Rita's table the night she had walked in and found Tony King there. Rita's table had been even more heartwarming with Ron Wybron at its head. Rita possessed the heaven-sent gift of knowing instinctively how to cope with the people in her life. It was a gift her mother envied. Perhaps this once she would borrow a little of her daughter's warmth and amiability to expend on her own immediate family.

She walked into the dining room, smiling pleasantly. "Hasn't this been a lovely day?" She looked directly at Bart and Bill. Usually, her glance traveled around the table in search of a possible omission or oversight on Mandy's part.

Bart's eyes widened in surprise. He had been expecting another tirade. A slow smile crept over his face.

"Did you enjoy it, Annie?"

"You've got a nice tan there, Mom," Bill commented. "Day on the beach?"

When the roast chicken was brought in, to the cook's delight, Anne complimented Mandy.

Bill had a funny college tale to tell. A girl in Creative Art had won a prize for an object. Everybody told her how great it was, but nobody had the nerve to ask *what* it was.

"That's art for you in this day and age," Anne laughed.

Bart had visited Rita's office that afternoon to size up the new manager. He had found him to be personable. "Seems to know his business." For once, Anne had something to contribute to the conversation, about her experience with Karen and her stepmother on the beach.

Bart had received a letter from his mother, Olivia Elsnar, who lived only miles away on Coquina Key but seldom visited her son's family.

"You ought to write to Mama more often, Anne," he said. "She gets lonely."

"I will," she promised.

When they left the table, Bill went happily to his room to "crack the books"; Bette Carey and her contract lessons were apparently forgotten. Anne wandered over to the piano in the west window of the living room. They had bought the instrument years ago, when small Rita had shown an unusual talent for music. Anne was no musician, but she could pick out a tune with her right hand and manage a bass line of sorts. She began to play some of the popular songs of her youth.

Bart sat down with the evening paper. A little smile played around his mouth as he listened to Anne's music making. It turned out to be an especially pleasant evening.

It's surprising how much a woman can learn from her children, Anne thought. She stood at the window, looking out at the pattern of lights and shadows made by the moon shining down on the trees in the grove. "Thank you, Rita, for this lovely evening," she whispered.

CHAPTER 9

Time hung heavily on Rita's hands in the weeks following her virtual banishment from the lumber business. She missed the mornings at her desk, talking over plans with Joe Lally. She missed the shrieking telephones, the busy clickety-clack of Edith's typewriter. There seemed to be nothing to do now, except walk from room to room, help Cindy, look after the children, write letters or try to become interested in her favorite magazines.

She took the children to the beach or for long rides. They loved it, but her life seemed rather futile. Cindy was efficient, and the children had been trained from babyhood to rely on themselves for diversion and entertainment. Rita preferred it that way. All this coddling and extra attention they were getting was bad for them. Then, too, the unrestrained delight with which she welcomed Tony King's visits was beginning to frighten her. She often wept during the long, sleepless nights, clinging hopelessly to Ron's unresponsive pillow.

On a cool November night, Cindy closed all the windows and built a fire in the fireplace. Rain sluiced against the panes, and the wind whistled down the chimney, goading the blazing logs to a frenzy.

Certainly, no one would venture out on such a night! After Rita put the children to bed, she went to her room and changed to a rose-colored housecoat and little flat red slippers. Her negligée clung to her slim figure and swung enchantingly when she walked. Ron had loved her in it. It was his last birthday gift to her. She took her book to the living room and settled down in a deep chair before the fireplace, but she found it impossible to keep her mind from wandering. The book dropped into her lap, and her eyes strayed to the blazing logs in the fireplace. It was fascinating to watch the long tongues of flame lick at the dripping pitch. The smell of burning fatwood filled the room with pine fragrance.

What was she to do with her life? It seemed futile to plan or dream. All the plans and dreams she and Ron had shared had died with him. There were the children, of course, but she couldn't give her whole life to them. She had seen enough of that in her own family. A long time ago, she had come to the realization that Anne, much as she loved her children, had never forgiven them for taking her from the career she wanted even more. *I don't want to be like Mother,* Rita thought. *She's a bitter, frustrated woman, and she takes it out on Dad and us kids. I like Daddy. I'm glad I'm Bart Elsnar's daughter!*

The sound of the doorbell startled her as Rita sprang

up. A joyous little tingle ran the length of her spine. Tony! It was Bart Elsnar's daughter who dashed impulsively to the door and stood there, shining eyed and expectant, all her barriers down.

She had no idea how lovely she looked at that moment until she saw the eyes of the man on the streaming portico light up.

"Rita!" he said softly.

The light went out of her, and she could feel herself shrinking. Sick with disappointment, she turned away from him.

"Come in, Jack," she said listlessly.

Jack Wybron shook the raindrops from his hat and topcoat and hung them on the hall tree. Rubbing his hands together briskly, he followed her back to the living room. He appeared nervous as he took a chair across the hearth from her.

"Nice and cozy here," he remarked genially. "Awful night outside."

Rita waited, tense and silent. Her brother-in-law hadn't called on her often since Ron's death. Jack had never concerned himself much with his brother's family. The children disliked him. He knew it and resented it.

"How are the kids?" he asked.

"Fine. They're in bed. Asleep, I suppose, by this time."

"Bobby doing well in school?"

"Yes."

Rita knew he was just making conversation, leading up to the object of his visit. She was determined not to help him.

"The kids miss their father?"

"Naturally."

He pursed his lips and nodded. "They should have a man to look after them. Help them over the hurdles, as the sayin' goes. 'Specially Bobby. You're a good mother, Rita, but I'm afraid you're not goin' to be able to handle that young man in a few years. Might be a good idea to send him to military school. Good discipline. Make a man of him."

Her heart began to quiver, but she sat still, waiting.

"The boy's education is important," he went on. "I think we agreed about that. So why did you refuse to sign the form for the trust fund? Or was Mark mistaken?"

"I'm considering another plan."

"Your lawyer's idea?"

"Does it matter?"

Surprisingly, Jack didn't pursue it. His eyes suddenly became shifty, "You'll need someone of your own to help you plan for the kids. You'll marry again, Rita. You're young and beautiful."

She shook her head. "I'm afraid not. Marriage with anyone else would be an anti-climax—after Ron."

"Have you ever thought that I might be in love with you?" he asked.

She stared at him. "You!"

His meager smile distorted his plump, dark face. "I can see you hadn't," he said, with an unusual quietness. "I always envied Ron because you were his wife. When he died, I felt I might have a chance."

The horror in Rita's eyes had stopped him. She stood up and walked over to the fireplace to stare into the flames. This was unbelievable. A nightmare. She wished she might wake up and find herself alone in her warm bright room. Her eyes lifted to the mantle where Ron smiled at her from a silver frame. *Oh, darling, darling, tell me I'm dreaming!*

"Well, what do you say, Rita?" the deep voice rumbled behind her.

She turned slowly. "I'm surprised, Jack, and touched." She was choosing her words carefully. "But I can't marry you—or anyone."

He was silent for a long moment. "Then you won't marry *anyone*," he said.

She turned to look at him. He stood behind a chair, one hand gripping the back until his knuckles showed white.

"When you came to the door tonight, you were expectin' someone else," he said. "I saw the look on your face. All dressed up like a—a— You thought I was Tony King, didn't you?"

Her eyes flashed. "You have no right to talk to me like that!"

"Except the right of a man who offers you *honorable* marriage—the man who promised your husband he'd look after you. There's too much gossip about you and King. You'd better put a stop to it."

"That's utter nonsense." She flushed angrily. "Tony is a married man. And he's my lawyer. Have you forgotten that?"

"You'd better not forget it. Your legal business with King isn't so pressin' that you have to see him every night in the week—in your negligee."

"That's not true and you know it." She dropped into a chair. All the defiance oozed out of her. It was no use trying to talk sense into this lunatic. A tear crawled down the side of her face. Unconsciously, she held out her hands in a pleading gesture. "Jack, I'm trying to put my life together. If I reach out to someone to help—''

Apparently misunderstanding, he dropped to his knees beside her, catching her roughly in his arms, his breath hot on her face. ''Rita, you're only human. I think I sense your need.''

''No!'' she cried, pushing at him. ''You don't understand. The only need I have is to be left alone to work things out.''

''If you'd give me a chance, you might get to like me,'' he pleaded. ''I'd be good to you—protect you and the kids. We'd build up the business. Travel a bit. Enjoy our money—the fruit of our labor, as the saying goes.''

Her heart began to jerk with fear. ''Let me go, Jack,'' she said firmly.

Terror mounted in her as she remembered she was alone, except for the sleeping children and the maid shut away in her room. She pushed at his wide shoulders with all her strength, but he was as solid, as immovable as a stone wall.

''Go away and leave me alone!'' she screamed.

''Yo' callin' me, Miz Wy'bon?'' said Cindy at the door.

They both looked up at the young woman whose usually smiling face was suddenly menacing. Her huge hands were doubled into fists. Under the threat of her flashing black eyes, Jack got awkwardly to his feet.

Rita smiled gratefully. ''No, Cindy, I didn't call. I thought you'd gone to your room to watch television.''

''No, Ma'm. I'll be right here in the kitchen, if y'll needs me. And I got me a good sharp mead cleaver,'' she warned as she turned away.

91

Jack's face was as grim as Cindy's when he looked down at Rita. "Just remember what I told you about King. You watch your step, Missy." He went out to the foyer and, rpesently, the front door slammed after him.

Rita sat where Jack had left her, while Cindy went about bolting the doors and windows before saying a cheery good-night and going back to her room. The house settled down to blissful silence, except for the crackling of logs settling in the fireplace and the rain spattering against the windows like shots from little machine-guns.

Rita shivered. The menacing presence of Jack Wybron still seemed to fill the room. He had taken her business out of her hands, and now he was curtailing her freedom. Jack was trying to wear her down. He watched her like a hawk. She knew the game he was playing, threatening to take Bobby away from her. He had it all figured out that she would marry him and turn her business over to him in order to keep her son from being sent away to school.

The telephone jingled and she jumped to answer it, hoping it was Tony. Or Daddy. Or someone she could confide in.

It was Bette Carey.

"Hello, Rita. Is this an ungodly hour to call?"

"No, of course not, Bette. I've been sitting here by the fire feeling lonely."

"Oh?" Bette's monosyllablic response carried understanding and sympathy. "Well, look darling, would the thought of a party cheer you up?"

Rita laughed. "it might. Tell me about it."

"The usual crowd. Saturday night. If I invite a nice man for you, will you come?"

Rita turned the thought over in her mind. This invitation was like a hand held out to her in her darkness, a respite from the emptiness of her life.

"It sounds like fun," Bette," she said slowly. "But if you don't mind, I'd like to come alone. Then, if I decide to slip away early, I won't spoil some nice man's evening."

"Whatever you say," Bette agreed.

The unpleasant image of Jack Wybron vanished from Rita's mind as she considered the pleasure of being among friends. If she knew Bette, there would be music and dancing, high-jinks, and hilarity. Tony would be there, and Margaret, of course. All the old crowd. If it became too painful without Ron, she had left herself an out. She would just slip away, and nobody would notice. Getting back into the swing of things would have to be faced sooner or later, and Bette's party would be a good start.

CHAPTER 10

Margaret King sat at her dressing table, staring into the mirror. Behind her, Tony was having his customary struggle with shirt studs. He hadn't noticed his wife's new dress, purchased especially for Bette's party. It was a slim column of flame that did nice things for her eyes. Her fresh permanent was the most successful one she'd ever had. It gave her an alive look, with its brown curls lifting high above her brow and ears. She was almost pretty. But Tony didn't notice.

Margaret dreaded this party. She was beginning to dread going anywhere. Every time she saw two heads together, she had the feeling they were gossiping about her and Tony—and Rita. Tony's guilty manner when he came home late, and his sporadic spells of irritability around the house made her even more suspicious. She would have an opportunity to see Tony and Rita together at the Careys' party. After tonight, she would know.

Tony shrugged into his dinner jacket and turned to her with a smile. "Ready? Is that a new dress? Nice color."

Margaret returned his smile wanly. *Nice color.* As she slipped the flame-colored stole around her shoulders, she wondered what he might say to Rita under similar circumstances.

A full moon was shining, making a white path out of the highway. Trees and houses stood out in bold relief. One could drive without headlights on a night like this.

Tony hummed a popular tune as he drove down Osceola Avenue and turned into Ocean Parkway. Evidently, he was looking forward to this party.

Lights glittered festively from the Carey house on the ocean front as Tony parked in the wide circular driveway.

In ruffled black chiffon, Bette looked the perfect hostess tonight. Margaret could see her and Dwight in the drawing room as she mounted the wide stairs to leave her wrap in an upstairs bedroom. Most of the guests had already arrived. She caught a glimpse of Bart and Anne Elsnar, but she didn't see Rita. Hopefully, Rita wouldn't show up. She hadn't been going out much since Ron's death.

Tony was waiting at the foot of the stairs, craning expectantly over people's heads, when Margaret came down. The orchestra was playing for the dancers on the polished floor. In another room, some older people were making up bridge foursomes at little tables.

"Dance?" Tony asked listlessly after they talked a few minutes with Dwight and Bette.

Margaret sighed with contentment as he took her into his arms. More than anything in the world, she liked to dance with Tony. She was lost in enjoyment when she felt his arm stiffen around her. Glancing over her shoulder, she saw Rita standing in the doorway. A little shiver went through her. In a glamorous blue-chiffon gown, with yards of satin ribbon circling the skirt, Rita outshone every other woman there. Margaret felt as though she were drowning in a sea of perfume and flowers and bright eyes and swirling silks, and she laid her head for a moment against Tony's shoulder.

He looked down at her. "Don't you feel well?"

"For just a second I felt a little faint," she said. "It's passing." An old, instinctive bid for attention, she thought. I mustn't let myself do that.

"Feeling better now?" Tony asked.

She nodded.

After that dance, he left her with a couple of other young wives. She had expected that, too. He didn't instantly appear with Rita, who seemed to be enjoying herself by dancing with one man after another, like a debutante at her first ball. Tony was at the bar, Margaret discovered a little later, washing away his disappointment. When he finally caught up with Rita, Margaret watched as he held her close, his chin resting on her head, as it had on that night three years ago when he had proposed to Margaret with a desperation she hadn't understood at the time.

Dwight Carey cut in. For a moment, Margaret was afraid Tony wouldn't surrender Rita. He pulled her closer, arguing with Dwight, laughing down into her face. Rita pushed Tony away playfully and he released her. He was putty in her hands. Margaret looked at him expectantly, hoping he would ask her to dance again. But he went back to the bar. He had forgotten about his wife sitting in a corner, waiting. She was alone now. The other husbands had long ago come for their wives.

The sound of hilarity, spiced with lively music, swirled around her in cacophony like a bad dream until she was unable to endure it—and Tony's indifference—any longer. She stood up and slipped outside. Stumbling against a chair in a dark corner of the breezeway, she dropped into it, glad to escape all those watching eyes.

The terraced walk to the seawall gleamed like silver, and the moon made an uneven path across the ater. White sails danced for an instant across the gold of the moon, then disappeared into silvery mystery. Down in the grove, where persimmons and tangerines hung heavy on the trees, a mockingbird sang. If only Tony would miss her and come looking for her here, perhaps the night and the moon would lend Margaret a little of their beauty and mystery to enchant him.

Then she heard his voice. Her heart leaped to meet it as she sat erect in her chair, smiling expectantly.

"This is more than I dared hope for," he was saying. "Getting you alone under a full moon."

Margaret started to get up. She started to say, "I was waiting, darling," but just then Tony walked into the moonlight. There was someone with him.

"Tony, please be serious for a minute," Rita pleaded.

"I've always been serious about you." His voice was not quite steady.

"Tony, Jack Wybron came to see me the other night. He was, well, to say the least, difficult."

"What do you mean?"

Rita walked over and leaned against the wide stone coping around the breezeway, her head thrown back, moonlight on her face. "He asked me to marry him."

Tony gasped. "Rita, you wouldn't!"

"Of course, not. You know how I detest Jack. He said something else, though, that made me shudder."

Margaret started to get up. She would have made her presence at once, only she had been so startled. This didn't seem the right time to pop out, either. Rita might be consulting Tony about some legal matter and would be annoyed at an interruption. If she just didn't listen. . . .

"Was it about you and me?" Tony asked.

"Yes. He said people are talking. He said it's got to stop. You can't come to the house anymore. If I have business with you, I'll have to go to your office."

"Look, honey," Tony's voice was low and tender, "you're not going to let that lug dictate to you?"

"I have no choice. He would stop at nothing. He even suggested I'm not competent to raise my son. He wants to send Bobby to a military school if I don't shape up. He's malicious and vindictive."

Her voice broke. With a little inarticulate murmur, Tony swept her into his arms.

Margaret, cringing in the shadows, wished the earth would open up and swallow her. It was humiliating to have to sit here and witness this. It would be even worse to confront them.

Her heart jumped into her throat as Tony cried savagely, "Why am I so helpless when I love you like this?"

Instantly, Rita was out of his arms. "Tony, you didn't mean that. It's just the moonlight. It's—it's my fault. One of my weak moments. I'm sorry."

He spoke slowly. "Rita, you used to love me. You still love me—a little. Don't you?"

"No, Tony. Please. Let's not be foolish. Just now, I needed a shoulder to lean on, and yours was handy. That's all."

"I understand. You're thinking about your children. No scandal—not even a divorce."

"Don't say that," she begged. "Don't even think it."

"All right," he said. "But don't expect me to give you up just like that. At least one kiss—"

"Tony, I came out here to have a serious talk. Why do you have to—?"

"Please, Rita."

"Tony, someone will hear you."

"I don't care if they do. I'd like to shout it to the whole world that I—"

Rita went to him quickly. "All right," she conceded, "but don't ever suggest such a thing to me again."

Margaret laid her head weakly against the back of the chair and closed her eyes. When she opened them, Tony and Rita were gone.

The rest of the evening passed like a dream. Margaret sat shivering in her hideaway, wondering if anyone else had seen Tony and Rita, had heard what Tony said. She wondered what people were saying about them. About her. Certainly, Tony's ardor was obvious tonight. There was no longer any question in her mind.

When she heard motors sputtering in the driveway, she went in. Tony was leaning over the bar, pushing a half-filled glass around and around with an unsteady hand.

"Shall we go?" she said.

He blinked heavily, his eyes on his highball. "All right," he agreed. "Might as well."

Rita was nowhere in sight. She must have gone home. Perhaps that was why Tony was so tractable. It was a relief to get out of the warm, bright house into the blessed darkness of the night. He offered no objection when she got behind the wheel of the car. He knew his driving was erratic when he drank. Tony slumped in the seat beside his wife, staring at the road ahead.

Quivering inside, Margaret drove the car home and into the garage. It was her key that unlocked the door, and it was she who led the way into the house. Driving home, she had decided not to say anything to Tony tonight. It was better to sleep on it and examine the situation in the clear light of day. It was too important to bungle, and she was still smarting from shock and pain. Besides, Tony was never himself when he'd been drinking.

As she turned on the bedroom light, she caught a glimpse of herself in the mirror. It was like a dash of cold water. Her high hairdo was flat and limp, and the flame-colored gown gave her skin a gray, pasty look. No wonder Tony had been tempted by the vivid freshness of Rita Wybron.

He walked in heavily. When he caught her eyes on him, he attempted an easy nonchalance. "Have a good time?"

Anger rose in Margaret like a smoldering flame whipped by a sudden gust of wind. "As if you cared!" She was unable to withhold her bitterness.

Tony's face darkened. "What do you expect me to do? Sit and hold your hand all evening?"

That tender little scene in the Carey breezeway was still a raging torment inside her. "I've come to expect nothing from you," she flared. "I'm just your wife."

He straightened with a jerk. "What's that mean?"

"Perhaps Rita Wybron could explain it in her loving little way." Margaret was appalled at herself, but she couldn't seem to stop. "You don't merely hold her *hand*, do you?"

He clenched his fist and she thought he meant to strike her. She shouldn't have started. Drink always made Tony quarrelsome. "Leave Rita out of this, you—you little spy!" His fist hit the dressing table and set all the trinkets dancing. "So now you know."

Margaret covered her face with her shaking hands. Instantaneously, Tony was on his knees beside her. "Oh, Margaret, I'm sorry. It's the drink. You know that."

"Tony, I love you," she cried.

He leaned closer as though he meant to take her in his arms, but he turned away without touching her. "Margaret," he whispered, "what have I done to you?"

She watched him get to his feet and walk away. He looked bewildered, beaten, as he stood there, thrusting long fingers through his thick dark hair. He walked to the door, laid an unsteady hand on the knob, and turned to look at her. His eyes frightened her.

"Meg, tell me you forgive me," he said in a strange, hushed tone that filled her heart with terror.

"I—I forgive you," she said softly.

He went out of the room then. She could hear his unsteady steps going down the stairs leading to the garage. Breathing unevenly, she wondered what he meant to do. A door slammed, then the sound of the car in the driveway came to her. Was he going to Rita now, in the middle of the night?

The sound of the shot seemed to shake the house.

Margaret sat there, petrified, knowing what it was, yet not believing. There was a rattle and clang of cans and garden tools, as though a body had fallen among them. It brought her to her feet. She ran screaming into the night, calling for help.

Margaret never knew how she reached the hospital that night. She remembered calling for help and bending over Tony's prostrate form, kicking aside the gun that lay smoking beside him. She recalled a buzz of voices, someone shouting over the telephone, bells ringing, sirens screaming. Confusion everywhere.

When she awoke in a hospital bed, foreboding struck her forcibly. She was wearing an oversized white gown and glimpsed the flame-colored dress hanging in the closet.

A nurse was standing over her, saying cheerfully, "You had a nice long sleep. How do you feel?"

"Tony!" Margaret gasped, struggling up from a drugged state. "My husband—is he—?"

"Mr. King is in the next room," the nurse explained.

"Is he—?"

"He isn't injured badly, Mrs. King. Just a scalp wound."

Just a scalp wound. His hand had been unsteady. If he hadn't been drinking. . . .

"May I go to him now?" she asked.

The nurse hesitated and glanced at her watch. "It's only six," she said uncertainly, "but I guess it will be all right."

She brought Margaret's negligée and slippers. How did they happen to be here? What had really happened last night? She remembered her neighbor, Grant Ellis,

102

helping her into the ambulance with Tony. She had apparently blacked out.

The nurse led her down the dim, chilly hall into another room. A nightlight glowed softly on the bedside table and a middle-aged nurse sat beside the bed. She arose as Margaret walked in. The two nurses whispered briefly as Margaret approached Tony's bed.

He was sleeping heavily, his head wrapped in bandages. Margaret stood looking at him, her lips grim. *This is my husband,* she thought, *and yet, as I look at him lying there, he's a stranger.*

"I won't be far away," one of the nurses said. "If you need me, just press the buzzer near his pillow."

Margaret nodded and sat down in a chair beside the bed.

"I'm so sorry about this, Mrs. King," said the older nurse. "Mr. King is my lawyer. How did it happen?"

Margaret sighed. That was the question everyone would be asking. How did it happen? With strangers, like these two women, who probably had no inkling of the real situation, she could save her pride by improvising.

"He was cleaning his gun," she said. "Evidently, he didn't know it was loaded."

"At three in the morning?" the younger nurse chirped.

"Men start out early in the morning on a hunting trip," Margaret said coolly. "I'd like to be alone now, if you don't mind."

"Of course, Mrs. King." They went out, their skirts whispering in the hospital silence.

The peculiar odors of anesthetic and sterile solutions fought with the lingering fragrance of her own perfume, the expensive scent Tony had given Margaret for her birthday. She had a feeling the nurses felt sorry for her; she cringed at the thought. Everyone who knew her and Tony would pity her now. Her name and Tony's—as well as Rita's—would be bandied up and down the streets, over teacups and across bridge tables. It was all in the open now.

How long, she wondered, would she be able to bear the humiliation? What would be the outcome? The nurses seemed to think Tony would recover. Then what? Divorce, probably, so he could marry Rita.

She stood up and walked over to the bed. His hand lay quietly on the white wheet. She touched it gently, and she touched his face. The dark bristles on his chin brought tears to her eyes. She liked to watch him shave, to see the boyish smoothness emerge through the thick cream he used. He had never used the electric shaver she had given him last Christmas.

"You're mine now," she whispered. "All mine. If you died, you'd still be mine. Always. Oh, why didn't you—?"

She turned away. *God! What am I thinking?* She felt that alive, he was really lost to her. Much as she loved him, she preferred divorce to living with a man who was in love with another woman.

In that gray, lonely hour, she tried to picture a life for herself without Tony. She could go back to teaching and a meager existence, alone in a small apartment—but not in Oceana Beach, and not right away. It might be a while before Tony was well again, and she would have to see him through that. Then they would talk about it. She would do whatever he wanted. There was no need to think of it now. It has enough for the moment that she was still his wife, that she still had the right to sit there beside him, to love him as much as she liked.

Presently, the sun poked its golden fingers through the venetian blinds and a nurse came in to turn out the nightlight and pull back the drapes. She coaxed Margaret in to going to her room to bathe and dress.

When Margaret got back to Tony's room, a breakfast tray and a magazine were brought to her. The magazine was the latest copy of *Beautiful Homes,* the one that had once featured their house in its pages. Tony had seemed so proud of her then. At that time, Ron Wybron was still alive. Tony had probably resigned himself to the fact that he had lost Rita.

"Someone to see you, Mrs. King," a nurse said at the door.

Margaret's heart jumped. She set the tray aside. Who could it be at this hour? She thought at once of Rita, and her hands began to shake.

The nurse stepped aside as Anne Elsnar walked into the room.

"Margaret!" she whispered, laying a sympathetic hand on the younger woman's shoulder. "I just heard about Tony's accident. Is there anything Bart and I can do?"

Margaret shook her head. With an effort, she pulled herself together and motioned Anne to a chair. This was the first of many ordeals she would have to face. Everything depended on how well she was able to carry it off. The pity in Anne's dark eyes made Margaret cringe inwardly, but she clenched her hands under the magazine and forced a smile.

"Tony's fine this morning," she said.

Anne's face brightened. "Oh," she said, "I'm glad it's not serious. I understood—" She seemed suddenly at a loss. "Are you staying on here?"

"For today, anyway," Margaret said. "I had no idea this hospital was so nice. Lovely view from these windows."

Anne wasn't looking at the view. She was looking around the room. Her eyes were wistful. "I'm more at home in a place like this than anywhere else in the world," she said.

It was Margaret's turn to feel pity. She knew that Anne had been a doctor. It didn't seem possible this morning, when she looked so frail and beaten and slumped tiredly in her chair. The fine lines in her face seemed to have deepened since she had come into this room.

Tony stirred and groaned. An alert, awake look came over Anne's face. She half arose from the chair just as the door opened and Dr. Emmett came in. The doctor was a big, vibrant, blustering woman, a bit awing, Margaret thought.

Dr. Emmett's fine gray eyes, behind their dark-rimmed glasses, lighted up when she saw Anne. "How do you do, Dr. Tallman?" she said with her hand out. A miraculous change came over Anne. She stood up, tall and straight, and grasped the other woman's hand. All of a sudden, Margaret looked young.

"Interested in this case, Dr. Tallman?" Anne might never have been married nor borne children for all the notice Dr. Emmett gave to that phase of her life.

"Tony and Margaret are my friends," Anne explained.

The older doctor motioned Anne to the bedside, where they discussed Tony's case in low tones. Margaret watched and listened, her ear confused by unfamiliar medical terms. She thought, *I'd trust Anne more, I think. She has the knowledge, but she also has something else: gentleness and understanding, something, as a wife and mother she has absorbed through the years. Something Dr. Emmett's cool professionalism lacks.*

The latter said to Anne before leaving, "You're talents are being wasted, Dr. Tallman. We certainly could use you here. Think it over."

Anne came back and sat down, looking bright and alert. For a while she had been in her element. Herself. Dr. Tallman. She smiled radiantly at Margaret.

"Watching you just now was a revelation, Mrs. Elsnar," Margaret said. "Mr. Elsnar must be a remarkable man to induce you to give up the profession you loved so much."

Anne shook her head. "He isn't remarkable, Margaret. Few men are. But we fall in love and we marry. That's supposed to be the Big Profession for women. We work harder at it than at anything else. We're not always successful. Sometimes, I get the feeling I might have been a better wife."

Margaret looked out the window at the palm leaves chattering in the strong breeze from the sea. The Anne Elsnars of the world probably never had to face a situation like hers.

As if divining her thought, Anne went on. "Bart hasn't been the easiest man in the world to live with. He's so big and strong and full of vitality, I've found it difficult to keep with him. He's always had an eye for a pretty woman, too."

Margaret glanced at her quickly. Anne's expression was innocent enough. "But that's a failing with a lot

107

of men, I guess," she went on easily. "It takes some of them a long time to learn that a good wife may possess qualities that make other things, like easy charm and superficial beauty, seem unimportant."

"But you have good looks, as well as the other qualities," Margaret said. "You wouldn't have any problem—"

"Oh, wouldn't I!" Anne was looking at the wall over Margaret's head, smiling. "Once there was a girl from Georgia. A preditory creature, if ever I saw one. I might have lost Bart that time. They were both pretty serious, but I didn't see why I should step aside."

"What about your pride?" Margaret broke in.

"Well, I guess I wasn't thinking about that," Anne admitted. "It was just before Bill was born."

"Oh," Margaret settled back in her chair. "That's different."

Anne shook her head. "Even if there hadn't been any children, I'm not the type to spinelessly sit back and hand over my husband to another woman."

"You were probably as pretty as the other girl," Margaret said.

"Pretty?" Anne repeated, as though that hadn't occurred to her. "Why, come to think of it, she wasn't the least bit pretty. But she was outgoing. Jolly. She had the sort of facile charm that is irresistible to many men."

"Charm," Margaret said dreamily. "That's something you have to be born with."

"Not necessarily. For a while there, I tried to ooze charm from every pore," Anne laughed. "It was the hardest thing I ever did. Of course, I knew I had the firmness of the marriage bond on my side, and it can be a very strong bond—if a wife is wise and patient."

Margaret wriggled uncomfortably. It was strange to be party to this woman's confidences. She was Rita's mother! Somehow, Anne didn't seem the sort who would blurt out her heart's secrets to another woman, not under ordinary circumstances. She must have a motive.

"About the Georgia woman, I mean, was it that serious? How were you able to forget? Oh, I know you couldn't forget." Margaret realized she was floundering, but she had to ask, "What I mean is, how could you forgive something like that?"

Margaret felt that Anne was advising her, in a roundabout way, to stick to Tony, to suffer humiliation and heartache if she had to, but to keep on trying. Rita might be Anne's beloved daughter, but Margaret couldn't help feeling that, in this situation, Anne was on the side of Tony's wife.

After Anne left, Margaret stood up and walked over to the bed. Tony still slept like a tired child. Lying there, he looked young and appealing and singularly guileless.

"You're mine, Tony King," she whispered, clenching her firsts determinedly, "and I'm going to fight to keep you."

CHAPTER 11

On her way home from the Carey party, Rita's conscience began to prod her. If she hadn't been there, Tony wouldn't have had the opportunity of declaring himself so strongly. She blamed herself for letting him get out of hand. She had known all along she only had to let down the bars a bit and Tony was ready to take advantage of her. That one kiss. She shuddered, exquisitely. It had been a mistake. Determinedly, Rita fought back its memory. In a more subdued frame of mind, she prayed that no word of the party, of that scene in the breezeway, would reach the ears of Jack Wybron—or of Tony's wife.

Her mind switched to another embarrassing moment. As she was fleeing from Tony, she had bumped into another man in the dark breezeway. His arms had closed around her slackly and, for a couple of heartbeats, she had rested against him, a haven in her sudden need. She seemed to have had one emotional upset after another tonight after pushing the man away.

"All right now?" he had asked.

"Yes," she whispered and hurried away across the moonlit drive to where her parked car. She had no idea who the man had been. It might have been any one of the guests, but Rita was grateful he hadn't taken advantage of her in a weak moment, as some men might whom she knew. She hadn't recognized his voice, but he had said only three words, "All right now?" His tone had seemed compassionate, and she had a feeling that, whoever he was, he would never mention the incident.

Cindy and the children were asleep when she Rita herself into her dark, silent house. She crept softly up the stairs, letting the moon shining through the hall window guide her. Even her bedroom was bright with moonlight; she didn't turn on the lights. She slipped out of her filmy gown and hung it in the closet. Her face was only a blur in the mirror as she sat down to remove her makeup. In ten minutes, she was undressed and in bed.

That night, for the first time since Ron's death, she did not cry herself to sleep. She was thinking of Tony holding her close and demanding of the peaceful night, "Why am I so helpless when I love you so much?" With those words ringing through her, Rita fell asleep.

It was morning, bright and sunny but cool, when she was awakened by the ringing of the telephone on her bedside table.

She reached for it sleepily.

"Rita?" It was her mother's voice. "Heard the news?"

She stifled a yawn. "What news, Mother?"

"Tony King shot himself last night,"

Rita stiffened. "What?" she gasped. "You mean he—?"

"No!, he didn't kill himself," Anne said. "He's

111

in the Oceana Hospital. Pretty scandal, isn't it? I'm going to see Margaret.''

"Oh!" Rita's heart began to beat wildly. "Ask Margaret if there's anything I can do."

"Perhaps Margaret feels you have done quite enough as it is," Anne said crisply.

There was a determined click in Rita's ear. She replaced the receiver and began to shiver. Even her teeth were chattering. If her mother understood the situation so clearly, then other people must also. How much had they noticed last night? Tony had cut in on her every other minute, like an infantuated boy. He quarreled good-naturedly about letting other men dance with her. Had people seen them go out on the breezeway together? What if someone had seen her in Tony's arms? "A pretty scandal," her mother had said.

Rita showered and dressed quickly and went downstairs. Cindy was in the kitchen getting breakfast ready. There was a fire blazing in the living-room fireplace, and a small table had been set in front of it. A pitcher of orange juice stood at Rita's place. She poured some into a tall galss and drank it slowly. It was sweet, tangy, and good, slipping down easily. Food, even Cindy's delicate hotcakes, would choke her this morning. She supposed she ought to go to the hospital, yet she felt guilty and uncomfortable about it. On the other hand, wouldn't people notice and comment if she didn't go? Would Margaret think it strange? She walked the floor unable to decide what to do, thinking, *Tony! Tony! Why did you do it?*

When it was time to get the children up, Rita told Cindy she would bathe and dress them herself. It would give her something to do. She couldn't rid herself of a feeling of guilt.

When she drove Bobby to school, she was surprised that the town, the streets, everything looked as usual. The sun shone brilliantly. It was a clear, cold day. She waved and called out to other young mothers of the "tote squad." They all returned her greeting, but they seemed too busy to stop and chat this morning. They just dropped off their charges and whirled away without a backward glance. Of course, it might mean nothing. Most mothers with several small children were very busy. It was Rita's first bad moment.

She had several errands to perform downtown.

Dave Elliott at the drugstore squinted his little pig eyes at her and said, "Funny thing about Mr. King shootin' himself, wasn't it? Must be tired of life."

"I just heard about it. Obviously, it was an accident." She strove for naturalness but felt the hot color leap into her face.

"Ye-ah?" Dave drawled the word out unpleasantly.

"I'll take some of Bobby's cough medicine, Dave," she said.

"Yes, Ma'am," he grinned.

Plump Mabel Corey at the cosmetics counter was more direct. "Wasn't that awful about Tony King? Someone said he was cleaning a gun. At three in the morning! You believe that, Miz Wybron?"

"He must have been going hunting," Rita said.

"I'll just bet he was," Mabel whinneyed. "He sure musta been planning on going hunting. You've heard the old one about a fella hunting d-e-*a*-r 'stead of d-e-*e*-r."

"That is an old one, Mabel," Rita agreed, hoping her smile looked natural.

She drove home swiftly. If she needed anything else downtown, she would send Cindy.

Around eleven o'clock, Rita heard a car door slam

out in the driveway. She was knitting a sweater for Babs and drew in her breath with a little gasp when Jack Wybron came briskly around the house and opened the door.

"Well, well, you look calm and cool this fine day," he said.

"Good morning, Jack," she sad distantly.

He sat down in a chair facing her and, for a long moment, there was silence except for the click of her knitting needles. She looked up nervously to find his eyes on her, his lips curled unpleasantly.

"Beautiful, cold-hearted Siren," he taunted.

Her heart jerked, but she went on knitting. "Whatever that means."

"You're a cool one, Rita. Your lover lies at death's door, and here you sit calmly knittin'."

She dropped the work in her lap and her eyes blazed. "What are you talking about?"

"Don't tell me you haven't heard about Tony King."

"Yes, I heard about Tony's accident."

"Look, Rita, let's stop beatin' about the bush. Tony King shot himself last night or early this mornin'. It was no accident, and you know it. People are talkin'. You can't pull the wool over people's eyes, you know. I heard Tony made a perfect fool of himself over you at the Carey shindig last night. And you let him."

"Whenever something unpleasant happens, the rumor-mongers get busy," she declared heatedly. "We go to parties to enjoy ourselves. Tony probably had a good time. I know I did. That's all there is to it. There were lots of other people there, you know. Tony's accident had nothing to do with me."

Jack shook his head.

114

Rita wrapped the small sweater around her hands so he couldn't see how they were trembling. "I'm not as heartless as you try to make out. Naturally, I'm sorry it happened. Tony and Margaret are friends of mine. They were friends of Ron's, too."

"And you didn't encourage him to hang around you last night? From what I hear, that's a joke. I can't understand what you were doin' at that party in the first place. You're supposed to be the sad little widow mournin' for her dead husband."

She heard Babs's voice singing, high and sweet, in a distant part of the house. Her hands closed convulsively around the little sweater. When she allowed herself to speak, she sounded hysterical, even to her own ears. "I don't know why I sit here and let you insult me!" She hoped he wouldn't guess it was stark fear of what he might do to her and her children, rather than injured innocence, that prompted her excitement.

Jack leaned over and clumsily patted her shoulder. "All right, Rita. Take it easy. Maybe King shot himself because he couldn't have you. That's understandable to any red-blooded man."

Rita restrained a shudder at his touch. "Please don't come to me with any more crazy gossip, Jack," she said. "It's been hard enough for me since Ron—" Her eyes filled with tears as she bit back the cruel words.

All softness vanished from Jack Wybron's manner. "All right. But I'm keepin' my eye on you. So watch your step, Missy."

Rita didn't see her brother-in-law go. Tears were blinding her, and she couldn't stop shaking.

Later, when she was able to think composedly again, she decided it might be wise to show up at the hospital and inquire after Tony. She needn't see him. She wouldn't even have to see Margaret. Just ask.

At the hospital, an insistent nurse piloted Rita firmly down the hall, assuring her Mrs. King would be only too happy to see one of her friends.

"Poor woman! She's so shook up," the nurse twittered. "Just sits by Mr. King's bed, looking at him." She opened a door at the end of the corridor. "A friend to see you, Mrs. King," she piped.

Margaret stood up. An odd look crossed her face when she saw who it wqs. Her eyes looked even bigger and sadder than usual. "Hello, Rita," she said coldly.

"Margaret, I'm so sorry about Tony."

"I'm sure you are."

Rita shrugged uncomfortably. "Is there anything I can do for you, Margaret?"

"No, thank you," the other woman retorted with icy courtesy. "There is nothing more you can do *for* me—or *to* me. You couldn't leave Tony alone, could you? With your looks, you could get *any* man, but you had to have Tony."

"I'll forgive that remark," Rita broke in gently, "because I know how upset you are."

"What wife wouldn't be upset after seeing her husband with you in the Carey breezeway last night?"

Rita caught her breath. So Margaret had seen them.

"I don't know what you saw, but if you heard our conversation, you know you have nothing to fear as far as I'm concerned."

To her amazement, Margaret burst into tears, but she recovered her composure quickly. "I did hear, Rita," she said. "And I believe you. I know that's the reason Tony tried to—"

Rita felt small and forlorn as she looked from the

116

weeping woman to the man on the bed. "Margaret, I have to tell you this. One day, I stood beside a hospital bed watching another unconscious man. His eyes never opened again. When I lost him, I lost everything. I buried my heart with him."

She felt the sting of tears as she turned and fumbled for the doorknob.

Behind her, Margaret said gently, "Rita, I'm sorry. I didn't mean—"

As Rita went out to her car, Margaret's big eyes seemed to follow her. The other woman's accusing words were like whips that lashed at her until she bled with guilt. She drove out to the highway, turning instinctively toward the causeway and the ocean. She was scarcely conscious of the scenery, the cars, or the people she met. There seemed to be swarms of huge black buzzards, their raucous sinister wails swooping low over the bridge across the causeway where fishermen dropped their catch. *Buzzards,* she thought.

Without realizing it, Rita was following a familiar pattern. Whenever she and Ron had needed to thrash out their cares, they had always gone down to the sea and sat close together in the car, watching the turbulent Atlantic gather the waves and fling them playfully against the shore. The wonder and the power and the majesty of it never failed to dwarf their problems, resolving them into satisfying solutions.

The parking space in front of the casino was empty today. Salt spray but the windshield as she turned off the ignition. With her head against the back of the seat, where once a warm shoulder offered tender support, Rita lay watching the waves until the sun dropped lower and lower and finally fell, like a great golden penny, into the sea.

117

CHAPTER 12

The excitement over Tony King's accident subsided, but it still continued to trouble Anne. Though she had heard it, she surmised there might be gossip involving Rita. She had seen enough at the Carey party to worry her. Every time she had looked up from her bridge hand she had seen Tony and Rita together. Other people certainly must have noticed, too. It wasn't seemly behavior for a young widow with two children. She meant to speak to Rita the next time they were alone.

As usual in the Elsnar household, another problem was already building toward a crisis. Even as she was thinking about Rita, Anne could hear the heated discussion between Bart and Bill in the library.

"I've been supplementing your allowance for weeks," Bart barked. "What do you do with the money? Light cigarettes with it?"

"Well, gee whiz, Dad, a fellow has to keep up his end," Bill argued. "I can't sit around and twiddle my thumbs. I have to have some social life."

"Meaning girls, I suppose. I've asked other fathers. Their sons seem get by on their allowances."

A chair clattered impatiently.

"Who is the girl, Bill?"

There was a little silence. "Well, look, Dad," Bill explained, "it isn't a *girl*. You see, Bette Carey has been awfully nice to me. I mean, she taught me how to do some old dances and play contract bridges, and she's going to do something about that song I wrote."

Anne closed her eyes and drew in a small, shuddering breath.

"Well, I'll tell you, son," Bart drawled, "we all get crushes on older women when we're young. Mrs. Carey is a married woman, so that puts her out of the running as far as you're concerned. She's been kind to a young fellow. All right, take her out to dinner just this once to show your appreciation."

Unable to believe her ears, Anne was on her feet and across the room while Bart was still speaking. He stopped when he saw her standing in the library door, white with anger.

"What is it, Mother?" he asked quietly.

Bill's color deepened as his eyes met his mother's.

"I overheard the splendid advice you just gave your son." she said. "Instead of taking away some of his privileges for chasing after a married woman, you urged him on!"

"Privileges?" Bart repeated. "Like what?"

"Like dating on week nights and using your car any time he feels like it. He needs to put more time into his studies. That's what we're sending him to college for."

Bart interrupted the excited flow. "As it happens, I didn't finish what I was going to say."

"You didn't have to. It was all very plain." Anne turned to her son Bill, who stood nervously kicking at the fringe on the rug. "Bill, I forbid you to see Bette Carey again. Is that plain?"

Bill looked dismayed. "But Dad said—"

Anne turned to look at Bart.

"I *did* tell him he could go this one time, Anne," he said, with a conciliatory grin. "But what I was also going to say, Bill is, I think it would be nice to ask Mrs. Cary out to dinner, but you're also to ask Dwight. Savvy? Take a girl from your crowd along and make it a foursome."

"Wouldn't that seem odd to Dwight?" Anne broke in. "The Elsnar kid taking the Careys out to dinner?"

"Do you have a better idea?" Bart demanded.

"Yes," she said. "Why not forget the whole thing?"

Bill took advantage of the argument to say "Thanks, Dad" as he ran out.

Anne felt sick while listening to her son's retreat. There must have been a financial transaction before she had arrived on the scene. She was so angry with Bart, she couldn't speak more than a minute. They never seemed to agree about how to handle the children. She favored a certain amount of discipline, and Bart favored what he generously termed "guidance." It was more like indulgence. If Anne tried to pin Bart down about his reasons for being easy-going, he would say he wanted his children to enjoy their youth and realize their father loved them.

She stood looking out a window. The westering sun was painting a glowing backdrop behind the palm trees and low, square houses. The faint sound of the surf came to her. In a few minutes, night would fall and blur the picture. In a few minutes, her anger would also fade. Perhaps, just this once, she and Bart might be able to talk calmly and sensibly about Bill and Bette Carey. About Rita and Tony. About what they could do about them, if anything.

Bart was in no mood for talk. His own quick anger had reached a peak and blazed out at her. "If you'd keep out of it when I'm trying to get something across to the kids, we could settle our little difficulties sensibly. But, no! You have to barge in and shoot holes in my arguments. Make me look a fool to the kids! That's what you want, isn't it? You're so afraid they'll respect me, you'd sink to any depth, I believe, to accomplish your purpose."

"I'm *always* considering the children," she said coldly. "*They're* the important ones. I'd fight for them to my last breath."

Bart slammed his book down on the desk and strode from the room. Standing where he left her, her hand holding her side, where pain gripped her again, Anne could hear him tinkering away in his workshop out behind the garage. The workshop did something for him. He could go there, angry, troubled or discouraged, and come back an hour later, smiling and affable. If only she had some such outlet! She thought of Dr. Emmett's hospital on the outskirts of town and sighed.

Something Bart had just said troubled Anne. "You're so afraid the kids will respect me, you'd sink to any depth. . ." Was she jealous of the children's love for their father? It was an appalling thought.

Darkness fell, and Anne went back to the living room. Mandy had turned on the lights, and a fire was blazing cheerfully in the fireplace. The lamps cast a warm rosy glow over the room that softened the fa-

121

miliar furnishings. She slected a favorite television program and sat down in a deep-blue chair before the fire. A quiet evening by herself might be a pleasant change.

On TV, a well-known columnist was talking about the Thanksgiving holiday just past. Funny, how distant the thought of Thanksgiving left Anne down here in Florida. Back home in New England, it had been one of the happiest times of the year. Snow was on the hillsides, and fat turkeys hung in steamy butchershop windows. Spicy, golden pumpkin pies and scarlet cranberry jelly were on pantry shelves. An air of festivity spread around the big rambling farmhouse. Friendly neighbors ran in and out in mufflers, red mittens, and galoshes. Frost was on the windows in the mornings as you looked out and heard the creak of farm wagons on their way to town. They were glorious, happy days she would never see again.

She wondered if her own children hadn't been cheated a little by never having known the joys of a northern winter. They seemed happy enough, excited enough about the holidays. But somehow it became increasingly difficult for Anne to call summon any feeling for Thanksgiving—or even Christmas—anymore. Was it a sign of age creeping up?

Sitting back, serene and comfortable, looking into the flames, she gave herself up to her memories. The sound of quick footsteps outside interrupted her thoughts. She shrugged impatiently, because she didn't feel like entertaining company tonight.

The door opened and closed briskly. Rita stood there, looking wistful, young, and unhappy beneath the sweetness of her smile. Poor lonely little thing! Perhaps she had come to her mother for comfort.

Anne straightened in her chair and smiled. "Hello, sweetheart," she said with unaccustomed tenderness.

"All alone, Mother? You look so pretty in red with your nice black hair. I wish my hair was that color."

"Your hair is much prettier, dear, with its golden highlights."

Rita drew up an ottoman close to Anne's chair and sat down, leaning back against her mother's knees.

Anne looked down at the bright head and reached out to touch it. "Anything wrong, dear?"

"Well, no. Not exactly. Just feeling blue."

"Worrying about something, Rita?" Anne wet her dry lips. "Tony King maybe?"

Rita turned quickly and looked up into her mother's face. "Why do you say that?"

"Well—"

"Do you think people are blaming me for what happened?"

"They might be. After all, you and Tony were not very discreet at the Carey party."

Rita's shoulders drooped. "I know we weren't," she admitted. "Tony's still in love with me. He told me so that night."

Anne's body tensed, but she kept her voice even. "I see. How about you?"

Rita shook her head. "There will never be anyone but Ron for me."

Relieved, Anne said crisply, "Then you owe it to yourself, and to Tony and Margaret, to send him about his business."

"I intend to."

"Do you think he shot himself because of you?"

"Yes, I think he did."

"But that's terrible! Suppose it had been more serious?"

The girl shuddered. "Can't you imagine how often I've thought of that?"

"Don't just think about it. Do something about it," Anne said a little impatiently. "What on earth possessed you to be so flighty at the party that night?"

"I guess it was in reaction to Jack Wybron. He upset me. He claims to be in love with me, too—if you can imagine Jack being in love with anyone but himself. I think he's in love with my property. Marrying me would give him the chance to take over. He's making life miserable for me. He even threatened to send Bobby away to school if I don't behave. I despise him, Mother. What am I going to do about him?"

Anne bit her lip. She had always been proud of Rita's beauty and charm. Now it seemed to her like a trap, a magnet drawing unscrupulous men to the child, like buzzards trying to devour her. Suddenly, fiercely, Anne hated all men. Yet, even though she could have strangled Jack Wybron cheerfully, she realized his high-and-mighty methods might prove to be Rita's salvation.

"I don't know that there's anything you can do, Rita, except follow Jack's advice and behave yourself," she said. "Your father and I are always here to help you when you need us. Would you like Daddy to speak to Jack?"

Rita reached for Anne's hand and squeezed it. "I know how you feel, Mother, and I'm grateful. But I don't want Daddy to get involved with Jack unless it's absolutely necessary."

"Why don't you spend more time at the lumber yard office? That would take up some of your time. Jack had no right to forbid you to go there. You should have spunk enough to defy him. How do you get along with the new manager, by the way?"

"Mark Roberts? I don't try to get along with him."

"That's foolish, Rita. He seems like a very nice young man. He was quite a favorite at the party, I noticed."

Rita turned quickly. "He was at the Careys that night?"

"I don't know how you could miss him," Anne said. "He was the handsomest man there."

"Handsome!" Rita scoffed.

"What have you got against him?"

"I don't trust him. He's Jack's protegé. Probably hand-in-glove with Jack to fleece me out of my business. Maybe he *is* handsome and charming. Some of the biggest crooks on earth are charmers."

Anne laughed. "Well, I can see he hasn't been able to charm *you*."

The telephone shrieked in the quiet room and Anne shuddered.

"I'll get it," Rita offered. It was Anne, and Rita carried the instrument to her mother's chair.

"Oceana Hospital calling," a brisk feminine voice said. "Please don't be alarmed, Mrs. Elsnar. I believe it's your son, William Elsnar, who was just brought in."

After she swallowed heavily, Anne gasped, "What happened?"

"Automobile accident. The boy isn't injured badly. Just a few cuts and bruises."

"Was he alone?" Anne asked.

"As we understand it, he was driving Mrs. Dwight Carey's car," said the crisp voice. "They were found at the sharp bend in the road on the county causeway."

"And Mrs. Carey—the others—were they—?"

"Mrs. Carey was more seriously injured. There were no others in the car."

"Get your father," Anne said briskly as she hung up. "Bill's in the hospital."

"What happened?" Rita's eyes looked frightened and anxious.

"Auto accident. Another scandal. He was driving Bette Carey's car."

Rita ran out to the shop to call her father. When she told him what had happened, he became white and shaken. He immediately went to his wife. They didn't speak, just exchanged a look. Sparks from their previous conversation seemed to be snapping and crackling all around them. Anne was shaking with terror and rage as she followed her husband out to his car.

CHAPTER 13

Bette Carey was bored. The excitement of her party and the events following it had died down. Even poking around in the embers was no longer any fun. She was restless and dissatisfied. Social life in Oceana, she had discovered, was a series of ups and downs. The ups kept her active and stimulated, but it was during the quiet periods she missed having something definite and enlivening to do. Before her marriage, her life had been a busy scramble, mostly for mere existence. Competition in the theatrical world had kept her on her toes. Now, there was nothing to do, nothing to think about or look forward to. Tonight, for instance, she had planned to see a movie with Dwight and drive over to the casino afterward for a drink or a dance or two, only to discover it was the night Dwight had dinner at his club. So she was at loose ends again.

Having nothing else to do, she dressed for dinner. She looked like a page from *Vogue* in her long black-velvet skirt and gold-lame jacket, a diamond star twinkling in her upswept blond hair. While waiting for Cassie's call to dinner, she paced up and down the small upstairs sitting room, smoking chain fashion, wishing she were in New York or Syracuse or Boston of Philadelphia. Anywhere at all where there was a little life! Anywhere else in the world, she thought frantically, she could pick up the telephone and, in a matter of seconds, hear a friendly voice, a *really* friendly voice. Someone who would honestly welcome her to anything the evening might offer.

She called up nostalgic pictures: Dal Garland's turbulent studio filled with shrieking people, and Dal and Bill Seilers utterly oblivious, composing a song at Dal's piano. Charlotte Hedden's apartment in Philly, always busy and crowded. What wouldn't she give for an hour of gossip with Charl tonight! If she were in New York, she would be a socialite in that group now. As Mrs. Dwight Carey. The fancy bistros. Celebrities popping in and out or crowded together at little tables. It might be different if she and Dwight lived in Miami or Palm Beach.

You'd think Dwight would see what this life was doing to his wife. But he couldn't see—or wouldn't. He was perfectly satisfied and happy to go on doing the same things, seeing the same old people, month after month, year after year. He didn't seem able to understand why she should find it less fascinating.

A bell rang faintly somewhere. Bette stood still, listening. She could hear the murmur of Cassie's voice downstairs as well as a man's. She patted her hair, pulled down her jacket, and adjusted a bracelet. The door opened, and Cassie's dark face popped in.

"That Elsnah boy wants to talk to you, Miz Carey."

Bill Elsnar? Bette didn't know whether she was

pleased or not. At least he was *somebody*. He might amuse her for a little while.

"All right, Cassie, send him up," she said.

Cassie had scarcely disappeared before Bill came in, smiling, young, eager. He was handsome. In a few years, when he had a chance to mature, he would be a heart breaker.

Bette held out her hand cordially. "Hello, Bill. Isn't that nice? I've been thinking about you."

"Oh," he said, "you're all dressed up. I ought to have phoned first. I wanted to take you and Dwight out to dinner."

This was new. Why Dwight? None of the youngsters had ever bothered about Dwight before. For one thing, he didn't encourage their friendship.

"Oh, I'm sorry," she said. "Dwight is having dinner at his club tonight." Her mind was working swiftly. This youngster wasn't much of a man, but he was a good imitation. He could get her away, out of this house, into a noisy place where there was a little life. She put every ounce of her charm into her smile. "Would you mind very much our being just a two-some?"

Bill looked startled and a little abashed. Slow color crept up from his cheeks to his dark hair and down into his collar. "Why, I don't know. I'm supposed to ask—, I guess not. I mean, I guess it will be all right."

Bette laughed. Funny youngster, blushing and stammering. Even girls had more poise in this day and age. This *would* be amusing.

"I'll get my coat," she said.

She went into her bedroom and opened the door of her well-stocked closet. In leisurely fashion, she selected a long, plain black-velvet coat. It was satisfying to have so many clothes that she was able to make a choice. She walked over to the dressing table and studied her face in the mirror. A bit more lipstick, perhaps. She looked a jot old and sophisticated for Bill. *Perhaps I'd better not go. This might start another scandal like the Tony and Rita affair that still has the town by the ears.* Unlike most people, Bette didn't blame Rita. It certainly would be nice to have a handsome man like Tony King in love with you. But beggars can't be choosers, and she was bored. Besides, she had accepted the kid's invitation.

She put indecision behind her and went back to Bill. "I've had the skip taken out of my car," she said. "It runs like a top now. Would you like to drive it?"

Bill's eyes were eager. "That would be great!"

They went downstairs. Bette spoke to Cassie about stowing the dinner away in the refrigerator. Cassie didn't seem pleased. She wasn't used to people who changed their minds a dozen times a day. Cassie was the third maid the Careys had had since September, and Bette had firmly resolved not to lose her. She just didn't care tonight.

"Come, Bill," she said.

Her long, low red sports car stood in front of the house with its top down, like a crouching greyhoud ready to leap into action. Bill helped her in and proudly took his place behind the wheel.

"Where are we going?" she asked idly.

"I thought the casino. Unless you have somewhere else in mind?"

"The casino will be fine. We'll have a dance or two."

Bill drove fast but expertly. He kept his eyes on the road and his mind on the car. Bette settled back to

130

enjoy the beauty of the cool and balmy night. A faint sprinkling of stars was overhead.

The casino was brilliant with lights. The two tall evergreen trees in front were generously spiraled with twinkling red and green light bulbs. It was almost Christmas.

Bette thought longingly of frosty nights up north. New York shop windows flaunting a million lovely gifts. Furs and diamonds and diaphanous negligées and fabulous bags and gloves. Crowds hurrying through falling snow, laden with prettily wrapped packages. Santa Claus standing beside a red chimney on every street corner. Cathedral chimes playing carols. And out in the country, icicles hanging from peaked roofs, with Christmas trees sparkling festively in farmhouse windows.

A warm breeze from the ocean ruffled Bette's hair as she walked into the casino.

She saw nobody she knew as she followed Pierre to a table. The orchestra was playing a tune that had been popular a long time ago. She had once danced to it, sung it, with high hopes that some day she would be lucky enough to see with her own eyes a tropical moon pouring its golden beams down on a Florida city.

Well, here she was!

The music was good, more sweet than swinging. That was all right. She was feeling lonely and sentimental.

As she looked around, it seemed to Bette people were only pretending to be happy. Their laughter sounded forced. Most of them seemed to be drinking more than they were eating. If Dwight were here, she might have suggested leaving at once. This was Bill's

131

party; was so proud and important about it, she couldn't spoil it for him.

"I'm going to have a steak," he said. "I suppose yours will be humming birds' tongues on toast."

For once, Bette was going to forget about her figure and enjoy a hearty dinner. "I'll have steak too," she said.

Bill looked at her approvingly.

She wanted a drink, but she didn't dare suggest it. Maybe the infant drank and may be he didn't. She picked up her glass of water and sipped somberly.

"Dance?" Bill asked.

She smiled and stood up. What would people think if she stepped out there and flung herself into the intricacies of one of her stage dances? She restrained herself with the greatest difficulty, admiring eyes followed her and Bill. At least the kid was getting a kick out of the attention they were attracting.

She wondered what people were thinking. That she was an older sister taking her kid brother out for the evening? Or perhaps mother and son. No, they wouldn't believe that. She looked much too young. They might despise her if they knew the truth. A married woman out playing with a boy.

Back at their table, Bill asked if she'd like a drink.

"No, thanks, Bill."

"Oh, come on. How about a martini? I'm having one. Waiter!"

Bette was glad when their dinner came. Bill ate with a healthy young appetite. She followed his example, down to the last morsel of the elaborate dessert. They didn't talk much. What could you say to a kid? Most of the time, Bill stared at her cow-eyed. She didn't think he was very amusing, after all.

After they had two more dances, she was glad it was time to go. Perhaps Dwight would be home when she got there.

Bill was not ready to go home yet. He drove her car to the darkest spot beyond the casino and stopped. "I guess you know this is a great night for me, Bette," he said.

She raised her eyes to high heaven. "Is it, Bill?" she asked patiently.

"Yes, and I think you know why."

She stifled a yawn.

"Because I'm with you," he went on, his voice shaking a little. "I guess you know I've fallen pretty hard for you."

She stiffened in alarm. "Oh, Bill, please. You shouldn't have had those drinks. You're not thinking straight."

"I've heard people say you and Dwight haven't been hitting it off too well. He isn't right for you, anyway. He's a stiff, and you're too young for him."

She laughed indulgently. "Of course, he's right for me. He's really very kind, and he almost never beats me."

"I don't believe you love him," Bill went on. "Or you wouldn't be here with me. This was your idea, you know. You do like me a lot, don't you, Bette?"

She tried to keep the facetious note in her voice. "Why, of course, Bill, I adore you, but—"

Before she could finish, his arms were around her, his hard young lips crushing hers. She was frightened now. She hadn't expected this. She had once caught Bart Elsnar's hot dark eyes on her and she had shivered instinctively; this young maniac who was crushing the breath out of her was Bart's son. Bette wondered if

133

there was any of Anne's cool good sense in this child to which she could appeal.

She struggled out of his arms and pushed him firmly away. "You're taking altogether too much for granted, Bill," she said coldly. "This performance isn't worthy of you."

"Why?" he demanded. "You just told me you adore me."

"Just as I adore all children," she shrugged.

She expected that to squelch him completely, but it didn't phase him at all.

"Oh, I may be a few years younger than you," he admitted, "but what difference does that make if we love each other? We don't have to stay here in Oceana. We could go away some place."

"Now just a minute, Bill," she began.

He didn't let her finish. "If it's money you're worried about, I have a small legacy from my grandfather. I could take care of you. Quit college and get a job. You can divorce Dwight."

She might have been amused if she didn't feel so guilty. "Bill, stop talking nonsense. I'm years older than you. I'm twenty-seven. Besides, I'm in love with my husband."

He sat back and stared at her, his eyes a little bleary. "In love with Dwight Carey?" he jeered. "I don't believe it. You married him for his money. Everybody says so."

White-hot, desperate anger arose in her. It choked her, filling her to bursting. She raised her hand and struck him smartly across the cheek.

She realized instantly it was a mistake. She hadn't meant to hurt the boy. In her anger, she'd been striking at everybody in Oceana Beach who had spoiled hers

134

and Dwight's love with their rotten gossip. They had even poisoned the minds of the children against her.

Bill sat there, stunned.

"I'm sorry, Bill. I didn't mean that," she apologized.

He didn't answer. The blow on his cheek hadn't hurt him physically, but it had gone deep. In youthful desperation, he backed the car out of the parking space, whirled it into the parkway, and caromed down the road.

Faster and faster he drove, until his foot was pressing against the floor board. The speedometer leaped to sixty, seventy, eighty. The wind whirled the pins out of Bette's hair.

"Bill!" she screamed. "Please slow down. You're coming to the bend!"

As her terrified cry died in her throat, the bend in the road beyond the county causeway rushed at them. She didn't know whether Bill tried to make the turn or just let go.

The car leaped into the air. It seemed to Bette they stayed up there forever, suspended between earth and sky. Then the car struck the ground with a terrific crash and swerved sharply.

Bette was thrown free. She could feel herself flying through space. Something sharp cut into her head and face. She had one last, lucid thought before being swallowed by oblivion: *So this is the way it ends for me.*

CHAPTER 14

For the first time in her life, Anne dreaded walking into a hospital. She knew that the soothing voice of a nurse or a doctor over the telephone frequently concealed the gravity of a case. Bill's injuries might be slight, as she had been led to believe, or he might be in serious condition. She had seen people brought into the emergency room after automobile accidents . . . but she mustn't think about that now.

Wearily climbing the hospital steps, she was reviewing memories of Bill from the minute he had been laid in her arms, until tonight, when she had watched him hurrying eagerly out into the night to—what? She would know in a few minutes.

Bart, beside her, looked as grim as a death mask. His hand shook as he reached to open the door. What was he thinking? Was he blaming himself for his indulgence—now that it was too late?

At the desk, he gave his name and asked about Bill.

"We've been waiting for you," said a nurse. "Right this way."

She led them down the hall, opened a door at the end of the corridor, and Anne and Bart followed her into the room.

Bill lay quiet on the narrow white bed. There was a patch across his forehead, and his right hand was bandaged. He opened his eyes. An expression composed half of fright and half of pleading crept over his face as he looked at his father, and then at his mother.

"Here he is," said the nurse. "A little slaphappy from shock. Otherwise, he's hardly scratched."

Anne dropped into a chair beside the bed.

Bart went around to the other side and took his son's uninjured hand in his. He said nothing, but his eyes were eloquent with sympathy and concern.

"You're sure you're all right, son?" Anne asked anxiously. "No pain? No discomfort? Inside?"

Bill nodded. "I'm all right."

"Can you tell me what happened?"

He shook his head.

"Were you driving the car?"

"Yes, Mom. Is—is Mrs. Carey all right?"

Bette! In her anxiety about Bill, Anne had forgotten about Bette. "Injured seriously," the nurse had said over the telephone. But that was an hour ago. By this time, anything could have happened.

Anne's knees shook as she stood up. "I'll go inquire about her," she said.

She went back to the desk and was directed to the second floor, where she found Dwight pacing the corridor, his face ashen. He stood still and clenched his hands when he saw Anne.

"Dwight," she faltered, "is Bette—?"

"She might be dead," he whispered tensely. "Your precious son might have killed her."

137

Anne paled. "I'm not upholding Bill, Dwight."

"I should hope not."

"But, after all, Bette is old enough to know what she is about," she retorted. "What was she doing riding around the country with my son? It isn't likely that he kidnapped her at the point of a gun. Bill is hardly more than a child."

Dwight's big shoulders slumped. "I know," he said. "I know."

At that moment, a door opened and Dr. Emmett came out.

"oh, Dr. Tallman," she said. "I'm glad you're here. This is an interesting case. Would you like to come in a moment?"

Shrinking a little, Anne followed her. She had never had less heart for anything. She couldn't forget that what she was about to see was probably the result of her son's folly.

The slim figure in the bed lay very still. At first, Anne couldn't see the coverlet move. The head and face were completely covered with bandages. One leg was in traction.

Anne heard Dr. Emmett murmuring, but she couldn't focus her attention on anything but that bandaged head.

The two doctors walked over to a window away from the bed.

"Will she be disfigured?" Anne whispered.

"I'm afraid so," Dr. Emmett murmured. "We're worried about that leg, too. Wasn't she a performer of some sort? A dancer?"

Anne nodded.

"Well, she will never dance again, I'm afraid."

"But she will live?"

"Oh, yes, we'll pull her through now," Dr. Emmett declared with professional satisfaction.

Bette, a cripple with a disfigured face! It was unthinkable. Anne turned away from the window and started for the door. Blinded by a sudden rush of tears, she stumbled against a screen.

"Dr. Tallman! What is it? Are you ill?" the older woman stretched out a steadying hand.

"No, I'm a little upset. My son was involved in this accident, too," Anne explained.

Dr. Emmett gaped at her. "Why, you poor thing! I'm so sorry. I didn't realize the boy was yours. Well, you don't have to worry about him. Just a few cuts and bruises. He can go home in the morning."

Anne smiled.

"Why do women like you marry and have children?" Dr. Emmett scolded. "Any woman can do that. Your gift was pretty special, you know. I think you made a great mistake, Dr. Tallman."

As she went back downstairs, Anne was inclined to agree with her old colleague. She felt utterly useless at the moment. It was true, as Dr. Emmett had pointed out, a doctor can't afford to have her mind divided; she cannot stand the strain when her emotions are involved so intensely.

She shuddered to think what life would be like for Bette now. Anne had seen similar cases. Only a very unusual personality could accept a crippled body or a disfigured face and remain stable and resigned. Bette wasn't the type. She wasn't big enough.

Bill came home the next day, very subdued. He couldn't return to his classes, he said, until he could use his right hand and see out of his left eye. He sat all day hunched in a chair, listless and silent. When the evening papers came, he went through them feverishly. He seemed relieved when he discovered his accident in the headlines.

Anne regarded her son coldly. She had been thinking all along of him being her little boy, but he was a young man who had escaped scotfree from a terrible accident, while the woman with him had had her beauty destroyed. It didn't seem to matter that the woman was Bette Carey, of whom Anne had so vigorously disapproved. Anne pledged herself to do everything humanly possible to restore whatever could be saved of Bette's grace and beauty.

The item of the was buried in an obscure section Oceana *Press*, among the classified ads. Mrs. Dwight Carey had been injured in an automobile ccident. Her friends would be happy to know she was recovering in the Oceana Hospital. No mention was made of her companion. The Careys had sufficient influence with the *Press* to keep all the facts from appearing.

Anne drove to the hospital every day. Bette's leg was giving them trouble, and Dr. Emmett was concerned. X-rays showed no fracture, but paralysis had set in. Massage and diathermy treatments were indicated. Anne insisted on doing all the work herself, which pleased Dr. Emmett. With endless patience and a constant prayer in her heart. Anne worked over the helpless leg, her back and arms aching with the effort. She vowed she would salvage everything possible from this pathetic wreck.

As the days went by, her feelings for Bette gradually changed. A doctor-patient relationship began to emerge, and Anne recognized the same empathy she used to feel when she was a dedicated young doctor. During some of these treatments, Bette must have felt acute discomfort, even pain, but she endured it without a whimper. This surprised Anne, turning her former derision to grudging admiration.

At home, she was silent about the work she was doing. She kept her family at arm's length, determined nothing her son and husband could do or say would swerve her from the path of duty.

Bart and Bill seemed to cling together. Their dark, intense eyes followed Anne wistfully. Bart had bungled the situation with appalling consequences. Bill had willfully disobeyed her request to keep away from Bette. He had accepted his father's indulgence. All right. Let him suffer, too.

In spite of her righteous feelings, Anne was lonely. As the short winter days flew by, Bart spent more and more time in his shop, while Bill either remained in his room with his books and his record player or went out with his friends.

Rita ran in occasionally, but she never stayed long and seldom brought the children. There was an odd expression in her eyes when she looked at her mother.

One day she ventured, "I feel sorry for Bill, Mother."

"Why?"

"He's really suffering."

"He deserves to suffer."

"I was just thinking," Rita said softly, "If it were Bobby, I think I'd try to pull him out of it. I'd remember he was just a kid that it was just a mistake he had made."

"A mistake!" Anne broke in. "You wouldn't think it was mistake if you could see that poor girl."

"Well, it was her own fault. She was more to blame

141

than Bill. A woman her age leading a kid around by the nose!''

''If Bill wasn't weak, he couldn't be led around by the nose.''

''Look, Mother. You insisted it was my fault when Tony shot himself. Now Bette's accident is entirely Bill's fault. You expect your children to be perfect and we aren't. We're just people, like everybody else. You can always find excuses for other people's mistakes, but you're like Vermont granite when it comes to us.'' Rita jumped up and dashed out to her car.

Anne lay still on the sofa, weary after her daily visit to the hospital. That afternoon, she had massaged and massaged Bette until her arms and back were in pain. Above and beyond her weariness, a pulse of triumph throbbed in her. She had so wanted to tell Rita, to tell all of them, to shout it from the housetops. *Bette had moved her toes today!* It was similar to painting a masterpiece. Like composing a symphony. Like writing a best-seller. And she had to keep it bottled up inside her because the rest of the family wouldn't understand or care. They were worried only about Bill.

On the wings of that thought, Bill walked into the room. His hands were free from bandages now, and the cut over his eye was almost healed. It didn't look as though there would even be a scar. Scot-free, she thought grimly. He was returning to class tomorrow.

''Tired, Mother?'' he asked, the charm of his smile enfolding her.

Looking up into his haunted eyes, Anne's defenses against her son crumbled. She had a sudden urge to do something, say something, to bring a little happiness, a little youthfulness, back into his face.

142

"Bill," she said, "Bette moved the toes on her injured foot today."

"Oh, Mom, did she?" He dropped to the floor beside the sofa, his eyes boring into hers. "Tell me about it. Rita told me that Natalie Kent, one of the nurses at the hospital, said you'd been there every day working over Mrs. Carey."

"Mom," Bill said, "I've wanted to tell you. I think it's great what you're doing. You're wonderful, you know it?"

Anne couldn't raise her eyes to meet Bill's. His boyish tribute was so unexpected, so heart-shaking, it was something you *couldn't* shout from the house-tops. It was something to hold close, to warm and uplift you.

"Thanks, darling," she said. "I wish I were worthy of it."

"There's something else I've been wanting to tell you," his words tumbled over one another in his eagerness. "I didn't deliberately disobey you and Dad about taking Mrs. Carey out to dinner alone. When I went over there, Dwight wasn't home, and she said, 'How about a twosome?' So what could I do? I had already invited her. I thought about going around to pick up Sally, but Mrs. Carey kind of took over. Maybe I'm not very hip, but I didn't know what else to do."

"I see."

"Mom, I wish you could understand the spot I was in."

Anne sighed. Just to understand—that's all he asked. To understand that he was young, and he hadn't learned yet how to handle a delicate situation or a woman like Bette Carey. To understand that he had been foolhardy and reckless and was now worried and contrite. That he had been punished enough.

Tears filled Anne's eyes. She waited until they subsided before looking up at him and smiling.

"I understand, son."

"So whose pal are you?" he grinned.

"Barnacle Bill, the sailor's," she chuckled.

They remained smiling at each other understandingly for a long moment.

CHAPTER 15

Rita had dreaded taking the children to the lumber yard after their father's death. When her husband had been alive, they had considered a visit to the office a special privilege. Ron had never been too busy to welcome and entertain them. He often took them on a tour of the buildings and explained to Bobby the way the business was conducted, as though he were talking to an adult. While they walked from building to building, he would carry Babs, who usually fell asleep on his shoulder. Rita felt certain it would be a shock to them to see another man in their father's place, particularly a stranger. The time was coming when they would have to face facts.

The time came sooner than Rita expected.

One day, when Bobby was home from school, he lingered at the breakfast table, playing with his cereal and looking troubled.

"What's on your mind, dear?" Rita asked.

"Know what I'd like to do today, Mom? Go down to Daddy's office."

"Why?" she asked.

"Just because."

"But, honey, it won't be the same, you know. There's another man there."

"It's still our office, isn't it? Yours and mine?"

She sensed the curiosity, the need to know what was happening in his old bailiwick and his father's. *Our* office. It was a request she couldn't treat lightly.

"All right, Bobby. As soon as Cindy has Babs dressed, we'll all go down to the office."

The drive downtown was quiet. Rita wondered what Bobby was thinking, but she didn't try to distract him. Was he frightened and apprehensive? She didn't dare ask. Whe just hoped that the situation would work out in an easy, natural way. She could trust Edith and Joe, but she wasn't so sure about Mark Roberts. When she drove up to the lumber yard building, she saw Bobby look over at the strange car.

"New York State," he said. "Isn't that what it says there, Mom?"

"Yes," she said.

Before opening the office door, Rita said a little prayer.

Mark Roberts was standng beside Edith's desk, evidently dictating a letter. They both looked up, startled.

It was Babs who made the first move. She ran across the room and threw her arms around Mark's legs. "Daddy!" she cried happily.

An arrow of pain shot through Rita. "She—she doesn't remember her father, I mean, how he looked," she tried to explain.

Mark lifted the little girl in his arms and she settled

against him. Rita's first impulse was to snatch the child out of Mark's arms and try to set her straight, but Bobby's hand crept into hers as if to restrain her.

"She's such a little thing," Mark said quietly. "She's just confused. Give her a little time, and she will work it out by herself."

They all stood watching quietly. Then Babs spied Edith. With a squeal of recognition, she wriggled out of Mark's arms to be caught up by Ede. The embarrassing moment passed, and Rita introduced Bobby.

"Mr. Roberts, this is my son."

Mark shook hands with the boy.

"I hope we aren't bothering you people at a busy time," Rita said.

"No, indeed." Mark's tone was casual and friendly. "I was just on my way to Sweetwater Oaks. Two new houses are going up there soon, so we decided to get in on the ground floor. Fellow named Carson is the contractor. Do you know him?"

She nodded. "Used to be one of our best customers."

"I know Mr. Carson," Bobby said. "I like him. Daddy took me—"

Mark broke the sudden silence. "Would you like to drive over to Sweetwater with me, Bobby?"

"I'm afraid not," Rita said. "You'll be busy, and Bobby would only be in the way."

"I'm willing to take a chance, if you don't object, Mrs. Wybron."

"Mommy, please!" Bobby pleaded.

It was the "Mommy" that won her over. She had been "Mom" ever since his Uncle Jack had warned Bobby he was "the man of the house now."

"Well, all right," she agreed reluctantly. "You be

147

a good boy and don't bother Mr. Roberts and Mr. Carson when they're talking business.''

After they left, Rita sat down at her dsk, opened the drawer, and took out the books.

"You don't like Mark, do you?" Edith said.

"Mark?" Rita laughed. "So you're on a first-name basis now. It isn't that I dislike Roberts. I just don't trust him."

"Why?"

"That's just it. I don't know why. Maybe because he's a protege of Jack's."

When Bobby didn't return home by the middle of the afternoon, Rita began to worry. All sorts of crazy notions marched through her mind. No one here really knew Mark Roberts—no one but Jack. Suppose Jack had conned Mark into handing Bobby over to him. She put in a frantic call to the office.

Edith said Mark had not returned. "But I'm sure everything's all right, Miss Rita. You know how long it someimes takes to close a deal."

"Yes, I know. I'll wait, Edith."

She would give him two more hours. Then she would call Bart and get in touch with the police.

It was late afternoon when Mark's car drove up to the house and Bobby came running in.

Rita tried to be casual as she greeted him. "How was your day?"

"Super. Know what I had for lunch? A big cheeseburger and milk, in one of them burger places. It was fun."

"How do you like Mr. Roberts?"

"Great guy. We had a good talk."

"About what?"

"Everything. What's for dinner?"

So Roberts was winning over her family as well as

148

her employees and everyone else in Oceana. Even hostesses had pounced on him as an attractive single man to add zest to their parties. He appeared to have a flair for attracting people without much effort on his part.

On a dour November afternoon, Rita answered the telephone and was alarmed by Edith's agitated voice.

"Miss Rita, I think you should come down at once. Mark and Mr. Wybron are having a terrible wrangle."

"What's the trouble, Edith?"

"I don't know. Something Mark did or didn't do, and Jack is threatening to discharge him."

"All right, Edith, I'll be right down," she promised.

She found Edith outside in the lumber yard, pacing back and forth and muttering to herself.

"Don't let him send Mark away, Miss Rita," she begged. "That way, Jack'd take over himself, and neither Joe nor I could put up with him. The whole business would go to pot."

Rita patted her shoulder. "Don't fret, Edith, I'll see what I can do."

When she walked into the office, the shouting stopped, as if it had been turned off by a switch. "What's going on here?" she asked.

"You keep out of this, Rita," Jack snapped. "It has nothing to do with you."

"Anything that goes on in this office is my business," she said. "Now what is it?"

Mark turned and walked over to a window. He looked angry and shaken.

"It's just that Roberts is getting a little too cocky, and I fired him," Jack said.

"What did he do?"

"Now, Rita—"

"What did he do, Jack?"

"He refused to carry out an order of mine."

She recalled the alleged trust fund, and wondered if Jack had hatched another scheme to get possession of the business. "He refused to carry out an order," she repeated. "Was it something in your favor rather than in mine?"

Jack began to bluster again. "It's between him and me. And it's all over. He's fired."

"I'm afraid not," she retorted. "He happens to be an employee of mine. This is my business, in case you've forgotten, and Mark Roberts is staying. I happen to like his work."

"I hope you won't be sorry for your interference, Rita," Jack shouted and stormed out of the office, like a black tornado.

Rita left with a limp wave of the hand. She realized she had been swayed by Edith's plea and hoped she had acted wisely. After all, she didn't know what the trouble was or who was to blame, but she meant to stand by her guns for the present.

Later that evening, when the door chimes sounded, she stiffened her backbone and prepared for trouble. It was probably Jack following up his threat with his usual bombast. When Cindy returned, she was carrying a long box tied with white ribbon.

"I declare, Miz Wy'bon, I believe they's flowers."

Rita was curious as she opened the box. Who would send her flowers? Wrapped in tissue paper were a dozen pink roses and a card.

"Thank you," she read aloud. "The roses remind me of you." It was signed Mark Roberts.

"Land o' Goshen, Miz Wy'bon! You got you'se'f a beau?" Cindy cried.

"No," Rita said. "Nothing like that. Just a thank-you gift."

"Um," Cindy said. "I was hopin'."

"Well, don't hope," Rita said sharply. "Not for anything like that—ever."

While Cindy disposed of the box, Rita stood with the roses in her arms, enticed by their beauty and fragrance. *That man*! she thought. *Now he's trying to win me over*. She shook her head. No, that wasn't quite fair. Why not accept the fact that he appreciated her standing up for him and saving his job? The roses were a token of his gratitude. Nothing more. He had never been presumptuous. If anything, he had gone out of his way to avoid her, which suited her fine. But she had to admit there were certain things about Mark she couldn't ignore, such as, how understanding he had been with Bobby and Babs that day in the office or the way Edith had pleaded with her to keep him on as manager. There was also his concern over Jack's plan to defraud her and her children. And now the roses.

Am I beginning to fall under the Mark Roberts spell, too? she wondered. *Patience! and shuffle the cards, Rita. But watch out for that possible ace up his sleeve*.

On a cold December morning, Edith called up to ask if Rita had heard from Mark. He hadn't appeared at the office for two days, she said.

"Have you called him? Do you have his phone number?" Rita asked.

"He has an apartment in the Chimes Building. I called him there a dozen times. He isn't there. I'm worried, Miss Rita. It isn't like Mark to just walk off without a word to anyone."

That was true. At least he had never given the

impression he was irresponsible. "Have you talked with Jack?" Rita asked.

"He's gone hunting. I called his hotel, and they said he and Lem Furgeson left this morning. Then I called Mrs. Fergeson, and she said Mark wasn't with Jack when he stopped for Lem."

"Well, it is rather strange. But don't worry, Edith," Rita said. "If Mark doesn't show up this morning, I'll go down to the office and take over until this is cleared up."

She wasn't able to take the advice she had given Edith. She couldn't help worrying. She had to admit Mark was dependable and dedicated to his work. He didn't drink. At least there had never been any indication of it, so it wasn't likely he was holed up somewhere with a hangover. The man was alone in a city where he wasn't very well known, so every possibility should be explored.

The first place to start the search was his apartment. She drove down to the Chimes Building and found his name listed in the vestibule. After ringing his bell several times without receiving an answer, she looked up the manager, a Mr. Gorman, who was watering plants at the rear of the building. He was a pleasant, elderly man, who squinted at her over his bifocals.

"Mr. Roberts?" he said. "No, Mrs. Wybron, I haven't seen him. His car is there in his stall. Come to think of it, that car hasn't been out this weekend."

"Mr. Roberts is an employee of mine," she explained, "and I'm worried about him. I wonder, could you let me into his apartment? I'm afraid something is wrong."

"Well, now Ma'm, I'm not sure. I never let anyone in these people's rooms, unless I'm called about the plumbing or something. I never enter an apartment myself. You see, the people trust me.''

She broke into his rambling with a crisp question. ''You do have a master key, don't you?''

''Yes, but I—''

''Mr. Gorman, you know me. You know I would never touch anything that doesn't belong to me. I feel that something is wrong, and I think we should investigate. You can go in with me.''

''All right,'' he agreed, ''if you insist. But it's very irregular.''

The living room of the apartment they entered was orderly, as was the kitchen-dining area. Rita approached the bedroom with Gorman at her heels. The door was closed, and she knocked. A strange, strangled sound that stopped her heart came from within. She flung the door open. Mark lay on the bed, looking white and ill. He was shivering violent, with a blanket pulled up around him. The strange noise she had heard was the rasping sound of his breathing.

''Oh, Ma'm, he's sick. Ain't he?'' the manager whispered.

''I'll call the hospital to send an ambulance at once,'' she said.

With the call completed and assured that help was on the way, Rita went to the clothes closet and found a robe and slippers. In a dresser drawer were clean pajams. Mark's electric shaver and toiletries were neatly arranged in the bathroom cabinet. She pulled a small traveling bag from a shelf in the closet and packed it with everything she thought he would need, choosing a blue suit for when he was ready to check out of the hospital.

When the ambulance crew left with Mark, she

153

thanked Mr. Gorman for helping, took the packed suitcase, and drove to the hospital.

A young doctor came to the desk while she was giving a nurse whatever information as she could about Mark.

"I'm Doctor Allen," he introduced himself. "What didn't this patient receive medical attention before this? The man has an advanced case of pneumonia."

Rita explained the situation.

"Have his relatives been notified?"

"I don't know who his relatives are, or if he even has any. He's from up north somewhere and has been in my employ only a short time."

"Health insurance?"

"I've no idea," she said crisply. "My lawyer, Tony King, will take care of everything until Mr. Roberts recovers."

"*If* he recovers," the doctor said.

Rita left for the office to take over Mark's duties.

Edith was almost tearful when she heard the news. "That poor boy! Oh, Miss Rita, I'm so glad you found him in time. They do think he will recover, don't they?"

"All we can do is hope, Edith. Did he ever mention parents? Brothers, sisters, anyone?"

"His parents died some time ago, I believe. He was an only child. Brought up by an uncle. But I don't know the uncle's name or where he lives."

"Maybe Jack will know when he comes back from his hunting trip. Seems to me, I recall Mark telling me his uncle was a friend of Jack's. Well, Edith, we might as well get on with the business."

Edith gave her an odd look as she returned to her typewriter. "You never did like the boy, did you?"

Rita didn't contradict her, but she recalled the feeling of panic that had set her heart spinning when she saw him lying there so white and ill—and that awful breathing.

In the meantime, it felt good to Rita to get back to the familiar routine. But the situation there had changed. Now, when the telephone rang, it was always "Mr. Roberts" or "Mark" people asked for. And then, "Oh, it's you, Mrs. Wybron. How nice to hear your voice again. May I speak to Mr. Roberts?"

It was frustrating and irritating, and she began to feel unwarranted antipathy toward Mark. Out of concern for him, though, she called the hospital to inquire about him every day. The replies were carefully vague, the sort of guarded information given to friends and acquaintances. She wasn't satisfied until she went to see for herself. There was a "No Visitors" sign on his door.

At the desk, she asked to speak to Dr. Allen. When he appeared, Rita demanded the truth.

"His condition is grave, Mrs. Wybron," the doctor said. "If we had seen him a day or two earlier—but that's water over the dam now."

"Will you call me as soon as he can have a visitor, Doctor? Perhaps it will help if he could see someone he knows."

"You will be the first to see him, when and *if*."

"The "if" bothered her. She wished she knew where to locate Mark's uncle. It would be a relief to turn him over to someone else. Edith would have accepted the responsibility gladly. As it was, she spent most of her spare time on her knees at St. Helen's Church.

The days wore on, and the gloom in the office could

be cut with a knife. Rita was busy at the work she loved, but she couldn't be happy about it under such unpleasant circumstances.

Even at home she couldn't get away from the thought of Mark. Bobby was concerned. The first question he asked every day when she came home was about Mark. He insisted on sending a get-well card. "You sign it, too, Mom," he said.

"No, dear, he will appreciate it coming just from you," she hedged.

The hospital called her at the end of the second week. She could see Mr. Roberts during visiting hours that afternoon. She didn't look forward to the visit, but she had insisted on it. There was no way out.

She found him sitting up in bed and reading the morning *Sentinel*. There was color in his face. A little-boy curl hanging over his forehead gave him an appealing look. When he saw Rita in the door, the brilliance of Mark's smile rivaled the sunshine outside.

"Mrs. Wybron!" he said. "How nice of you to come. You're the most beautiful sight these eyes have beheld in weeks."

"With all these pretty nurses around here?" she teased.

"I guess I've given you plenty of trouble. Dr. Allen told me you had me brought in. He said you saved my life. I don't know how to thank you."

"No need for thanks." She sat down beside the bed. "I'm glad I was able to help."

"Tell me about everything," he said. "About *you*."

"I'm fine. Trying to take your place at the office. But I love it, so take your time getting well. And don't worry about a thing. Edith misses you."

"Good old Edith. She's a great girl." There was an added sparkle in his eyes, as he added, "I hope you miss me a little, too."

This was becoming embarrassing, a little too cozy. She didn't want to encourage it. However, there was no need to answer. Someone knocked at the door. Before either of them could speak, it burst open and a pretty girl of about twenty came gushing in.

"Mark, darling! I thought they'd never let me in to see you. I just rushed right by them, and here I am."

She ran to the bed and kissed Mark on the cheek, leaving a smear of scarlet lipstick like a wound on his face.

He looked embarrassed, "Mrs. Wybron," he said formally, "Miss Stover."

"Oh." The girl's expression was more of a pout than a smile. "This is your boss? And such a pretty one. How kind of you to come visit Mark, Mrs. Wybron."

"I'll leave now that you have company, Mr. Roberts," Rita said.

He looked disturbed. "I'm sorry. I mean, I hope you'll come again. We hardly had a chance to talk. But thank you—for everything."

Driving back to the office, Rita didn't know why she was annoyed. It was good to know Mark was on the mend and had friends who cared about him.

Edith greeted her eagerly. "Tell me about him. How did he look? You didn't stay long."

"Didn't have to. Some girl named Stover came barging in, mushing all over him."

Edith's eyes had a mischievous twinkle. "Well, what do you care, honey? You don't even like him."

Beats me. You've been keening over him like a little mother hen ever since he took sick.''

Rita laughed to let Edith know the teasing didn't bother her. "I would have done the same for anyone sick or in trouble.''

Then why, she asked herself a dozen times that day, am I so upset about that girl? I should be glad he has someone who cares about him. And I am glad. I *am*.

When Mark was ready to leave the hospital, Dr. Allen called her. "Mr. Roberts mentioned a taxi, but I thought you might like to pick him up and see that he gets settled in. It will be a few days before he's ready to go back to work.''

Rita would have opted for the taxi, but since the doctor made such an issue of it, she drove over to the hospital. At the desk, she learned all financial matters had been taken care of, so she went directly to his room. Mark was dressed in the blue suit. His bag was packed and ready.

"This is an imposition, Mrs. Wybron,'' he said, as they were driving away. "I don't know why they didn't call a taxi as I requested.''

"We wanted to make sure you will be properly cared for,'' she said.

"It's all been arranged,'' he said. "I phoned Mr. Gorman and the little German lady who cooks and cleans for me. She will be waiting at my apartment. The doctor shouldn't have bothered you.''

"It's all right,'' she said, but she was glad her obligation stopped at the entrance to the Chimes Building.

Mark came to work the following Monday morning. Rita remained at the office just long enough to fill him in on what had taken place during his absence.

158

When she was about to leave, he stopped her with a hand on her arm. "Could we have dinner tonight? You've been so kind. It's small thanks, I know, but—"

Rita was about to decline, but she caught sight of Edith's eyes daring her to refuse.

"You don't have to thank me," she said, "but dinner would be nice."

"May I pick you up around seven?"

"Seven will be fine."

While she was dressing for the evening in a becoming blue dress Ron had liked, it occurred to Rita that this was a date with a man. She had never had less heart for such a thing, but she would be as pleasant as possible. Afterward, she would give Mark to understand that this dinner would end all future socializing between them.

The evening wasn't as difficult to get through as she had expected it to be. The corsage he sent her was made of pink baby roses that looked lovely on the blue dress. The dinner at the exclusive Riomar Club was excellent and the conversation lively. She caught herself laughing more than once.

On the way home, Mark stopped his car two blocks from her house.

"It's such a beautiful night, would you mind walking the rest of the way?" he asked.

The request was surprising, like the man himself, but Rita agreed to it readily. That way, she could avoid a possibly awkward moment in the car.

They strolled along the quiet street among lights and shadows cast by the full moon.

"I miss the winter nights up north," he said. "One wonderful night, the stars fell all night long. Hundreds

159

of them, like golden snowflakes falling from the sky. Meteors, I suppose they were. I stayed outdoors until three in the morning, watching. I never saw anything like it. And on moonlight nights like this, you could look out and see a buck and a doe, or a doe and her fawn frolicking in the snow. And the dark, leafless trees stood out against the white world like a Japanese print. Other nights, the aurora borealis entertained us, waving colored lights across the skies.''

Rita stood still, enshrouded in Mark's dream. If only she and Ron had taken a winter vacation up north to see all those wonders—stars falling like golden snowflakes, the snow, the deer, and . . .

She came down to earth with a dull thud when she heard Mark say, "I'd like to show you our winter wonderland sometime.''

She started walking briskly. She was almost home.

"Well, here we are,'' she said. "It has been a very pleasant evening, Mr. Roberts, but I mustn't keep you out too late. You need all the rest you can get.''

"I've enjoyed every minute of it,'' he said.

As he came closer, she held out her hand. "Good night,'' she said, "and thank you. I've got my key, so I'll just run on in.''

He stood in the street until she closed the door.

The dying embers in the fireplace filled the room with a rosy glow. Rita curled up on one of the small sofas by the side of the fire. It had been a pleasant evening. Mark was good company. Then why hadn't she asked him in for a nightcap, as she would Tony, for instance? Was this man creeping into her cold heart and warming it just a little? Was she afraid to let him get close to her?

"Oh, no!'' she moaned, springing up and turning

on a lamp. She had been stirred by the magic of the night, the laughter they had shared, the dreams he had aroused of a world she had never seen. In the bright morning light, she would be able to think rationally, to put the events of this evening in their proper perspective.

CHAPTER 16

Green wreaths tied with red bows hung in downtown shop windows. Lighted trees glittered in Florida rooms up and down Oceana Streets in the evenings. Fat red Santa Clauses grinned from the walls of supermarkets. Velvety-red poinsettias blossomed in front yards and gardens. And the blazing sun laughed down on it all in sheer unbelief. Christmas in the land of sunshine.

It seemed odd to Anne, as it had for years, to be sending out cards picturing snowy doorsteps, fur-wrapped skaters, and horses and sleighs racing down drifted country lanes. She helped trim a tree with tinsel and bright baubles and wrapped gifts in holiday boxes with the usual feeling of unreality, as though Christmas had somehow changed place with the Fourth of July.

The mouth-watering aroma of roasting turkey and spicy pumpkin pie filled the house. In the kitchen, there were scarlet cranberries and silver turnips and golden winter squash to prepare. For the children, there were curls of old-fashioned hard candy. Anne closed her eyes and thought she was back on a Vermont farm in December.

She and Bart and the children always went to church on Christmas Eve. Inside the church, candles burned, and a spirit of joy prevailed, just as Anne remembered from back home in New England. The carols and the flowers brought her close to the feeling and meaning of Christmas.

St. Helen's was filled to capacity this Christmas Eve. Rita and the children sat in the Elsnar pew this year, huddled close to Anne and Bart. It was their first Christmas without Ron. Margaret and Tony came in. Tony still looked rather wan. Margaret held her head higher these days. She seemed to have acquired a new dignity. Down in front, Dwight Carey sat in the family pew with his parents. Bette was still in the hospital.

Bart moved restlessly beside Anne as though groping for something upon which to anchor his life and energies. She wondered if he would ever find it. He had been chasing will-o'-the-wisps all the years she had known him. It would be a mercy if, in this coming year, he would find himself.

One thing had become apparent to Anne. Since the night of Bill's and Bette's accident, the mysterious pains that had mystified doctors and made a semi-invalid of her through the years, were bothering her less and less. In her zeal to help Bette and try to counterbalance Bill's culpability, had she proved what Dr. Gordon had once said: "Mrs. Elsnar, I believe it's just your imagination." Had her New England conscience and mental healing worked together? Perhaps her pain had been the bulwark she had erected against the stress of an unsatisfying life.

They knelt for the benediction and then went out

of the church singing carols, as was the yearly custom at St. Helen's. It was a lovely custom, Anne thought. The sound of clear, triumphant voices and organ music followed them down the street. It seemed strange not to feel the tang of frosty air and hear the squeak of snow underfoot. Instead, there were palm fronds rattling in the warm wind that gently caressed their faces and the salty smell of the sea.

Rita and her family were staying at her parents' house over the holiday. *Poor child*, Anne thought. Rita was trying hard to appear happy for the children's sake. She and Mary Louise Reagan, her friend from Orlando, were playing a game with Bobby and Babs, racing down the street.

They were to have the gifts as soon as they arrived home. Bart and Anne had laid all the gifts under the tree in the library that afternoon, so everything would be ready. Anne watched Rita as they walked in. She was unnaturally pale and her eyes were very bright, but she was trying to smile.

Mary Louise went into the library and came dashing back shouting, "Guess what, Bobby! Santa Claus has been here already!"

"He hasn't!" Bobby gasped, incredulous.

"Come and see."

"Come on, old girl," Bill said, lifting Babs to his shoulder. "Hop up on my other shoulder and I'll carry you, too, Rita."

"Listen to Wonder Woman," Rita jeered.

The children shrieked their delight at the sight of the tree. Bill distributed the gifts with silly little speeches that sent the youngsters into gales of laughter.

Rita was kept busy untying ribbons and exclaiming and explaining so that she seemed to forget herself.

Anne sighed with relief when she saw the color creeping back into her daughter's cheeks.

Bart, Bill, and Bobby lay full-length on the floor, playing with Bobby's electric railroad. It would be difficult to decide, Anne thought, which of the three was the most enthralled. Babs promptly set up housekeeping with her new dolls and the little furniture Bart had made for her. Rita and Mary Louise couldn't refrain from making suggestions and trying to participate in the child's activities.

"I wanna play with my own toys!" Babs shrieked at last.

Almost at the same moment, Bobby demanded, "When do I get to run my own railroad?"

Everyone laughed, and Bart declared he'd certainly have some toys of his own next Christmas.

Mary Louise offered to help put the children to bed when they began to nod over their treasures. Anne heard her say, as the two young women climbed the stairs, "Rita, will you come to my room with me? If you're not too tired, there's something I'd like to discuss with you."

Blessed Mary Louise! She would probably talk up a storm, but she'd see that Rita didn't cry herself to sleep tonight. It had been an inspiration to invite her to spend Christmas with Rita.

Anne sat before the fire for a while after everybody else had wandered off to bed. The house was fragrant with the smell of evergreens, blazing pitch, and good food. She was thankful for her home, her children, and her grandchildren. The world would be a barren place for her without them.

The doorbell rang softly. For a moment, Anne wondered if she had imagined it. All of her own family were in bed. Who could it be at this hour? From the front hall she could see somone standing on the porch.

As she cautiously opened the door, a familiar brisk voice said, "Dr. Tallman, is this a weird hour to call?"

"Why, no, Dr. Emmett." Anne flung the door wide. "Come in."

"I was on my way home from the hospital and I saw your light. Just thought I'd stop and wish you a Merry Christmas."

Anne understood. The poor lamb had nobody of her own, just an empty apartment waiting for her; she was lonely.

"This house looks as if a cyclone struck it."

Anne laughed. "We had our tree tonight on account of Rita."

The older womn looked puzzled. "Rita?"

"My daughter. She lost her husband some time ago. Ronald Wybron?"

"Oh, yes. That lovely young man. What a pity."

"I was very fond of Ron," Anne said. "He was like my own son. It's hard to believe. He was so young, so bubbling with life. It seems as though he should be bursting in that door, calling out, 'Merry Christmas, everybody!' "

Dr. Emmett nodded. "Wasn't there a child?"

"Two children. A boy and a girl. Come see our tree."

The two women went into the library. Anne opened boxes and demonstrated toys, telling amusing anecdotes about the children.

"Well, I declare. I wish I'd come earlier," Dr. Emmett said.

"Come sit by the fire," Anne invited. "You don't have to go home yet. I'll get us some fruitcake and wine."

166

The wine was sweet, but it had a pleasant tang that warmed and mellowed them. Mandy's spicy cake, thick with fruit and nuts, would satisfy the most fastidious gourmet. The two women sat relaxed over their little repast. For the first time since they had known each other, they didn't talk about lesions and incisions and cardiac cases but of their own childhoods and girlhoods in two little towns up north.

It was long after midnight when the elderly doctor arose to leave. "This has been so pleasant," she said. "I don't know when I've enjoyed myself so much."

"Why don't you have Christmas dinner with us?" Anne asked impulsively. "I like you to meet my family."

"That's kind of you," said Dr. Emmett, drawing on big, masculine-looking gloves. "I'd like to come."

Christmas Day dawned bright and warm. The children shouted excitedly at their play all day. Friends of Bill and Rita ran in and out. A group of them played tennis all afternoon: Anne was glad Rita had gone along.

After they left, she relinquished the babies to Bart's care and drove over to the hospital to see Bette. The sun felt warm and invigorating after the recent cold snap. Anne could feel it penetrating through her light coat as she walked up the steps of the hospital.

"Please, no treatment today, Mrs. Elsnar," Bette pleaded.

"All right, dear," Anne agreed.

Was Bette becoming discouraged? Only her eyes, big and blue and unnaturally bright, were visible through the bandages, and Anne was unable to read them.

Bette's pretty, slim hands rested on the white spread. On one of them, a beautiful dinner ring glittered and sparkled. "See what Santa Clause brought me?" she asked with a twinkle in her eyes.

"It's lovely," Anne said. "I do want to thank you and Dwight for that gorgeous brooch. I've never had anything so beautiful."

Bette shook her head. "You deserve much more for all you've done for me."

Now and then, Bette moved her hand in a graceful arching gesture to admire her ring. How thoughtful of Dwight to give his wife something to enhance the one beauty left to her. The room was filled with flowers. Exquisite silks and laces foamed from open boxes. The girl in the bed seemed unmoved by all this richness. She was quiet. Two quiet.

Anne's nerves twitched unpleasantly. Poor child! Lying there waiting for the fog of doubt about her condition to clear away and reveal what the future held for her. Anne told Bette about Dr. Emmett's visit. "She's having Christmas dinner with us," she said.

At last, Bette broke her heavy silence. "Dwight is having dinner with me today, too."

"How nice," Anne said. "I hear someone coming now. Perhaps it's Dwight."

He came briskly through the door with his shy, one-sided smile, shook hands with Anne, and wished her a Merry Christmas. Then he took his wife in his arms and kissed her lingeringly. She touched his cheek. He turned her hand over and held it there.

Anne went quietly out and closed the door. What if all this had happened for the best? Anne, like everyone else in Oceana, had known that Dwight and Bette had been close to parting before the accident.

When the Elenor family was gathered around the

168

table that night, Anne thought of the Cratchits' Christmas dinner, as Bart carved the turkey and the smell of the savory dressing gushed out, bringing squeals of delight from the children.

Ron's chair, beside Rita, was occupied by Dr. Emmett tonight. As though she understood, the forthright old doctor was particularly attentive to the young woman at her side. She had a thousand reminiscences with which to entertain them all.

"I had just finished my internship while the First World War was raging," she said. "I went blithely off to France to care for the wounded soldiers. They were exciting days for those of us in the service. We went across in a camouflaged boat to try to fool the enemy. It was a long journey, if you know what I mean, but we landed safely. For a while, I was stationed in a hospital at Le Havre."

"Did you meet many celebrities?" Bill asked. "Who were they in those days?"

"Bill, you make it sound like the Middle Ages," Anne protested.

Dr. Emmett laughed. "Sometimes, it seems that long ago to me. Well, let's see. There was Elsie Janis, who was lovely and amusing. And Padwerewski, who never had a peer. General Pershing. The king of Italy. And soon after I went to Nice, President Woodrow Wilson came over. They all turned up at the front lines at one time or another."

"What fun!" Mary Louise piped.

"Oh, it was far from fun, my dear," Dr. Emmett declared.

She had spent a year in China, and had once been invited to lecture before a group of medics in England.

Tonight, even Bill, whose short stay at the hospital

169

had led him to believe she was a gruff old tyrant, hung on Dr. Emmett's every word, enthralled.

Anne was glad she had invited the doctor to share their day. Irene Emmett had made it a memorable one for all of them. After her departure to go back to her duties at the hospital, the family sat on in the softly lighted living room. Bart was still smiling over some of the doctor's stories.

"Damned interesting woman," he remarked. "She must be crowding eighty."

"Could she be that old?" Rita said. "She's so vivid, so alive. She makes you forget everything—almost."

Bill said, "I'll bet she wasn't bad looking in those war days. Funny, one of those soldiers didn't grab her up and marry her."

"Dr. Emmett?" Rita hooted. "They wouldn't dare. She'd slay any lovesick swain with one look from those steel-gray eyes."

They all laughed at the picture of Irene Emmett and a lovesick swain.

You're probably comparing her to Natalie Kent, Bill," Rita teased. "She has quite a crush on you since she took care of you at the hospital."

"You get the zaniest ideas," Bill scoffed.

Anne noticed the warm little glow in his eyes at the mention of the young nurse's name, and it pleased her. She remembered seeing the Kent girl, a pretty brunette about Bill's age. It would be a blessing if he would become interested in someone like Natalie. Anne was in for another surprise when her son came out of a dreamy silence with the firm declaration, "I've been thinking about it for a long time, but now I've decided. I'm going to study medicine."

Anne regarded her youngest with startled eyes and

a lump in her throat. Bill a doctor. It was like looking back at her youthful self, that strong, militant self, filled with glowing plans and dreams. Bill could carry on for her. Her son might ascend to heights she had never scaled, except in her imagination. Together, she and this once-unwanted child might build a dream and see that dream come true! Anne couldn't have asked for a more glorious Christmas gift.

CHAPTER 17

A cold wave struck the coast towns after the holidays. The grove owners were busy keeping smudge-pots and sprinkling systems going. Mornings were frosty, most days gray and lowering. People became restless after a week of staying indoors with log fires blazing all day.

On a cold, windy night, Margaret King sat in a deep chair before the fire, so engrossed in a historical novel she could almost hear the clop, clop of horses' hoofs and the squeak of carriage wheels on the flagstones of a southern mansion. Her heart twisted when she looked up and saw Tony walking the floor, like a caged lion. Now and then he ran a hand through his thick dark hair until it stood up in little peaks. She could almost read his thoughts. They had never discussed the events following the Carey party. She realized it had been a mistake, but the pleasant, uneventful weeks since had dulled her concern. It

172

might clear the air if they could talk about it, but the words froze on her lips every time she tried to bring up the subject.

"Something wrong, dear?" she asked.

He turned and regarded her with a speculative look. "Well, yes. I understand a client of mine feels guilty about pushing me into a stupid move I made a while back. Actually, it was my own fault. I feel I should straighten out the situation. Would you mind if I went out for a little while?"

She forced calmness into her voice. "Why, no. I wouldn't mind, if it's that important."

Relief spread over his face and he became brisk. "I won't be long," he said and went to the bedroom for a warm jacket.

When he came back, his hair was slicked down, and Margaret caught a whiff of his tweedy cologne as he bent down to brush her cheek with his lips.

I understand all right, she thought. *Little Rita must be reassured that your attempt at suicide wasn't her fault*.

The sound of the racing motor was like a fist against Margaret's heart. He couldn't wait for the car to warm up. She could hear its protesting bark as Tony took off down the street. The wind whistled down the flue and blew the logs in the fireplace into a flaming frenzy as she sat there, her book lying forgotten in her lap.

An hour crawled by, and still Tony had not returned. Restlessness turned to panic. Margaret thought, *I've got to find out if he's with her*. Any kind of action was better than sitting and seething with suspicion and worry. She went to her bedroom to get her coat. A glance in the mirror gave back an image that was almost pretty. After the holidays, she had had her hair cut short, forming a sleek cap for her well-shaped head. Red always brought a sparkle to her eyes, and she was wearing the scarlet blouse she had received for Christmas.

When she went outside, the icy wind whipped Margaret's skirt against her legs. Her hands trembled on the wheel as she backed her car into the street. *Here I am again, back in the whirlpool,* she thought. Her foot pressed heavily against the accelerator as the car flew down the boulevard.

Over on Royal Palm Drive, she slowed down and peered through the darkness until she spotted Rita's pink brick house. Tony's car was in the driveway. There was another car parked in the street between Rita's house and the house next door.

Margaret sat there pounding her hand on the wheel. Over Tony's sick bed she had promised herself she would do everything possible to save their marriage. Even walk in there and face them? Well, why not? She might never have the opportunity—or the courage—again. She stepped out of her car, walked briskly up the walk, and rang the bell.

Rita's maid opened the door. "Evenin', Miz King," Cindy said. "Come in. The folks are there in the livin' room."

Margaret took a deep breath and preceded Cindy. She was unfamiliar with the house, having been here only once before, at a luncheon. Pinning a bright smile on her stiff face, she walked toward the lighted living room beyond the foyer.

Margaret stopped when she heard Jack Wybron's rough voice. "I warned you, Rita. Entertainin' a married man here in this house night after night proves to me you ain't a fit mother for Ron Wybron's children, and you don't deserve to keep them."

Margaret caught her breath. Was that man threatening Rita and her children because of Tony? It wasn't true that Tony was with Rita night after night. This was the first time he had left the house alone since his—accident. Suddenly, Margaret knew what she had to do.

She walked briskly into the room.

Rita, in tears, sat curled up in a big chair. Tony stood behind her, protective and defiant. "Now just a minute, Wybron!" he was saying. Jack Wybron stood with his back to the fire, leering at them triumphantly. Two other men, looking uncomfortable, sat on a sofa across the room. Margaret didn't recognize either of them. All five of them turned and stared at her with varying expressions of surprise and bewilderment.

"Oh," she said. "I didn't know you had company, Rita. How do you do, Mr. Wybron? I promised Tony I would stop by after he and Rita finished discussing their business. I hope I'm not intruding."

Rita was the first to recover. "Come in. Margaret," she said. "Of course, you're not intruding."

"Isn't it a wild night out?" Margaret said.

Somebody mumbled something polite.

"What is this?" Jack Wybron demanded, looking at Rita.

She rallied magnificently. Margaret marveled at her quickness. "A couple of my friends have dropped in to call," she explained. "Is there anything wrong with that?"

Jack's florid face grew redder. "Well, why didn't

you say so?'' he asked angrily. ''You let me make a fool of myself—''

''I had nothing to do with that,'' Rita said impudently. ''That was something you accomplished long before I ever laid eyes on you.''

Margaret was as astonished as the others. Not over five minutes ago, Rita had resembled a small trapped animal fighting for her life. Now she was the picture of a misunderstood queen.

''You could have stopped me,'' Jack said sullenly.

''It's hard to stop a cyclone.'' Rita stood up. ''Now, get out of my house and stay out, Jack.''

His manner became ingratiating. ''Now, Rita, don't fly off the handle. Anybody's liable to make a mistake.''

She ignored him. ''Come on, Margaret. Let's go out in the kitchen. I have some ice cream in the fridge.''

The other two men were on their feet. ''Well, Wybron,'' one of them said, ''you'd better go home before you have any more bright ideas. We were witnesses, all right, but if I had to testify in court—''

''Oh, shut up!'' Jack barked.

Outwardly calm but quivering inside, Margaret followed Rita. She was almost reluctant to see the three men leave. It was easier to have a crowd around than to have to face Rita and Tony alone. If only she could continue to appear easy and natural. That would be the only way to keep the upper hand and save her pride.

The kitchen door swung open to a bright, spotless room. Tony stood leaning against the snack bar, his hands deep in his trouser pockets, his expression a mixture of guilt and anger.

Rita walked over to the refrigerator and took out a carton of ice cream and a chocolate layer cake. Her hands were shaking.

Margaret wondered if "the wronged wife" was expected to burst into an angry tirade. Instead, she said casually, "Let me help. Could you find some plates, Tony?"

Rita choked and reached for a drink of water.

Her surprise gave Margaret a glimmer of satisfaction. But a cold hand closed around her heart when Tony walked unerringly to the right cupboard and reached for the plates, as though he had done it a dozen times before. She doubted if he was as familiar with the cupboards in his own kitchen. That, she supposed, was because she always jumped to wait on him. Evidently, Rita didn't. She would expect *him* to fetch and carry for *her*.

Margaret found a knife in a kitchen drawer and cut three portions from the brick of ice cream and arranged them on the plates. She could feel the eyes of the other two boring into her back, and thought, *I'll see that they eat this if it chokes them—as I'm sure it will me.*

"Here you are, Rita, Tony." She passed the dishes and they took them automatically.

For a few minutes, there was silence in the kitchen, except for the tinkle of silver against china, as all three attempted to force down the confection.

At last, Rita set her dish carefully on a cabinet, as though she could no longer endure the silence. "Margaret, I hope you don't think—," she began.

"This cake is delicious, Rita. Won't you have some?" Margaret broke in eagerly.

"No, I—"

"Tony? You love chocolate cake."

He gave her an odd look and helped himself.

Rita's eyes widened, and she looked at Tony questioningly. She seemed about to speak again, but Margaret said quickly, "There's something about Jack Wybron I dislike. I can't explain it. He's always pleasant enough when we meet."

"He's a scoundrel!" Tony exploded.

"Tony!" Margaret said. "Don't forget, dear, he's Rita's brother-in-law."

Clearly, both Tony and Rita were puzzled by her attitude. Perhaps it was spiteful of her, but Margaret had no intention of explaining to either of them—ever—how she had happened to walk into this house tonight at such a crucial moment. Let them guess and wonder and speculate, as she had had to, night after night, for nearly a year.

"Goodness, Tony, look at the time," she said as she began to gather up dishes and spoons. "We should be on our way."

Rita still seemed to feel that some sort of explanation was expected. "Margaret," she began, as they walked toward the front door, "I hope you don't think—"

"I couldn't come with Tony," Margaret broke in. "I was busy, so I told him to run along and I'd come later. Give you time to talk over your business."

She thought, *I wonder if she thinks I'm as idiotic as I sound.*

Tony was following her meekly. He seemed as amazed by her chatter as she was herself. A wave of hysteria was building up inside Margaret. She clenched her teeth and balled her hands into fists as she fought it down.

She and Tony walked out to their cars in silence.

He opened the door of her car and touched her arm briefly as she stepped in.

"You go ahead and I'll follow you," he said. "You shouldn't be out alone at night."

Her starter whirred, the motor answered lustily, and she took off down the street. Tonight, she decided firmly, when she and Tony got home, they would have a showdown. Win or lose, it would be final, as far as she was concerned.

She settled down in the seat. She could be herself now. She began to wonder about that self of hers. It seemed suddenly as drab and as uninteresting as her plain face and thin, unattractive figure. Margaret realized there was little about her to inspire love in a man, particularly a man who for years was in love with a girl like Rita Wybron.

There had been something arresting about the wife who had walked boldly into Rita's house and taken the center of the stage with a *savoir faire* nobody had dreamed she possessed. Margaret had felt it herself. She had seen it in Rita's eyes. In Tony's. Even in Jack Wybron's. They were all seeing someone they had never seen before. She *had been* a different person back there in Rita's house.

She had been a shy introvert all her life. Her plainness and colorlessness had made her apologetic, self-effacing, humble. She had never demanded anything for herself, always waiting on other people, grateful for the merest crumb of praise or appreciation. That, she could see now, had been stupid.

She had once read an intriguing story about the wife of a great statesman. As a youngster, this famous woman had been conscious of her lack of beauty and had set about cultivating charm to offset it. Margaret thought now of that woman's tall, straight figure, her lovely manner and warm friendly smile. When looking at her picture in the papers or watching her on television, you realized she possessed a power that most beauties lost with their first gray hairs.

Margaret smiled to herself in the darkness. She possessed that power, too. She had discovered it less than an hour ago. It was her last weapon in her fight to hold Tony. It was what Anne Elsnar had been talking about the day she advised Margaret, in her subtle fashion, to cling to him. If she could just hold on to it while they had their talk tonight!

The wind was blowing hard, furiously swinging the tattered veils of Spanish moss that hung limply from the oak trees along Osceola Avenue. Palmettos in a vacant lot rustled their fluted green skirts as they bowed before the wind. Burton's grocery store and gas station was closing for the night. Lights winked off in a house far back from the street. The shuffleboard courts were empty, and one of the park alligators lay as dark and immovable as a rock against the wire fencing of its pen. Margaret wished she had put another log on the fire before going out.

The moment she drove into the garage, she opened her car adoor and stepped out. Tony was right behind her.

"I think I'll drive around a while before I turn in," he said.

Margaret's eyes, bright and alive in the dimness, commanded his. "Not tonight, Tony. I want to talk to you."

With a little sigh, he shut off the ignition and followed her into the house.

She slipped off her coat and hung it in the hall closet before going into the living room and turning on the lights. A rosy log fell apart in the fireplace with a shower of sparks. She was about to kneel and replace it but drew back quickly.

"I think you'd better build up the fire," she said.

Tony glanced at her briefly before he complied.

No, I'm not sick, Tony. Nor out of my mind. I'm through being a slave and a doormat, that's all.

He sat down across from her and kicked off his shoes. "Where are my slippers?" he mumbled, looking under the chair and then helplessly at her.

"In the hall closet," she said crisply, thinking, *You knew where to find the plates at Rita's.*

He stood up and shuffled out of the room. She could hear him fumble around, bump his head, and swear under his breath, but she sat firmly in her chair. He might as well learn where his slippers were kept so he could find them the next time.

He came back into the room wearing the slippers. His lips twitched nervously as his eyes met hers. "I suppose you want to talk about that mess tonight," he began uncomfortably.

"I want to talk about you and me," she said. "I think it's high time, don't you?"

"What do you mean?"

"Let's not make a mystery out of a situation that's town talk."

His face flamed.

"I know you're in love with Rita. You always have been. Everybody else knows it, too. What do you intend to do about it?"

He looked at her helplessly, not denying the accusation. "What is there to do?"

"There's divorce." Her heart quaked at the mention of the word, but she kept her head high, giving no quarter.

Tony shook his head. "If you mean divorce you and marry Rita, that's out. She wouldn't have me. She's always talking about her heart being in the grave with Ron Wybron."

Margaret winced. So they *had* discussed it.

"Tony, why did you marry me?"

He looked startled. "Why, I—I—what are you getting at?"

"Try to think back to the night you proposed to me. We were dancing at the Riomar Club. Rita and her husband were also there. You danced with her, and then you two went out together somewhere. When you came back, you seemed angry. On the way home, you asked me to marry you, remember?"

He nodded.

"Why?"

He shrugged and dropped his head in his hands. It was characteristic of him not to lie to her.

"I'll tell you why," she said, her voice quiet and controlled. "You were frantic over losing Rita. Perhaps you quarreled about it that night. I don't know. You decided to marry someone, anyone, just for spite. I was there, handy. So—"

Tony shifted ipatiently and raised his head. "Margaret, you make it sound so calculating and cold-blooded."

"Well, that's the way it was," she said, fighting back the panic that seized her every time she thought about it. "Didn't it occur to you that I might be in love with you?" she asked quietly.

He lifted troubled eyes and stared at her.

"No, of course. You hadn't thought of that," she accused. "You never thought of me at all. If you had, you might have realized I wouldn't—I couldn't marry a man I didn't love. Not even," she added, her voice breaking, "for spite."

Margaret turned her brimming eyes toward the fire. With a hiss, the log turned over on the brass andirons and sent a shower of sparks up the chimney. Tears of fire, like the tears that were burning against her lids. She hadn't meant to give way like this. She had felt hard as nails when beginning this discussion; she had been certain she could carry it through. She might have known.

"Meg," Tony was on his knees beside her, holding her hands in his. "I'm sorry. What do you want me to do?"

She pulled her hands away. "Go back and sit down, Tony. Let's keep it unemotional. I didn't mean to be such an idiot, but do let's have—everything—settled tonight, one way or another."

He went back to his chair. "All right, Meg."

"You've admitted a divorce wouldn't do you any good. It wouldn't do me any good. It would only embarrass Rita."

He nodded soberly.

"Then why can't we start over?" she went on. "Plenty of marriages have been successful, even happy, built on something other than love. Respect, I mean, and companionship, a goal of some kind."

He was thoughtful for a long momet. "Yes," he agreed, "I guess that's true."

"If you'd concentrate on something like building up your business, or—or—"

"Raising a family," he broke in.

Margaret's face flamed and her heart seemed to fly up in her throat. "Yes. Raising a family," she repeated quietly.

She stood up and leaned an elbow on the low mantle. "Meg," he said, "I'm beginning to realize that marrying you was the best thing that ever happened to me. I'll try to be worthy of you. I'll really try."

She looked up at him with a misty smile. "That's all I ask. I'll try harder, too. We just might make a go of it."

CHAPTER 18

On a warm morning in late February, Bette Carey was awake early. The hospital was quiet at this hour, just an occasional sussurus of sound as ghostly figures sped up and down the corridors. She had slept little all night. This was the day the bandages were to be removed for the last time. She was frightened but determined to brazen it through, whatever the outcome. People wouldn't expect her to do that. They'd expect her to collapse or tear up the sheets and go violently berserk over the scars lurking under the bandages.

She smiled to herself, a smile as revealing as a mirror. She could feel the twisted muscles of her upper lip pulling and straining. Her heart began to beat faster and she clenched her hands. She mustn't break. After all, she had received more than one knockout blow during her life, and she had never failed to come up fighting. This was a cruel blow, but she was determined not to bat an eyelash—provided she had an eyelash left to bat.

Outside her window, a cardinal fluttered up into the green branchesof a lime tree and stood for a moment, preening its scarlet wings. The bird lifted its head proudly, its black crest glistening in the sunshine as its high, sweet song rippled and soared.

"You beautiful thing," Bette said softly. For a moment, tears threatened, as she thought, *I looked as pretty as that in my red dress.*

Her slim body stiffened under the sheets as she forced back the little burst of emotion. "Idiot!" she muttered.

Bette moved her left leg back and forth across the bed, stretching and bending the toes. Dr. Tallman—as that old buzzard, Dr. Emmett called Mrs. Elsnar—had done that much for her. Everyone believed she would walk with a limp, that she would never dance again. Well, she would show them. Before she was through, she would walk as gracefully as ever, and she would dance, too—or die in the attempt. It would be good to get home, to get away from this plain, ugly room and the smell of disenfectants, not to mention the flat-tasting hospital food.

A pretty, bright-eyed nurse came into the room with fresh towels and bath water. Bette thought she had never seen such a flawless complexion, the skin like a ripe peach, a perfectly shaped red mouth, clear eyes, and rich chestnut hair. Hundreds of girls looked like that. Why had she never noticed before? Probably, because her own mirror once gave back a similar image. She turned her head away and stared into the thick branches of the lime tree. *Come on, old girl, snap out of it.*

"Are we ready for our bath?" the nurse asked
186

brightly. "We have to get all fixed up this morning. We're having quite an audience. Mr. Carey and Dr. Emmett and Dr. Glencoe from Atlanta."

Bette seethed inside. The nurse worked briskly as she babbled away. You'd think she was trying to bolster the courage of a dying gladiator.

At last, Bette broke desperately into her chatter. "I never in my life saw anyone as cheerful as you are."

The nurse blushed.

"I'm sorry. Kent," Bette apologized, "but don't try to cheer me up. Not this morning. Don't strain yourself. It's not going to get me down, if that's what is worrying you."

Natalie Kent smiled at her. "Good for you, Mrs. Carey. You've been so jolly and easy to care for, all the nurses like you. We're all rooting for you."

"That helps, Kent," Bette said.

The nurses liked her! Bette had never thought much about nurses except to consider them slightly unhinged for electing to put up with the goofiness of sick people. Maybe some of them fancied themselves as doctors' wives and had gotten in on the ground floor, where it was easier to land that kind of man. But she could also see that these girls really loved their work. Most of them were deft and efficient. Many things could be done to make their work easier, though, particularly in this little hospital. Dwight and his friends had he money. She would have the time, and later the energy, to do something for them. It was a plan for the future.

"Who's Dr. Glencoe?" she asked.

"The famous plastic surgeon," Natalie explained. "According to Dr. Emmett, he's a wonder of the world."

"Oh," Bette murmured, "the plastic surgeon."

187

For the next hour, the hospital routine kept Bette so occupied she didn't have time to think of the ordeal before her. There was no waiting this morning between bath and breakfast. The instant she laid down her coffee cup, someone was there to help with her hair and to tie on her pink quilted bedjacket. The maid came in to dust the room and arrange her flowers, and everybody chattered as though they were robots turned on for the occasion. It was considerate of them, but nothing could quell Bette's mounting excitement and apprehension.

Dwight came in early, as falsely cheerful and reassuring as everyone else.

"Dwight, I want you to do something for me," she said.

"If course, honey, anything you say." He took her hand and held it tightly.

She wrapped her fingers desperately around this thumb. "There's a mirror in the compact in my purse. When I ask for it today, I want you to bring it to me—without any argument. Will you do that?"

As he hesitated, two bright spots burned high on his cheeks.

"All I'm asking is that you treat me like an adult, Dwight. I've been one, you know, most of my life."

"All right, Bette," he agreed.

He looked nervous and anxious. In spite of his unease, his presence gave her courage.

She clung frantically to his hand. "I'll probably be quite hideous," she said.

"I'm not so handsome myself," he grinned.

Dr. Emmett came in with Dr. Glencoe, a tall, graying man, brisk and authoritative. When a nurse brought in the tray of supplies, Dr. Emmett began gently to remove the bandages. It seemed to take hours, Bette thought. When the last bandage came away, a little shiver went through her.

The four people standing around the bed looked at her with controlled expressions. A muscle jumped in Dwight's cheek. Dr. Glencoe moved her head from side to side and bent close to examine her face. Not a word was spoken in the quiet room.

"Hmm," Dr. Glencoe said finally. "Not bad. Not bad at all. In time, these scars will practically disappear. I can graft here. Lift the nose and narrow it. No sir, not bad at all." His cheerful professional smile enveloped Bette.

She thought: *He's not fooling me. I'm a holy horror. I know it.* Aloud she said, "Dwight, the mirror, please."

Dr. Glencoe shot a glance of alarm at Dr. Emmett. He cleared his throat and said gruffly, "Mr. Carey, I wouldn't—"

"The mirror, Dwight," Bette said firmly.

Dwight's hands shook as he took out the mirror and placed it in Bette's hand. They were all watching her, fascinated.

She braced herself and looked, clenching her teeth to keep them from chattering. Not bad, the doctor had said. An ugly red welt ran the length of one cheek. A pitted horror of an upper lip. A depressed nose. *Not bad?*

"The map of Europe isn't the only one that's changed," she said tremulously, handing the compact back to Dwight.

Bette's hand didn't shake. There were no tears of self-pity. The faces surrounding her were just a blur, and there was a roaring in her ears. For an instant, the

189

vision of a dimpled face, pretty as a pink rose, smiled above closed eyes. *Dead, Bette Carey is dead. And who am I?*

A little whimper started in her throat, but she remembered the people watching her, and she turned it into a cough. She even forced a smile, knowing its effect was hardly one of beauty and charm. It would take everyone, herself included, a long time to get used to the grimace she would have instead of a smile from now on. A long, shuddering sigh quivered through her, but the smile shook only a little.

Dr. Glencoe patted Bette's shoulder without a word, the two doctors and the nurse walked out of the room. After a moment, Bette's vision cleared, and she saw Dwight standing there, looking down at her with an enigmatic expression. The only calamity that could befall her now would be for him to find her repulsive.

"Dwight?" she whisper.

"Yes, darling." He took her in his arms, his lips tender against her scarred cheek.

Relaxing against him, she said, "You're the real thing, Dwight." Her voice shook. "Nothing as trivial as a few scars could change you. Or is it that love is blind?"

"Love isn't blind, honey," he said. "It sees all and has an endless capacity for forgiving."

Her glance fell away from his. His meaning was clear. She had reason to thank God for the Carey superiority and strength of character that she had once scorned. Respect for the Careys and all they stood for suddenly filled her with humility. She knew she had only to play the game according to the rules, and Dwight would never let her down.

That afternoon, Bette had a caller.

"It's Bill Elsnar," Natalie Kent said, her color high.

Noting the girl's confusion, Bette thought, *She's crazy about Bill*. The other half of her mind was fighting against seeing anybody she knew, particularly Bill Elsnar, who had been a special admirer. Why had he come. Today of all days? No, she said, she wouldn't see him.

"I could arrange the veil over your face," Natalie suggested hesitantly.

A white veil. It was a symbol of purity, of cowardice, of vanity, things foreign to Bette's forthright manner. The nurses had brought a graceful length of nun's veiling in that afternoon. It made her look like a mysterious, romantic figure lying languidly among her pillows.

"It's for when you have company," one of the nurses had explained. "Just until your face heals."

Bette pulled her thoughts back to Bill, and she decided to get it over with. "All right, I'll see him," she said. Natalie draped the veil over her head and face and hurried out of the room.

When Bill opened the door and walked in, looking young and embarrassed, he smiled expectantly. Then he saw her. A strangled gasp escaped him as he became as white as the veil around Bette's head.

"Hello, Bill," she said. "It's nice of you to come. Won't you sit down?"

He dropped down in a chair and sat looking at his hands. They were shaking. He lifted them to grasp the arms of the chair, and his knuckles were white.

"How are you getting alone?" he gulped.

"Very nicely now. Dr. Emmett says I'll be able to go home in a few days."

"You *will* be able to walk, won't you?" he stam-

191

mered.

"Oh, yes, eventually. Thanks to your mother. She has been wonderful, Bill."

"I—I'm glad of that."

They faced each other starkly, speech strangling in their throats.

"It's a lovely day, isn't it?" Bette managed after a moment. "It won't be long before Dwight can carry me down to the beach. It'll be nice to sit in the sun again."

She stopped abruptly. Bill had dropped to his knees beside the bed, his face hot against her hand. "I didn't mean to do this to you! It was my wretched temper. Oh, Mrs. Carey, if there was only something I could *do*!" His shoulders were shaking, and Bette felt a tear drop onto her hand.

All of a sudden, she too was crying. She hadn't forseen this exaggerated, youthful remorse. She had merely meant to discourage any interest she might have possessed for him. But the shock of seeing her like this had been too much for Bill.

"Please, honey, don't," she said. "It was just an accident. Anybody can lose control of a car. It wasn't your fault."

He shook his head hopelessly. "I'll never forgive myself."

She stroked his hair, her fingers gentle. "It was my fault. Really, Bill. I'm older than you, a married woman. I had no business going out with you that night. I got what was coming to me. Sometimes it takes something like this to teach us we can't play with fire without getting burned. But it's not all bad. As my grandmother used to say, when God closes a door, He opens a window."

Bill raised his head and looked at Bette hopefully. "What do you mean?"

"Dwight and I were drifting apart, just as you said that night. I guess that was what made me so mad. But my illness has brought us together again."

Bill's face brightened and he stood up. "You mean that? You're not just saying it to make it easier for me?"

Bette shook her head. "No, Bill. I'd rather have Dwight Carey's love than all the beauty in the world."

With an awkwardness that was endearing, Bill raised Bette's hand to his lips. "If there's ever anything I can do for you, will you let me know?" he asked.

"Yes, Bill. Thanks. And now you'd better run along," she said with an attempt at their old camaraderie. "I'll bet Natalie Kent is loitering out there, hoping to get another look at you."

The color came back in his face and he grinned.

"Come again," she invited politely.

"I will," he promised.

Better knew he never would. No man would ever look at her with admiration and longing again. It was like seeing the last sweet semblance of her youth walking out that door, never to return. Her eyes filled with sadness as she turned toward the green freshness of the lime tree outside her window.

Down in the plaza she could see Dwight stepping out of his long blue car. He, too, had a gentle, expectant smile on his face as he looked up. But with Dwight she knew it was real. She knew she could count on the love and devotion of her husband. And some day, if she was lucky, her son.

CHAPTER 19

The end of winter heralded the annual visit of Bart's mother. Anne stiffened her backbone and geared for battle. Olivia Elsnar made waves wherever she appeared. She still lived on Coquina Key, a little island off the Gulf where Bart had been born. A widow for many years, she lived alone. Except for visiting her son and his family each spring, she seldom left the log house she and her husband had built with their own hands. She loved the Key and was as free and easy in manner as the birds and animals of her wilderness home.

Bart met his mother at the bus on a balmy February evening; she had been on the road all day. He watched her step down carefully from the lumbering vehicle. It seemed to him she had slowed down considerably in the past year; but for a woman in her late seventies, it was to be expected. Her gray hair sprayed out untidily from under a flat dark-blue hat she had worn for years. Her shapeless blue dress made no pretension of simulating current fashion.

Her raucous "Hey, there, son!" lacked none of its old spirit.

"Gee, Mama, you look great!" Bart said, greeting her with a bearhug.

She would stay in Oceana her usual four days, but it looked to Bart as if she had enough luggage to last all summer. As he gathered it up, she warned him to handle it carefully as she had some things in there for all the children, as well as for his wife. Bart thought, seashells and bits of driftwood probably, and hand-made aprons and scarves, most of which usually ended up in his shop.

Olivia's eyes missed little as Bart drove along Osceola Boulevard.

"Cardboard city," she muttered. "All painted up and preening like a child's play toy. Son, don't you ever miss the real things, the bayous, the wild cats bayin', the birds singin' up a storm in the morning?"

"Well, yes, Mama," Bart conceded reluctantly. "I suppose I do. The Key is a great place for young ones, but a man has to make a decent living, educate his kids. I can't do that way off in the sticks."

"'Course not. And you cain't dress Annie up in the latest styles and buy her a mansion unless you make a mint of money."

Bart remained silent. There was no way his wife and his mother would ever see eye to eye. They came from two different worlds. Olivia seldom backed down from an issue, but Anne's tolerance could be amazing. Even now, she would be at the front door one minute, where her mother-in-law would expect a hearty greeting, and the next minute in the kitchen reassuring Many's justified complaints, "That woman comes in my kitchen orderin' me around. I go out the door and you won't see me no mo'."

Anne braced herself and sent up a silent prayer when she heard the car door slam. Olivia came puffing up the steps and offered her cheek for Anne's kiss.

"How are you, Grandma?" Anne said. "Did you have a pleasant trip?"

"I'm dead on my feet and hungry as a bear," Olivia declared. "Supper about ready? I s'pose you still got a woman doing your work for you. Maybe I ought to go speed her up a bit."

Anne's lips firmed. She darted a look at Bart, and he took his mother's arm to pilot her to the stairs.

"Dinner will be ready in five minutes or so, Mama. You get yourself cleaned up and ready." His firm order was accompanied by his most winning smile.

A gamine grin spread over Olivia's broad face. "You let *your* son talk to you like that, Annie?"

At dinner, everything seemed to have settled down. Olivia was full of questions about the family. She wanted to know why that little girl of hers wasn't here the first night her grandmother was in town. Anne explained that Rita had two children of her own to care for now, but she would be making lunch for them the next day.

"What business you in now, Bart?" Olivia inquired.

Selling real estate didn't seem to his mother to be much of a job for a big, strappin' man like Bart. He should have a business of his own at his age. As she explained to one and all, "Bart always was a lazy critter. Nothin' like his father, God rest his soul. That man of mine really bucked the odds.''

She turned her attention to Bill, her pride and joy. ''College! Well, bless my soul. You were always smart. Remember when you used to visit the Key when you was a little tyke, Billy?''

''Sure do, Grandma. I learned a lot about nature from you.''

Olivia chuckled. ''You keep on, you'll amount to something one of these days, love.''

Luncheon at Rita's the next day went along smoothly. Rita was more adept at handling her grandmother than Anne was. Besides, Olivia adored Rita's two children and knew a dozen ways to enchant them. Their favorite was with bird calls. Olivia's whistle was as clear as a teenaged boy's; she could imitate the songs of all the birds that inhabited her wilderness.

''My gosh, who'd ever believe I'd be a great-grand-mother!'' she chuckled, quickly shifting her attention. ''I thought you had a lumber business, Rita. You give that up?''

Rita explained how her brother-in-law had insisted she stay home while her children were small, which drew scorn from Olivia.

''Some of these men think a woman's made outa marshmallows. I'd tell your Jack a thing or two. How about us goin' down to the lumber building, Rita? I always enjoyed visitin' there. I'd like to meet this feller that's doin' your work for you.''

Rita was well aware that one of the highlights of Olivia's former visits was a call at the lumber office. Olivia had doted on Ron Wybron, who knew how to handle her remarks and field her question. She would probably overwhelm Mark, but there was no way Olivia could be put off. She had made up her mind.

Anne wisely remained with the children while Rita drove her grandmother downtown. As soon as they entered the lumber office, Olivia took over. Mark's eyes widened with surprise as the two women, so unalike, converged on his desk.

"Mark, this is my grandmother," Rita said proudly.

He stood up and offered his hand. "This is a pleasure, Mrs. Elsnar."

His charm enfolded her, and her manner softened. "Mark?" she said, "That your name? Well, I declare. Matthew, Mark, Luke, and John. You're in good company, young man. This young lady doesn't need you around here no more'n a cat needs ten tails. She can run this business blindfolded, one hand tied behind her back."

"I'm sure she could," he agreed. "Does this mean I'm getting my walking papers?"

"Of course not," Rita intervened hasity. "Grandma likes to have her little joke."

"Well, I'll say this," Olivia said, "You two would make excellent partners in any situation. Ain't they a handsome couple, Edie?"

"Grandma!" Rita's face took on the tinge of her strawberry-colored dress.

"Business partners, I mean," Olivia amended, sensitive to her granddaughter's embarrassment. Then she turned her attention to Edith. "My, you don't change a bit, Edie. You still workin' every day and takin' care of your mother? You're a good girl, Edie. Where's that Joe Lally?"

"Out making a couple of deliveries," Mark explained.

198

"There's one fine man," Olivia declared. "If I was twenty years younger, I'd set my cap for old Joe."

They all laughed, but Rita was relieved when her grandmother said, "Well, we must be goin'. Anne's waitin' at Rita's to take me home with her, so I'll bid you both goodbye, and the Lord be with you."

Before she left the house with Anne that evening, Olivia walked into Ron's study and looked around, her keen eyes missing nothing. Not many changes there, she noted. The best thing Rta could do was clear out his things and redecorate the shrine. The boy was gone. Why not face it?

By the time her four-day visit was over, Olivia Elsnar had left her mark on all of them. Bart was advised to settle down and make something of himself, get into a good business and stay there. If Anne had any spunk, she'd get out and cure the sick, since she had the knowhow, instead of layin' around cosseting her own aches and pains. Her grandmotherly advice to Rita was to clear the decks and have her eye out for a man; she and those little children needed someone to look after them. Only Bill passed muster. Olivia felt her grandson had inherited some of her own vigor and good sense.

In spite of her relief at seeing Olivia off, time seemed to drag for Anne after her mother-in-law left. She couldn't shake off her suggestion. Was she really wasting her life and her knowhow? In any case, Anne felt the need to get away by herself in order to think it through, and she knew just the place.

There was an old Spanish mission a few miles out from Oceana, and Anne decided to drive there, where she could be entirely alone to come to grips with herself. A long time ago, she had taken the children there,

199

and she still had pleasant recollections of the beauty and peace that had pervaded the old mission.

The noble old building—sun drenched and bathed in a golden light, surrounded by palm trees and beautiful, well-kept flower gardens—stood like a mighty fortress in its quiet setting this late winter day. Anne tried all the doors in the front of the building. To her dismay, they were all locked. She walked around the back and finally found an unlocked door in the shade of an old oak tree dripping with Spanish moss. As she crept into the silent church, she had to wait a moment for her eyes to become accustomed to the dimness. The aromatic fragrance of incense lingered in the air. Above the altar, votive lights twinkled like jewels, giving her a feeling of joy that was almost ecstasy. She slipped into a pew and sat there, looking at the altar and letting the deep peace surround her.

A sudden light from behind her indicated a door had been opened. It was a young priest in his long black cassock. He looked startled when he saw Anne, but he made her welcome with a smile as he walked down the aisle, genuflected before the altar, and disappeared up a side aisle. Presently, the sweet strains of an organ filtered into the nave. Anne recognized Bach's *Sheep May Safely Graze*. As the music swelled her, she began to feel strong and confident, as though blessed by an unseen hand.

Finally, she arose and left the church. She knew what she had to do. It was as clear as though the words had been spoken aloud. Driving swiftly back to Oceana, she headed across town to the hospital. Morning quiet pervaded the place as she entered the familiar building. At the desk, she asked if she could see Dr. Emmett.

Irene Emmett seemed glad to see Anne. "What a nice surprise. You look positively radiant. Good news?"

"I hope you will think so," Anne laughed. "Ever since our conversation following Mrs. Dwight Carey's accident, I have been thinking over what you said about needing another doctor here."

Dr. Emmett nodded, adjusted her glasses, and leaned back in her chair, looking expectant.

"Just recently, I learned that my son is interested in a medical career. It has come to the point where something must be done." Anne could feel the color rising in her face.

"And you want me to take him—under my wing?"

"Not at all," Anne protested. "Bart is managing to get Bill through college. But, well, I have to confess that my husband might not be entirely reliable over a long period of time. Bart is a dreamer, and Bill's career is the most important thing in his life, as it is in mine, too. I would like to make sure nothing interferes with it."

Dr. Emmett nodded. "I think I'm beginning to understand."

"The point is, I could take care of Bill's education, if you still feel I might fit in here."

The doctor leaned forward, her face beaming. "I've been hoping for this for years. In fact, some time back, I even looked into your record. Vermont, wasn't it? Mother of Mercy Hospital. I was delighted with what I learned, not to mention the way you took over Mrs. Carey's case and almost had her on her feet before she left here. That was little short of miraculous, Anne."

"Well, I think I should make myself clear about that, Doctor. I have to admit that treating her almost

201

floored me. I'm afraid, at this stage of my life, I couldn't keep up that kind of pace indefinitely.''

"Oh, no, no. I wouldn't expect it. What I have in mind is something entirely different. Ever since Christmas, I've been thinking about your beautiful healthy children and grandchildren. I know it requires wisdom and understanding to bring up a healthy family. Many cases here prove what ignorance and neglect can do to children. We need a dedicated physician to look after our little ones and advise their parents. Would that interest you?''

Anne's heart lifted. "It's an answer to prayer. I was hoping for something like that. I feel confident I could handle it.''

Dr. Emmett stood up and offered a warm hand. "When do you think you could start? I don't want to rush you.''

"Give me a month to get my affairs straightened out and my family used to the idea.''

CHAPTER 20

It was warm and balmy by the end of February, like early June up north. Bart had been away in Miami for several days. As usual, he was looking for "something by which a man might make a little money." Anne doubted his ability to find the Utopia he was seeking, but she was enjoying the peaceful interlude. She liked to sit in the sunshine with a book or her needlework on a velvety strip of green in the middle of the grove. She was there one afternoon when Bart came tearing out the back door, calling to her excitedly.

"I'm out here, Bart," she called back. "What's all the commotion about?"

He came lumbering through the grove, his bellow preceding him. "Anne, I think I've run into something. A real thriving business. Down near Miami. There's a scad of money to be made down there."

Anne frowned. "What kind of business?"

He dropped, panting, on the grass at her feet. "Well, I know it's a long way from here, but I tell you, Anne, there's *money* in it. The feller owns it has made his pile and wants to sell out and retire. And he's only forty!''

"For heaven's sake, Bart. Get to the point,'' she said. She had an uneasy feeling this was just another of his wild schemes.

"It's a restaurant,'' he explained hesitantly. "Meals. The feller has a liquor license, a juke box, and a couple of waitresses.''

"A restaurant?'' Anne sat still, considering. If it was any kind of place at all, he might be able to do something with it. She pictured a big, bright room with an inviting air. Small cozy tables, candlelight and flowers, and some good southern cooking. Attractive waitresses in blue uniforms, courteous and pleasant, making the patrons comfortable and happy, so they would return often. She hoped he would eliminate the juke box.

If they were to get Bill through medical school, Bart might be able to help out. "Why, I don't know. Bart,'' she said cautiously.

His eyes began to sparkle. "Anne, why don't we drive down there and look the place over together?''

"By all means,'' she agreed. "I'd want to do that.''

"And while you're forming an opinion of it, try to remember the money a feller could make there. We could retire in five years and live comfortably the rest of our lives.''

She looked down at him, wondering how many times she had heard the same story through the years. "I wouldn't consider going down there to live,'' she said.

"Why not? We could close this house. Or rent it.

204

Might as well make some money on the winter tourists."

Anne shuddered at the thought of strangers walking through her rooms and using her things. "For one thing, I have other plans. I'm going to have to discuss with you later. When do you plan to go back to Miami?"

"How about tomorrow morning? I thought we might take Bill and Rita along as a treat."

"All right."

He stood up and patted her shoulder. "Good girl, Anne. I knew you wouldn't fail me."

She refused to get excited about it. It might be just another of Bart's brainstorms. It had been a long time, though, since she had seen him so excited about anything remotely connected with hard work. That, at least, was encouraging. He needed to settle down to something permanent soon.

Early morning of the next day seemed to have been touched by the hand of Midas. The highway stretched ahead like a shining golden rope, uncoiling gracefully along the coastline. There were glimpses of the sea and swooping gulls. After a while, the road wound closer to the shore, where the thunder of the waves was still audible. The dark shapes of ships, rising and dipping with the swells, flung plumes of gray smoke from their tall smokestacks to smudge the perfect blue of the sky.

In the back seat of the car, Bill and Rita laughed, sang, and bickered good naturedly. Bart whistled a monotonous, tuneless melody. Anne's spirits, too, were caught up by the morning and the pleasure of the trip. She enjoyed traveling, although she tired easily now. They would have to go down and back in one day.

As they drove through Fort Pierce, West Palm Beach, Hollywood, and other coastal towns, the streets teamed with happy-looking people. It was easy to distinguish the native girls. Nearly all of them had exquisite pink-and-white complexions. Anne thought they looked much prettier than the heavily tanned tourists. The doctor in her thought it a pity for girls to destroy their lovely soft skin.

It was noon and uncomfortably hot when they reached the outskirts of Miami. Bart turned off on a macadam road leading into a wilderness where houses were few and far between. The macadam ended as they struck a sand track.

"Where are we going?" Anne wailed. "Is this a shortcut?"

Bart laughed. "Now, Annie, don't get excited. You'll soon see."

The wild Florida outlands never failed to send the shivers through Anne. There were cypress trees and Spanish moss with deep irrigation ditches on either side of the road. Wild alligators were said to hide there, as well as huge snakes, coiled into fat, shiny ropes. The wilderness depressed her.

"How much farther is it?" she asked.

"Not far now," Bart said cheerfully.

A wildcat leaped nimbly across the road in front of the car. Anne glanced at Bart, but he looked unmoved and entirely happy.

"Isn't this a rather out-of-the-way place for a restaurant?" she asked.

"We could fix Susie's Place up real swanky," Bart declared, but there was a nervous twitch in his cheek.

"*What* place?"

"Susie's Place. That's its name. We can change it, of course. Maybe to Annie's Place."

The cold hand of doubt clutched at Anne suddenly, and she settled back limply. The picture of a charming restaurant on a well-traveled highway had faded.

"Just wait till you see the place, Anne, and realize its potential."

"I'm all agog."

They presently came into a clearing. In its center stood a long, low rambling building with a sloping roof and a wide veranda surrounded by a rough log railing. A circular driveway led up to the building. As the scorching noonday sun beat down on it, there wasn't a sign of life around. A brown tent leaned drunkenly in the side yard.

"That's where the waitresses live," Bart explained.

In that tent?"

"Yes. What's wrong with that? The couldn't very well live inside. There isn't room."

Anne's shoulders slumped as she followed the others out of the car.

Bill stood looking around at the wilderness of rough palmettos and scraggly scrub pines stretching away bleakly in every direction. "Be nice and spoky here at night," he remarked. "You're not thinking of taking over this joint, are you, Dad?"

Bart didn't answer. He strode up on the veranda and opened the door. The others followed gingerly, their eyes busily alert to every feature of Susie's Place.

They first went into a long, narrow dining room with a waxed floor. The juke box was silent now, and there was soiled napery on the small wooden tables. A hard-looking, frowsy-haired girl came through a

207

door at the end of the room and stared at them from dark-circled, blue eyes. Her skin was pasty, and she wore a wrinkled blue shirt and slacks that looked as if they had been slept in.

Anne laid an arm around her daughter's shoulder, as though to shield Rita, in her crisp green linen, from contamination.

"This is Queenie," Bart said. "Queenie, my family. Mrs. Elsnar. Rita. Bill."

"Glad to know you," the girl simpered. Her large eyes remained fixed on Bill. Like a vulture, Anne thought.

"Where's Tessie?" Bart asked.

"She's doin' her washin'," Queenie explained.

Anne saw Tessie through a window. A frowsy blond, as plump as Queenie was thin, wearing tight brown slacks. Tessie was hanging skimpy feminine apparel on a clothesline.

"These are the waitresses?" Anne asked pleasantly, while she thought, with an inward groan, of the crisp, smartly groomed young women she had expected to see.

"Ah, yes." Bart's face flushed as he hurried through the doorway in which Queenie stood.

The girl turned in at the door as Bill passed her and smiled straight up into his face.

The "lounge" was a big square room with a bar across one side, with well-stocked shelves of wines and liquors. A good-looking man of about forty was pushing a wet rag around the top of the bar. He was clean shaven and well dressed.

"This is Dan, Susie's husband," said Bart.

Anne felt like saying, "Don't any of these people have last names?"

"I'll call Susie," Dan said. By this time, Anne

208

knew about what to expect. Susie wouldn't be much of a surprise.

She was a thin woman with vivid lips and cheeks and bold eyes. Her nails were long and pointed and blood-red. She wore a clean blue shirt, slacks, and glittering earrings.

Anne turned away, wondering if Bart had lost his mind.

"Come along, Mrs. Elsnar, and I'll show you around," Susie offered cordially.

They went first to a bedroom beyond the lounge. It was furnished with a bed that sagged in the middle and was covered with a wrinkled cretonne spread. There was a scratched dresser, a chair, and limp curtains at the window.

"You and Mr. Elsnar could snatch forty winks here, like Dan and me, when business is slow." Susie smiled.

Anne swallowed painfully and stared at the woman, speechless.

"Now, here is the real *peece de resistunce* of Susie's Place." Susie explained proudly, leading the way into another large bare room. "This is where the money is made. And plenty of it, I might add. Look at Dan and me. We've made our pile. Now we're goin' back to Chicago to live. Enjoy ourselves. I'd just like to see a nice couple like you and Mr. Elsnar walk right in here and pile up the dough, just like us."

While Susie talked, Anne looked around the room. A sagging sofa and two armchairs stood near the door. In the middle of the room was a long, narrow table surrounded by straight wooden chairs. The table dipped in at on end, and Susie pulled out a circular drawer. It was empty, except for a shiny revolver.

"This is where Dan sits in on the games," she

explained. "So's he can pull out his take from each pot and drop it in this drawer. The fun comes when you count the night's take—or mornin's, 'cause sometimes the boys play all night."

Anne's mouth sagged open. A gambling house! Susie didn't seem aware of Anne's reaction. the young woman seemed to take it for granted that she knew.

"Don't you have trouble—?" Anne waved her hand expressively.

"Oh, you have to grease a few palms here and there," Susie admitted easily. "Just be friendly and generous with the deputy sheriff. He's the only one bothers us anymore. He comes in only once a month. You see, we're quite a ways from town. Sit down, Miz Elsnar, and ask me any questions you like."

Anne dropped limply into one of te armchairs. Through the open door, she saw Dan sliding two drinks across the bar to Bill and Rita. She cringed.

Susie was trying very hard to convince her this was the opportunity of a lifetime. "That right there," she said, pointing at the long table, "is a gold mine. I've seen Dan take in five, six hundred at one session. Cross my heart and hope to die. Our customers are all fine, upstandin' businessmen from town. As I said, they play all night sometimes. You get so you sleep through it. *I* do. It's a bit hard on Dan. He has to sit right there, eagle eyed. Some men have terribly short memories when they win a pot."

"I can imagine," Anne murmured.

"You could keep Queenie and Tessie on if you wanted," Susie went on. "They know the ropes." She winked.

There was more advice. About the way to deal with souses, when Mr. Elsnar wouldn't be there and Anne

210

was behind the bar, and how Susie's chili was so popular she made it in quantiies. She was generous about passing on her recipe.

"So now," she finished briskly, "I guess you know as much about running the place as I do."

Anne smiled wanly. "Yes, indeed. You've been most enlightening." She was thinking about the revolver she had seen in Dan's drawer. She couldn't wait to get out of there. The drab walls seemed to be closing in on her, smothering her. This certainly was Bart's craziest project yet. It was also his last.

"Are you ready to go, Bart?" she asked.

"Well, what do you think of it, Anne?"

Dan and Susie watched her expectantly.

"I'd like to think it over," she said with a polite smile. "Could we let you know in a few days?"

Susie shot a look at Dan. "Well, don't take too long," she warned. "There's a couple other parties really interested. We'd like to see you nice people get it, so don't wait too long."

The four Elsnars walked out to their car in silence.

Bart was bristling with excitement. "Chance of a lifetime, isn't it Anne?" he asked, as they whirled down the drive. "You needn't worry about being able to swing it. Their price is a bit steep, but we'd get it back in no time. I'm sure we could get a loan frm the Oceana bank. You wouldn't have to live there. We'd rent an apartment in town. Fact is, you wouldn't have to take any part in the operation, if you didn't want to."

"Bart, sometimes I wonder if you are entirely sane," Anne said.

"That's no attitude to take," he shot back. "You're always harping about needing money. Well, there's

211

our chance to make plenty of it, and make it in a hurry. We'd be on Easy Street in a couple of years. We could all have anything we wanted. Cars for everybody. Summer cruises.''

Anne had to admit Bart was right about one thing. There was money to be made in that place, but it took a shrewd, hardheaded operator, like Dan, to swing it. Those ''fine, upstandin' gentlemen from town'' would annihilate easygoing, indulgent Bart in no time at all.

Anne turned to the back seat. ''What do you children think about this project?''

''The place is a dump,'' Bill said. ''I was wondering what I'd say when my friends ask what my father does.''

Rita shuddered. ''It gives me the creeps just to think about it. Those awful girls!''

''There's your answer, Bart,'' Anne said.

His lips tightened and his face flushed. The arrow on the speedometer climbed to seventy. He didn't speak. To Anne, who knew him so well, his thoughts were almost audible. She wondered if she and Bart would ever see eye to eye on anything. After a quarter of a century they were still poles apart.

On the way home, they stopped at a roadside restaurant with a canopied walk up to the entrance. This was the sort of place Anne had pictured when Bart had first broached the subject of a new business. It was dimly lit inside, with spotless napery on the tables and beaming young waitresses in natty uniforms.

Anne couldn't resist saying, ''This is the sort of place I thought you had in mind, Bart.''

He harumphed impatiently and picked up a menu.

"I wouldn't mind working in a place like this—nights and weekends," Bill said, his eyes on a waitress.

Rita just smiled and refrained from comment.

A wasted day, Anne thought. Or was it? This was the first time in years the whole family had been out together. She could see Olivia's fine hand in this situation. His mother had prodded Bart into getting into a business of his own, and evidently this seemed to be the answer—for him. Actually, there was such a wide gap between her values and Bart's, there seemed little hope of them getting together in understanding at any level.

CHAPTER 21

Anne knew Bart's restlessness had reached its peak when he decided to go deep-sea fishing with Luke Ainger, skipper of the *Gray Gull*. She and Bart needed to be apart while cool feelings existed between them. Bart would come back refreshed by the sea air, rubbing his big hands together gleefully. He loved the sea, and Luke's fishing boat cut through the waves like a big white pelican. Bart gloried in the tug of a wahoo or a tarpon, a red snapper or a sailfish on his line. That was a battle he knew how to win. It always filled him with an almost childish joy when he came home with a good catch.

She welcomed this quiet interval, too. She had just about decided on the lesser of two evils, having endured about all of Bart's idiosyncracies she could take. When he returned, she would be ready with her plans and proposals.

The morning dawned gray and sunless, the sort of day that needed time to awaken. The few clouds in the sky didn't look like impending rain, but the atmosphere had a yellowish tinge that bothered Bart as he stood at a window puffing on a cigar.

"Oh, well, if there's any danger from the weather, Luke will know," he said at last. "See you tonight, Anne."

"All right," she replied.

The *Gray Gull* always left its dock at eight sharp to clear the sand bar in the channel before the tide went out. Anne could hear a faint echo of its bell as the *Gull* took off for the open sea.

At nine, heavy clouds rolled up from the direction of the Keys, and the wind began to moan around the house with a tropical wail that never failed to chill her. By noon, it was raining hard, and the wind had risen to almost hurricane force. Pellets of hail beat against the windows. Lightning ripped out of the gray clouds, followed by crashes of thunder that rolled around and ended by shaking the ground until the house trembled.

Anne cowered in a dark corner of the living room.

At four, Bill came dashing in, his rain gear drenched.

"What a gale!" he said. "Good thing the shrimp fleet didn't go out today."

Anne's throat suddenly felt hot and dry. "How do you know the shrimp fleet didn't go out?"

"Ken Louder's father said so. Mr. Louder owns the fleet, so he knows. He drove down to the college to pick up Ken and brought the rest of us home."

Anne stood up so quickly she banged her elbow against the sharp edge of a table, but she hardly felt the pain. "Your father went out on the *Gray Gull* this morning," she said.

Bill jerked around to face her, water dripping from his raincoat onto the rug. "But, Mom, Luke wouldn't—are you sure?"

She nodded. "I heard the bell."

"What time?"

"A little before eight."

"Are you sure? It's almost impossible to hear the bell from this distance."

"I heard it. Besides, your father would have come home long before this if he hadn't gone."

They stood staring helplessly at each other. Neither of them heard Rita drive into the yard.

"The phone," Bill muttered, just as a ball of fire ripped out of the gray sky on an ear-splitting crack of thunder.

"No!" Anne cried. "Don't touch that phone. It isn't safe with all the lightning."

"Isn't this a riot?" Rita came in, shaking the rain from her coat. "What's the matter? You two look like a couple of ghosts."

Bill explained, his words tumbling over one another.

"I'm going to drive down to the docks," he said.

"I'll go with you," Anne said.

Rita shrugged into her raincoat again. "Me, too."

"Come on," Bill shouted.

"I'll get your raincoat, Mother," Rita said.

They dashed out to the garage, and Bill started Anne's car with a punishing roar that would have drawn a protest from her under ordinary circumstances. Today she hardly noticed.

As they drove down the flooded streets, rain slashed against the car, slowing the windshield wipers almost to a stop. A howling wind tore through the palm trees in the parkway, bending their straight trunks almost double, their green fronds stretched out like pleading hands. A tall old oak tree crashed with a ripping, slow-motion groan across Hibiscus Avenue, just missing them. Bill had to turn around in the narrow street and take another route.

Anne sat forward in the seat, nervously clasping and unclasping her hands. The deafening roar and whine of the wind made the trip to the inlet seem to take an eternity.

As they approached the dock area, the wet sand road was slippery. They slid around precariously, sloshing through puddles that covered the car with yellow mud.

On one covered dock, a few women, bundled in raincoats and sou'westers, huddled together like fright-ened gulls. Laurel Ainger, wife of the *Gull's*'s skipper, stood apart, clinging to a wet post, her eyes wild, her young face crumpled into an aging mask.

Bill pulled up beside her, and Anne opened the window. The rain sluiced down in knife-sharp, slant-ing sheets that raked her face. "Did the *Gull* go out, Laurel?" she asked unnecessarily.

Laurel came over to the car and leaned against it, her raincoat whipping against her legs. "It went out." Her cry was an echo of the wind and was carried away on it's wailing roar. "Luke radioed the Coast Guard that they were in rough seas. That was hours ago. There's been nothing since."

A ball of fire rolled across the sky and crashed into another one coming from the opposite direction with an explosion that seemed to split the heavens.

John Edgerton, whose little store was close to the docks, came out, bent double against the wind. He took Laurel in his arms. "Come on, Laurie. You cain't do no good to Luke standing out in this storm. Was Bart on Luke's boat, Miz Elsnar? Too bad. Well, there's no use stayin' around here. You just go on home and take it easy. We'll call you when the *Gull* comes in, the minute we hear anything.''

Take it easy, Anne thought, as Bill turned the car around and headed for home. Bart's very words. ''Take it easy, Annie,'' he had said a thousand times when she was annoyed or worried. Hot tears were flooding her eyes, but she winked them away so the children wouldn't see them. She knew they must be asking themselves the same question that was tugging at her. Suppose something happened to the *Gray Gull* out there and Bart didn't come home? Never before had Ann considered the possibility of anything happening to Bart. So strong, so full of energy, he seemed indestructible.

Her children were unnaturally quiet, and Anne knew how frightened they were. The car, even in Bill's strong young hands, was like a leaf in the wind, weaving from side to side down the flooded streets. Anne knew this was nothing to what was happening out there on raging sea. She could almost see the angry waves leaping over the top of the small boat, the powerful weight of the water smashing the *Gull* below the surface, like a giant hand, and holding it there until all on board would perish.

Bart's face, looking white and strained, swam before her eyes, and she could see him disappearing into the sea, one hand held high, as though in farewell—the hand with the garnet ring she had given him that first Christmas. A wave of nausea washed over her.

When they were safely home again, she went into the library and closed the door, where she could pace the floor without the children knowing. She wondered how many miles worried wives had paced through the years. On a vacation in Kennebunk, Maine, she had been intrigued by the lovely old houses of former sea captains, with their widow's walks, those high balconies facing the ocean, where the wives of seafaring men had paced and prayed and suffered through stormy weather. The carpeted stretch between the bookcases and the door became her widow's walk today.

The word widow hit Anne like a lightning bolt. She had never thought about it. She had always thought of herself as the first to go. She was now face to face with a new concept. What would life be like? What would this house be like without big, noisy, good-natured Bart?

The storm outside raged on, leaving Anne weak and shaken. Now and then she wondered if the thunder might be drowning out the ring of·the telephone. She sat down in Bart's chair, fingering his pens and the picture of herself and the children on his desk. She rubbed her hand over the green blotter with the doodles he had scribbled on it while composing a letter or struggling with his check book. As she leaned back, she could feel the shape of his body in the soft leather of the chair. In that moment, she knew something of the aching despair that tore at little Rita's heart every time she touched something that had belonged to Ron.

Funny, the things that run through one's mind at a time like this, she thought. Bart's booming laugh. The gleeful way he rubbed his hands together when he was pleased. Gentle hands on her shoulders. "Now, Mother, take it easy." In spite of his blustery, noisy ways, Bart was a gentleman. Gentle with her. Gentle with the children. Memories of the way she had leaned on him when the children were born came to her. After the pain and the stress, she had always awakened to find his hand holding hers, his face anxious, love and gratitude in his twinkling brown eyes. It was so long since she had thought of all that. She could even smile now as she recalled how often she had heard his old refrain, "It might be a way by which a fellow could make a little money." Bart had never found that sweet Utopia he had dreamed about.

Anne's faith in her husband had first been shaken by his affair with that girl, Celia. Cute little thing. Cuddly and deft. What a delectable dinner she had ready that day I walked in! "Oh, you're Bart's *wife*? Pleased to meetcha. Won't you say and have supper?" *The way I sailed into her. Scared her to death. But could I really blame Bart? He was alone all week on the road, and I was miserable that summer. That little rascal, Bill, was making life unbearable. I thought he'd never arrive.*

Anne stood up and began to pace the floor again. Once, she opened the door and looked out at her children. They were slumped in chairs, looking white and stricken. *They love him so much. I love him, too. And now he may never know.*

As abruptly as it had begun, the storm subsided. The sudden silence gave Anne the hollow sensation of falling into a deep well. The sun burst forth, and through the east window she saw a perfect double rainbow arched across the sky. There might be news of the *Gray Gull.*

The scream of the telephone stopped Anne's thoughts and she ran across the room and seized it eagerly.

It was John Edgerton. "The *Gull*'s in, Miz Elsnar. Everybody's safe."

She opened the door and called to the children.

"The *Gull*'s in. Your father is safe."

Rita and Bill grabbed each other and began to shout and dance around the room.

When Bart walked in, looking drawn and weary, Anne's heart raced to meet him, but all she could say was, "So you're back."

"Yes, I'm back," he replied stiffly, his face blank with disappointment.

Inwardly, Anne cursed the coldness that held her rigid in such moments. She had never been demonstrative. Even now, she couldn't seem to force warmth and gladness up from her rejoicing heart, but the children made up for her. They hugged and kissed Bart and bombarded him with questions.

"It was pretty grim out there for a while," he said. "Seemed as if the wind and the sea were fighting over us to see which would destroy us first. The *Gull* was like a toy boat on a windy lake. The gale would blow us one way, then turn and slap us back the other. Then we'd go into a deep trough and the waves would wash right over us. More than once, I thought we were swamped. That thunder and lightning was something to behold. Gave a fellow an idea of what the end of the world might be like. The lightning struck us once. I think the ship-to-shore system went out that time. Nobody asked. Nobody wanted to bother Luke. He had all he could handle. Luke's a good skipper."

"If he's so good, why did he go out on a day like this?" Bill asked. "The shrimp fleet stayed in."

"Well, it didn't look too bad this morning. Besides, the shrimp boats are small and old. They're not equipped like the *Gull*."

"Daddy, what were you thinking? What were you doing all that time out there?" Rita asked.

"Doing what I could to help. Praying, mostly, I
221

guess. I wasn't making any plans for the future," he chuckled.

Anne sat there listening. She couldn't get a word past the lump in her throat. She knew Bart was minimizing the danger for the children's sake, but the trembling of his hands and the quietness of his voice were more revealing than his words.

Now was the time to go to him, to tell him how happy she was that he had returned safely. She couldn't. She seemed glued to the chair, the words strangled in her throat. She wondered why Bart couldn't read her as she read him. Why couldn't he see the gladness in her eyes when she looked at him? But the day went by without a sign from either of then that their situation was any different from what it had been.

That night, alone in their room, Anne tried again. "You'll never know how glad I was to see you walk in today, knowing you were safe, Bart."

He gave her a long look that said, "Show me."

She just looked back at him, her hands locked together across her stomach.

"It might have been better if I hadn't come back," he said. "You don't have to put up with me any longer, if that's what you want. I know it's been running through your mind ever since Bill's accident. There was a time I worried about our marriage breaking up, because I was afraid the kids might grow away from me. Now I know there's no danger of that."

He took clean pajamas from a drawer and walked into the bathroom. Anne stood there, staring at the closed door.

CHAPTER 22

Bart's sullen mood, following the fruitless trip to Miami, was not surprising. He spent hours puttering about his workshop. Anne knew he would snap out of his unpleasant frame of mind in a few days. His workshop was a panacea for all his ills. In the meantime, life in their house was not too harmonious.

As far as Anne was concerned, their marriage had reached its lowest ebb. There was only one solution she could think of, but it upset her to think about it. It would scandalize the children, but she had had about all she could take of Bart's notions.

For months prior to her recent agreement with Dr. Emmett, she had thought about the profession she had given up years before. Now that she had committed herself, she knew it would not be easy. She had to tell the children but kept putting it off. For the present, she decided to wait a little longer and catch up on some calls she had to make.

She had seen little of her daughter and grandchildren

lately. Rita had told her about the night Margaret had walked into her house at the most auspicious moment to rout Jack and his cohorts. It seemed to Anne she had seen Tony and Margaret around town together more often lately. She decided to drop in on both young women today.

Rita's house looked serene and lovely, the sun shining down on its red roof and glinting rainbows from its sparkling windows. The trees in the grove with their glossy green foliage hung heavy with fruit. Orange and grapefruit blossoms were bursting out all over, filling the early spring atmosphere with a heavenly sweetness. After years of Florida living, it still seemed miraculous to Anne that citrus trees should burst into the blossoms of a new spring while still laden with last year's fruit.

She found Rita and the children in the study. As Anne stood at the door, her heart skipped a beat. She had often found her daughter sitting at Ron's desk, with her head buried in her arms. Today, all that was changed. Ron's desk and the red sofa were gone from the study. So were the red drapes. The room was all blue and gold now. Rita's Queen Anne desk replaced the heavy oak one Ron had used. The room no longer looked like a shrine to the departed, and Anne was glad.

A table and three chairs stood beside an open window, where Rita and the children were sitting, so absorbed in what they were doing they didn't see Anne until she spoke.

"What goes on here?" she asked.

They all looked up, and the children flung themselves on her with whoops of joy.

"Get a chair for Nanny, Bobby," Rita said.

"Why, Rita, you're making sand pictures again," Anne said. She picked up one of the finished pictures in its little gilt frame and studied it: a beach, the sea, and two palm trees, and an orange moon. It was lovely.

"This is better than anything you ever did, honey," she said.

Rita looked pleased. "Do you really think so, Mother? I've decided to go into it on a large scale. I met Mrs. Dwain the other day. She has a gift shop in Vero Beach, and she told me the tourists snap these up so fast she can't keep them in stock." Anne remembered when Rita had started making sand pictures in her teens, but there were so many demands on her time then, she gave it up. Rita pushed aside her saucers of tiny shells and varicolored sands and stretched her arms above her head. "I had to do something. I was getting desperate. There were some things I had to stop doing, too." She looked around the transformed room.

"I'm glad, dear," Anne said.

Rita was a changed person. There was a new dignity and purposefulness about her. She looked contented, even happy this afternoon. The fact that she had begun to work at something creative was a healthy sign. Olivia had scored again.

"The children are getting as much of a bang out of my artistic flair as I am," she laughed. "We've walked miles, and driven even more miles, in search of shells and different colored sand. When I finish several pictures, I'll have an exhibition at the Art Club downtown."

"It makes me happier than I can tell you to see you like this again, dear."

Rita colored self-consciously. "Notice the way I've

changed the room?''

Anne nodded. ''It's bright and gay now. More like you.''

I decided that keeping Ron's things around wouldn't bring him back. This room tore me to pieces, yet I couldn't keep out of it.''

''Yes, darling. I hated seeing you so morbid. It wasn't like you. This is much better.'' Anne's gesture took in the redecorated room, the busy work table, the interested children.

''Stay to dinner?'' Rita asked.

''Not today. I have some other calls to make, so I won't bother you. You'll want to get back to your work.''

Anne felt a definite lift of the spirits as she walked through the cool, clean house and out to her car. Somehow, Rita had groped her way back from the dark grave where part of her heart was buried. She seemed to have found a substitute for Tony King.

Anne hoped Margaret had fared as well. She found Margaret on the shady east porch, hemming curtains.

''How nice to see you, Mrs. Elsnar,'' she said. ''Come up and sit down.''

''Nice and cool here,'' Anne said, selecting a chair in the shade of a climbing flame vine. ''I just came from Rita's. I'm so happy about her.''

Margaret looked up inquiringly.

''I think she's settled down to living again,'' Anne went on. ''She's made up her mind to stop grieving for Ron. She and the children were busy as bees working on sand pictures. Rita always had a flair for art.''

''Yes,'' Margaret said placidly. ''So I've been told.''

''Perhaps,'' Anne began, feeling her way carefully,

"she owes some of her present contentment to you, Margaret. She was so grateful that you called at the house the night she was in such a spot. That Jack can make her miserable."

Margaret smiled and nodded. "It seems to have worked out well for all of us. Tony and I had a definite understanding that night after we came home. Tony has settled down. He seems more contented than I've ever known him. We both want a baby now," she added shyly.

"That's good news, Margaret," Anne said. "I'm so glad for you. I have to make one more call this afternoon. I haven't seen Bette Carey since she left the hospital. I really haven't much heart for it, but thought I'd run over for a few minutes."

Margaret's face sobered. "I haven't seen her either. I hardly knew what to do. She'll think it strange if her friends don't call, and yet I wonder if she really wants to see people."

"Perhaps she won't mind seeing me. I was with her so much in the hospital. But I'm really afraid for Bette." Considering Bill's part in Bette's misfortune, it was a difficult subject to discuss with anyone. "I'll give you a ring and let you know how I'm received."

As she drove down the street, Anne passed Tony coming home from his office. He smiled and waved to her. He looked happy. Anne thought that everything seemed to be working out for them.

It was with considerable trepidation that she drove up to the Dwight Careys' brick and coquina house on Ocean Drive. She had been there only once before, on the memorable night of Bette's party. At that time, she hadn't approved of Bette.

Mrs. Cary was at home, the maid said, leading Anne

227

to the shady breezeway where Bette lay on a chaise longue. It was the first time Anne had seen her without the bandages covering her face. She was thankful for her physician's training as she clenched her teeth and assumed a pokerfaced expression to conceal her shock.

"What a nice surprise," Bette said cordially. "Mila, pull up that rocker for Mrs. Elsnar."

It was beautiful there as the late afternoon sunshine cast shadows across the terrazzo floor of the breezeway and intensified the brilliance of the flowers in Bette's tropical garden. Beyond the sea wall, the ocean was as blue as the sky, except for he frolocking whitecaps.

As she settled herself in the comfortable chair, Anne realized she was more nervous and ill at ease than her hostess. There was something poised and dignified about the still figure with the strangely disfigured face framed by soft, golden hair.

"I hope you're feeling much better," Anne ventured.

"Practically back to normal. I take a little walk every day. With Dwight's help, of course."

Anne smiled warmly. "That's fine. Do you have much trouble with that leg?"

"No. Thanks to you, I manage. By the time I'm through with this leg, it will be as good as the other," she said firmly.

Anne settled back in her chair. It seemed funny now to think she had expected hysterics, self-pity, even reproachful allusions to Bill. She had never really known this girl at all.

"Some day, when you have the time, Mrs. Elsnar—or should I call you Dr. Tallman?"

Anne laughed. "Poor Dr. Emmett. She's a good

228

soul, but she hasn't much use for men. Not as husbands, anyway. They ruin a woman's career, she says."

"Yes, I know. She's a funny old girl. What I wanted to ask is about her hospital. It isn't too well equipped, is it?"

"No, I suppose not. They lack a number of the newer developments there."

"That's what I thought. One of these days, I'd like to go over a list with you," Bette said surprisingly. "Maybe there's something we could do about it."

"That's very thoughtful of you," Anne said.

"And while we're on the subject, what about you? Look what you did for my leg. You could do a lot for other people, too."

Anne was silent. She couldn't tell Bette she had gone home completely exhausted after every one of those treatments that had been so successful.

Bette sat up in her chair and looked Anne directly in the eye. "Tell me, Mrs. Elsnar, why did you bother about my leg? You didn't approve of me. Not that I blame you. I was so rude to you."

Anne was startled. "Oh, now, really!"

"No, I mean it," Bette said. "Why did you do it?"

"Well, if you must know, I felt it my duty to do snything I could. Bill was driving your car that night."

"I thought that was the reason. He came to the hospital to see me. Did he tell you?"

Anne shook her head.

"Poor kid, he was sick with remorse. I told him the accident wasn't his fault. I wasn't quite fair to Bill. I've never been quite fair to anyone, I guess. That's the story of my life. I've always had to learn the hard way."

Anne remained silent. If confession was good for the soul, she might be able to help by listening.

"I'm learning, though," Bette went on. "In these months, I've suffered for every wrong I ever did." Her voice shook, but she recovered her poise instantly and went on talking. "It isn't as bad as you may think. Of course, I don't have to look at my own face, but I don't mind as much as I expected to. Besides, for the first time since our honeymoon, Dwight and I are really happy."

Was e? Anne thought of her own youthful suffering due to Bart's roving eye. She recalled Tony King's devotion to pretty Rita while neglecting his plain little wife. Dwight might pity this pathetic wreck of the beauty he had married, but would he love her enoug to make her happy now?

As if in answer to her thought, Dwight came briskly into the breezeway and went straight to Bette. "Hellow, sweet." He bent and kissed her lingeringly. Then he turned and shook hands with Anne. "How good of you to come, Mrs. Elsnar," he said.

"I'm amazed at the progress this young lady is making, Dwight. She tells me she is walking now."

"That's right," he beamed. "Isn't she a wonder? Let's show Mrs. Elsnar how nicely you can toddle about, honey."

Bette laughed. "You'd think I was an infant." She reached for his hand, and together they walked slowly down the path toward the sea wall.

Anne caught her lip between her teeth and bit down hard. The distant roar of the surf seemed intensified in her ears. Little beads of perspiration stood out on her upper lip as she watched. There was grace in every line of that erect young figure. Not once did Bette drag her left foot. She lifted it and set it down firmly, although Anne knew that every movement must be excruciating agony. She thought again, *I never really knew that girl at all*.

They turned and came back, and Bette went on smiling. But her face was so white that the scars stood out, red and angry looking. Otherwise, she gave no sign of what that short walk had cost her.

"Isn't she wonderful?" Dwight asked again, and his eyes bright with pride as they rested on his wife.

"Yes," Anne said, "she *is* wonderful, Dwight. You must be proud of her. Now I've got to run along."

To her surprise, she bent and kissed Bette's cheek. Tears misted her eyes as she walked out to her car. She believed Dwight and Bette were happy now, if she could read the looks that had passed between them. Only once before had she seen such a depth of affection. Between Ron and Rita.

As she turned into Ocean Drive, Anne thought back over her afternoon. Rita, happy with her children. Tony contentedly coming home to Margaret. Bette and Dwight. All of them seemed to have solved their problems. She thought, *What ails me? I helped the others to happiness. Why can't I help myself? Or is there no help for Bart and me?*

The word separation sprang at her like a clenched fist. She remembered how often she had thought of it, longed for it, and fought against it through the years when there were young children depending on her and Bart. But now that the children were grown up, Bart would never change. Anne's respect for him had dwindled. The love they had once shared was like a worn-out garment. It might be a relief to discard it, a relief to both of them to go their separate ways. No more straining at cross purposes.

231

The day after the storm Bart was unable to shake off his black mood. He had half expected Anne to take him up on his offer to get out and leave her alone. Maybe she was thinking it over. The bomb still might drop at any moment.

One panacea that seldom failed to lift his spirits was puttering in his little shop behind the garage. On this humid March day, while fitting tiles into the top of a cocktail table he had designed, he thought back to the spring morning years ago when he lay convalescing in a Vermont hospital. He had heard a brisk voice out in the corridor, a challenging voice that sent little electric shocks all through him. Then he saw her, the dark-haired, slender young woman coming down the hall. Reed-slim and tough-fibrered, but bright-eyed as a kitten, she had come to his door and asked, "How is the patient this morning?"

"Just fine," said the nurse, who was fixing his bed.

Bart couldn't say a word. All he could do was look. She was so vibrant, so happy, so in tune with life. She was on her way to a successful career. He remembered how surprised he had been when the nurse said, "That's Dr. Tallman."

Bart's big hands fingered a smooth tile absently as his dark eyes became dreamy with memories. Anne had been fun then, with a merriness in her eyes and a dry sense of humor. She hadn't been the least bit vain about her youthful success.

Their courtship hadn't been very satisfactory. Bart was convalescing, and his leg gave him plenty of trouble. He couldn't sit still long enough to give it a chance to heal properly. But there had been pleasant intervals when she had time to talk, and they seemed to think alike about almost everything. They had been swept

232

off their feet and into a marriage that had seemed ideal in the beginning.

He banged his fist on the table in front of him. Maybe Anne should never have married at all. Or she should have married another doctor, or a business tycoon with the same drive and ambition she possessed. *But not me*, he thought. *Not a lazy man who is contented only when he's dreaming up a new gadget or making a lot of useless junk. I can't help it if I despise conventional jobs, where a fellow has to punch a clock. That isn't living, to my way of thinking.*

If a fellow didn't have to keep up with the tycoons, he could make enough to live comfortably selling citrus from a small grove and maybe selling fancy gadgets he makes. The family could go off on little trips and beach parties, where they could be pleasantly lazy. Have a few congenial friends who could be happy with a mandolin and a song, a stein of beer, and some interesting hobbies to talk about. Keeping your nose to the grindstone every minute to have a big house and educate your kids in the same schools as the bankers and the rest of the big shots is the bunk. Doesn't give a fellow a chance to live. Anne was always driving him, always finding an opening in some prosaic line of work, practically forcing him into it.

Maybe he should have married someone like that little red-headed gal from Georgia. *Celia*. He smiled as he thought of her. Little vivid, laughing Celia. There was a girl who knew how to live.

He never saw Celia again, but he couldn't forget her. Bring Celia flowers and she was as excited as a little kid. She'd break off a pink rose and pin it in that mop of red curls, chirping like a bird. Bring Anne flowers and she'd look at you with an exasperated sigh that seemed to say, "Oh, Bart, how could you spend money so foolishly?" Anne was always looking for price tags. Her people must have had a tough time of it on that Vermont farm. Well, the Elsnars hadn't been wealthy either, but Bart recalled with nostalgia the carefree life in his father's house on the Key. Warm humid days when he walked barefoot on the hammocks with his fishing pole and a can of worms. It always pleased his mother when he came home with a mess of fish for supper. He loved the eerie quiet of the marshes, the lazy alligators coming up to snap at a fish or sliding out of the water to lie in the sun on a strip of land. And the birds. Cardinals with their brilliant red bodies and blue jays in the trees. Mockingbirds filling the air with music and statuesque herons standing for what seemed hours on one leg.

He had gone back to visit now and then. The one time he took Anne, they had to leave after one night. She had been terrified of snakes and alligators, especially the whistle and scream and bark of night birds and animals. She had clung to him all night, and in the morning she had insisted on leaving, vowing never to go back.

There was a scuffling on the shell drive and Bart looked up expectantly. Rita came rushing across the threshold and flung herself in his arms.

"Hi, Daddy! It's so good to see you in your shop again and know you're safe."

"Hello, Baby," he said. "What are you—?"

Over Rita's shoulder, he saw Anne standing in the doorway, and his heart turned over. Something was up.

234

CHAPTER 23

The day after the storm, Rita was unable to settle down to her usual routine. She still felt shaken and depressed, after those grueling hours waiting for news of the *Gray Gull*. She couldn't understand her mother. When Bart came home in a state of shock from his experience, Anne had just stood there, wooden. All she had said was, "So you're back."

If that had been Ron coming back to me, I'd have flung my arms around him, and they'd never have pried me loose, Rita thought. *Poor Daddy! He looked so disappointed.* There had been something frightening about the way her parents stood facing each other, rigid, unyielding, as though everything was over between them. Yet, Rita was certain her mother cared for her father. Anne had walked the floor for hours in anxiety until the call came that everyone on the *Gray Gull* was safe. It probably was her strict New England upbringing that made Anne seem so stiff and cold.

The idea that her parents' marriage was tottering nagged at Rita. She had to find out.

Now that her house was quiet, with Bobby off to school and Cindy and Babs on their way to the club for Babs's swimming lesson, Rita showered and dressed in a becoming new mauve suit and drove downtown.

The wind and rain of the day before had left their mark all across the city. Branches and fruit had been blown from citrus tres and strewn about lawns and gardens. An oak tree had penetrated the roof of a flat-topped house. Crews of men were everywhere cleaning debris from the streets. The downtown area had escaped much of the damage, except for a few broken plate-glass windows. Edith had called earlier to say that the office and lumber yard were intact.

At the post office, where she stopped to mail a couple of letters, Rita ran into Mark Roberts at the stamp window.

"Good morning, Mark," she said.

He looked surprised. It was the first time she had called him by his first name.

"I see you survived yesterday's gale," she added.

"Wasn't that a heller?" he said. "I've seen thunder storms up north that were bad, but never anything as wild as that."

"There was a double tempest in our family," she said, feeling the need to talk to someone. "My father was out on the *Gray Gull*. You know, Luke Ainger's fishing boat?"

"I heard about that," he said. "I didn't know your father was on board, though. Can't we go somewhere for coffee? I'd like to hear about it."

236

Rita surprised herself by suggesting, "There's the Sweete Shoppe next door."

Over a little white table in the Sweete Shoppe, she told him about driving down to the docks, the pandemonium down there, and the hours they had waited at her mother's for word.

"If anything had happened to Daddy," she choked up and was unable to go on.

Mark reached across the table and folded a warm hand around Rita's. Her cold fingers turned and clung to his for a moment. When she looked up, she was alarmed by the expression in his eyes. She pulled her hand away and picked up her purse.

"I didn't mean to get emotional," she said, brushing at her eyes and trying to smile. "I guess I just had to talk to someone."

"I'm glad I was around. It's nice to know everything turned out all right for you and your family, Mrs. Wybron."

"Rita," she said.

"Rita," he repeated, with a smile so warm it rivaled the spring sunshine.

Driving to the Elsnar home, she was amazed at herself for confiding Mark Roberts. She knew it was unwise and unkind to encourage anything beyond a casual friendship. But from his expression when they parted, she was afraid she had gone too far.

She realized that one of her failings was a tendency to lean on someone. First, it had been her father. Then, Ron. More recently, Tony. Since the night Margaret had come to her rescue with a puzzling pretext, Tony hadn't stopped in or even phoned. *There's nobody*, she tought. *I feel so alone*!

Was she trying to lean on Mark Roberts now? It would be so easy. She was beginning to see him as others saw him, a thoroughly nice person with her best interests at heart. She determined not to toy with his emotions. The night they had had dinner together last winter drifted into her thoughts frequently—the way they had laughed and talked. But the way he looked at her sometimes bothered her. She'd have to be more careful.

At the Elsnars', she found Anne in the patio with the morning paper. Her mother looked pretty to Rita, serence in a flowered-print dress, her dark hair becomingly arranged with a center part.

"Where's Daddy?" Rita asked.

"Out in his shop, puttering about, I suppose," Anne said.

"Guess I'll go see what he's up to."

Anne surprised her by throwing aside the newspaper and reaching for her hand. "I'll go with you," she said.

They walked through the kitchen where a delicious aroma tickled the senses pleasantly. Mandy stopped Anne. "This stew 'bout done. You want to thicken the gravy, Miz Elsnah?"

"Not today, Mandy. You can manage it, can't you?"

"Yas Mam'," Mandy said.

"I suppose the gravy will be lumpy," Anne remarked to Rita as they walked down the driveway. "Maybe the men won't notice. If they do, they can grumble to Mandy."

Bart was putting the finishing touches on a table. Rita rushed at him and enveloped him in a bear hug.

"Hi, Baby!" he said. "What are you doing out so early?"

Then he saw Anne.

"Mother, look at this table Daddy's been working on."

Anne moved closer.

"Just look at all these lovely things, Mother." With youthful enthusiasm Rita brought out more tables, book ends, magazine racks, and shell novelties. All of them were original in concept and showed skill and imagination. "Some of these things are much nicer than the pieces that sell at fabulous prices I've seen in coastal towns. Where do you get your ideas, Daddy?"

"What's the use of having an art student in the family if a feller can't study her books?"

The two women exchanged a look of amazement.

"Do you see what we have here, Mother?" Rita said. "An artist. Bill and I have been nagging him for years to open a gift shop."

"Aw now, honey bun, you know your mother would never approve," he protested. "First off, I'd have to rent a place downtown or on the beach. No, we'd better just forget it."

"You people know it's lunch time?" Bill said at the door. "I've got to get back to classes. Hi, Rita."

"Bill, you interrupted something," Rita said. "We were talking about the gift shop idea again. "Weren't we, Daddy?"

"Well, you kids know how I've always felt about it. Once or twice I mentioned it to your mother and she seemed to think it was the wrong thing for a big, healthy feller like yours truly."

"What do you think now, Mother?" Rita asked.

Hot color flamed into Anne's face, but she spoke quietly. "Why not? If that's what you want, Bart. I had a long talk on the phone with Dr. Emmet this morning. As usual, she had a story. This one was about the eagle and the prairie chicken. I'd like to tell you about it."

"We're all ears," Bill said.

Anne sat down on a bench beside the door. "It's an old Indian legend," she began. "It seems an Indian brave once found an eagle's egg and put it in the nest of a prairie chicken. All his life, the changeling believed he was a chicken and did what the other prairie chickens did. He clucked and cackled and scratched in the dirt for seeds and insects to eat. He never flew more than a few feet off the ground. Then, one day, many years later, he saw a magnificent bird soaring on golden wings far above him. Asking a neighbor what it was, he learned it ws an eagle. 'But you could never be like that bird', the neighbor said, 'You're just a prairie chicken.' "

"Interesting," Rita remarked. "Does it have some particular significance here, Mother?"

"Yes." Anne stood up and faced them, her shoulders straight and her head held high. "Irene Emmett reminded me I've been an eagle all my life, I have forgot how I should soar."

Bart's face went white. "What are you getting at?" he muttered.

"The significance, my dear child, is that I have decided to join the staff at the hospital," Anne said surprisingly. "When Bill starts medical school, we will need more money. Much more. I don't want anything to interfere with his caree, and I shall see that nothing does.''

"But, Mother, are you sure?''

"Yes, I'm sure. Sometimes, all of a sudden, the reason for everything becomes clear, and crooked paths look straighter. That's how it happened for me one morning in a little mission church not far from here. But to tell you the truth, it was your grandmother who opened my eyes in the first place. She suggested, in her inimitable way, that I was wasting my time and talent and became a grumbling invalid.''

"Oh, now Annie, she didn't mean it,'' Bart said. "You know how Mama is.''

"Bart, I agree with her.''

"But, Mom, you don't have to go back to work to help me,'' Bill objected.

Anne turned at the door. "I'm not doing it just for you, son. It's for me, too. Some day when you're at the height of your profession, you will understand.''

They were all quiet as they started toward the house, in answer to Mandy's call.

For the moment, discussion of Bart Elsnar's gift shop would have to be put aside while everyone absorbed what Anne had told them. The discussion was delayed only slightly, though. Male eagles as well as female eagles can soar, as Anne came to know.

CHAPTER 24

William Tallman Elsnar had finally gotten himself together. He had avoided the drug and liquor habits that proved so destructive to some of his fellow students, probably thanks to his mother.

On this bright spring afternoon he strode across the campus, swinging his briefcase and whistling a popular musical comedy tune.

"Hi, Elsnar!" someone called. He swung around to face Kevin Cloonan. "You're always in such a sweat lately. Where are you headed?"

"My dad's gift shop," Bill said. "He just started a new venture, and the whole family's getting into the act. All except Mom."

"She's the new doc at the hospital, I hear."

Bill nodded. "When anything goes wrong with the Elsnars, we don't have to yell for a doctor in the house?"

"How does your old man feel about it?"

242

"Dad's motto is: Never trouble trouble till trouble troubles you. He seems proud of Mom, really."

"I suppose you got the idea of med school from your mother. You know how many years you have to put in before you can hang out your shingle?"

"I've faced it, and it doesn't scare me."

"You'll be cooped up batting your brains out while the rest of us guys are whooping it up. What are you going to do about girls?"

"Well, with some of the agressive females I've met lately, I can do without. But there's one, a cute little doll, different. While I was in the hospital, I reached for her hand one day and she jerked it away as if I'd sunk my teeth into it."

"A nurse? I don't envy you, Elsnar.. Or do I?" Kevin stopped in the path and looked up at his tall companion, "You know, Bill, I haven't the slightest idea what I'm going to do with my life."

"Don't worry about it, Kev." Bill slapped him smartly on the shoulder. "You'll find yourself some day, just as I have."

They parted after sparring with a flurry of blows that never landed.

The bus stopped at the sand road leading to the beach. Bill slipped off and hurried away in the direction of the Tropical Gift Shop. He and Rita were aware that Bart's idea of running a business left something to be desired. Bill thought bookkeeping was for the birds. Take in the money, spend it, and enjoy it. Rita had different ideas. Her experience with the lumber business was an asset. She started the shop off with a set of meticulously kept books. Bart grumbled about the check rein on his financial activities, but he had

243

been heard boasting about his smart kids who were making him into a respectable business man.

As he approached the shop, Bill could see Rita decorating one of the plate-glass windows with an attractive array of gifts. The kid really had an artistic touch. People were standing outside admiring her work. Most of them ususally ended up inside to browse or buy.

"Where's Dad?" Bill asked, breathless from his sprint down the beach.

"Working in the back," Rita said. "He had an order for one of those magazine holders shaped like a fireplace woodbasket. Can you wait on those customers, hon? I'll be through here in three shakes."

The gifts were selling fast, even though Rita wasn't at all hesitant about asking prices that seemed exorbitant but that people paid cheerfully. After wrapping a sand painting for a customer, Bill turned to find a pair of enchanting blue eyes watching him. His heart jumped. It was the girl he had been telling Kevin about, Natalie Kent.

"I'm looking for something for my mother's birthday," she said.

He could feel his face getting hot and red. "Did you have anything special in mind?" he asked, attempting to appear self-assured and businesslike.

"No. Everything here is so beautiful." The blue eyes lifted to his. "Does your father make all these lovely things?"

He nodded, "Except for the sand paintings. My sister does those."

"What a talented family! You're Doctor Elsnar's son, aren't you?"

"Yes. Mom and I are the practical ones in the family. Dad and Rita are the artists. I guess it takes both

244

practical and artistic people to make the world go round." He stopped, embarrassed. He was acting like an ass, trying to impress this girl. "Does your mother have any hobbies, like knitting or gardeing? Perhaps I could suggest something."

"She likes to sew." Natalie seemed amused by his confusion.

"How about a sewing box?" he said. "We have several over here. Different styles and colors."

She opened one of the boxes. "They're all so lovely, I hardly know which to choose." She finally selected a blue one with a pattern of shells on top. "I know Mother will love this one."

Bill fumbled with the wrapping until Rita came to his rescue, took the money, and made change with her usual deftness and charm. She invited Natalie to come again.

"I will," Natalie promised, but she was looking at Bill.

"Well, Butterfingers, what happened to you?" Rita laughed, after his customer left. "Or shall I guess?"

"Yeah, oracle. Guess."

The door opened again and Natalie stood there. "I forgot to ask. What time does the next downtown bus come by?"

Rita looked at her watch. "Another half hour. Where do you live?"

"Osceola Avenue. My car is being repaired."

With a mischievous twinkle, Rita said, "Bill, why don't you take Daddy's car and drive her home?"

His smile thanked her. "May I?" he asked Natalie.

"That would be very kind," she murmured.

They were a little shy with each other at first. After a few observations about the weather and how pretty the azaleas were this year, Bill knew he would have to act quickly if he were to take advantage of this opportunity.

"Now that you know who I am and that I'm quite respectable, how about dinner some night?" he blurted out.

When she turned to look at him, his face flamed. Was she remembering that he and Bette Carey had been brought in to the hospital together after that auto accident? She might not consider him particularly respectable.

"That would be nice," she said after a moment.

Relieved, he asked, "Where would you like to go?"

"The casino?"

He shuddered. Not there! That was where he had taken Bette that gruesome night. Was Natalie remembering that, too? "I was thinking of that new place out near the country club. Chastain's?"

"Oh, yes. I've heard it's very nice."

With the day and the hour agreed upon, he let her out at the small white house where she lived with her parents. He was in heaven as he drove back to the gift shop to pick up his father and drive him home to dinner.

These days, everyone was relaxed and amiable around the Elsnar dinner table. There was so much to talk about: the hospital, the gift shop, college. Tonight, a new topic was introduced—Natalie Kent.

"She's a nice girl, dear," Anne said. "An excellent nurse, so good with the patients. Even the disagreeable ones. She has adopted Dr. Emmett's we. She never says I or you. How are *we* feeling this morning? It's quite amusing."

"Glad to see you're interested in a nice girl, son," Bart said. "Will you need some cash for your date?"

Bill lifted his head proudly, "Not this time, Dad. I've got what you pay me at the gift shop."

With immense satisfaction, he saw his parents exchange a pleased look.

The first date with Natalie led to others. A Saturday afternoon at the beach. Evenings at the movies. And finally, Sunday dinner at Natalie's home with her parents.

As spring vacation approached, Bill struggled with his feelings for Natalie and his interest in medicine. Sometimes, he wondered whether she should go into business with his father. Then he could marry his girl in a year or two. Dad would probably approve, but Mom would be disappointed. Not only that, but years from now, would he regret that decision and take it out on Natalie? In trying to resolve the situation, he knew it was no use trying to discuss it with his parents. Mom would opt for medicine. Dad would advise marrying the girl. He needed to get away by himself to think it through and come to a decision.

"I think I'll spend spring vacation at Gram's," he said one night at dinner. "That mob from the northern colleges will be swarming on the beaches like a flock of locusts. It used to be fun, but this year, I don't know."

"But why Grandma's?" Anne asked.

He shrugged. "Just a notion. I haven't been there in years."

"I know one thing," Bart put in, "Mama will be delighted to have you."

On a mild spring day, Olivia was waiting for her grandson's bus to arrive in Coquina. It seemed to Bill she must have corralled everyone in town to be on hand to greet him. They gathered around, old and young, to shake his hand, as though welcoming a celebrity. He was amused to see the people on the bus staring out the indows, probably wondering what this was all about.

"Over here, Billy," Olivia said, after greeting him with a bearhug. "Alex Huntly, this is my grandson. Alex brought his car to take us home. You couldn't walk all the way toting that heavy grip. Well, how are you, love? How're the folks? I'm so glad to see you I could bust. How long you stayin'? Here, Alex, put his grip up there in front with you."

"Gram, simmer down," Bill laughed. "You'll have a heart attack."

Her reaction startled him. "What possessed you to say that?" She had turned white under her tan.

He took her arm and helped her into the back seat of Huntley's car. "I didn't men anything by it, Gram. Just an expression."

"This is a great day for your grandmother, son," Huntley put in quickly. Switching his cud of tobacco to the other side of his mouth, he regarded Bill with a toothless smile.

On the way out to his grandmother's, Bill delighted in recognizing old landmarks. "That cabin is where the naturalist lived. We called him the Bird Man, remember, Gram? And up there in those woods you showed me an old abandoned still where they made moonshine during Prohibition. And over there is the road we used to take when we went fishing."

"I'm surprised you remember all that." She looked

248

pleased. "We're going to have a good time this week, Billy."

When they drove up to the old house, it looked just the same, the logs silvered by time and weather, sturdy under a canopy of ancient oaks.

Bill thanked Alex for the ride and asked him to give his regards to Mrs. Huntley.

"You recall Maudie? Well, I swan! Wait till I tell her."

"I remember her cookies," Bill said.

"Oh, pshaw!" Olivia sniffed. "Her cookies ain't no better'n mine."

"I know, Gram." He kissed her on the cheek and she grinned up at him, mollified.

As Olivia had promised, they did have a good time that week. They went fishing and shelling. The west-coast shells were different from those on the east coast; Bill had promised to bring back some for his father.

On his last night in Coquina, Bill had just jumped into bed and pulled up the patchwork quilt when there was a knock on the door.

"May I come in, Billy?"

"Sure, Gram. Please do."

She came into the dim room, lighted only by the pale moonlight. Bundled into a long robe, she sat down in the rocker beside the bed.

"I have a feelin' you didn't come over here just for a good time," she said. "Is there something on your mind I can help you with, love?"

"Well, yes, Gram. Maybe you can help me. I had to get away to do some thinking. You're right. I have a problem. You see," he propped himself up on one elbow. "More than anything else in the world I want to be a doctor. But you know how long it takes."

"For you, an eternity, I suppose. For me, a short span as time goes. Surely, you've got the time. What bothers you?"

He cleared his throat. "Well, I'm in love. Maybe you don't think that's very important."

"Of course, love is important. I was young once myself. I gave up a lot of chances when I married your grandfather, God rest his soul. Not big opportunities, like doctorin'. Just chances for a rich marriage."

"I'm afraid my girl won't wait, and I don't want to lose her. Mom and Dad will see me through medical school, but I could hardly expect them to finance a marriage, too. I wouldn't be able to work at a job and put in all the time I'd need for study at the same time. Natalie is a nurse. She said she could take care of our expenses, but somehow, I find that distasteful. Pride, I suppose."

"Well, love, let's take a look at this situation." The chair began to rock, a soothing sound in the quiet room. "A person's work is for as long as he or she lives. It's tough if he don't like what he's doin'. Would runnin' a gift shop quiet the gnawin' inside you in the years to come? After your father's gone, what would you do? After all the things he made were sold, you'd have to stock up with the usual junk most gift shops sell. How would that set with your customers? You saw what your Ma went through till she got back to the thing that was life and breath to her. She was a fussin', unhappy woman.

"Suppose you went to medical school and married your girl and let her support you. I'm not bein' delicate, you see. What if she found out she had to take time out to have a child, with all the expense that means these days. Then what would you do? Fall back

250

on your parents? Quit in the middle of your study, with the goal only a piece down the road? If love is the real thing, it can wait. The waitin' can bring strength to both of you. How strong is your Natalie? How strong are you, love?''

Olivia stood up and pulled the quilt up around Bill's shoulders, as she used to when he was a little boy. ''You have to make up your own mind, Billy. I can't make it up for you. Just remember to be true to yourself.''

''Thanks, Gram.'' He pulled her face down and kissed her. ''I love you, and I'm glad I have you.''

She went quietly out of the room, but he thought she was crying.

Back in Oceana, he had a heart-to-heart talk with Natalie and convinced her that their happiness and his success in life depended on his reaching his goal in medicine.

When he finished, Natalie said simply, ''Your grandmother must be a wonderful woman. And a wise one. I'm looking forward to meeting her.''

''Thank you, honey, for understanding,'' he said. ''You do agree with me, then?''

She reached up and kissed him, then settled back down in his arms. ''I'll wait for you, Bill,'' she said.

He looked over her head at the moon shining down through a palm tree. ''If you ever find the waiting tedious, I'll understand. You might meet someone else, you know.''

She shook a finger at him. ''Don't count on it, darling. But this is *tonight*, so let's just be happy.''

Only the night breeze heard his answer.

CHAPTER 25

Olivia Elsnar died on the twenty-fifth of May. It was a shock to the family. Though there had been little communication between her and Bart since the night of the storm, Anne felt she and the children should accompany her husband to Coquina Key for the funeral. Rita left the children in Cindy's care, but Edith promised to look in on them occasionally, and Mark said he would take them to the beach.

The funeral was the largest ever in Coquina. Everyone knew Livy Elsnar. They knew the sting of her tongue when she disagreed with the town board or disapproved of the conduct of a transgressor. Other remembered that, in sickness or trouble, Livy was the first to appear with food and comfort. Little children wept for the Bird Lady.

A young man at the cemetery singled Anne out to tell her Mrs. Elsnar had given him his first pair of boots.

"It was colder than usual that winter and I was

running around barefoot. I guess she felt sorry for me. I'll never forget those boots and that wonderful lady.''

All this was a revelation to Anne. Later, walking through the spotless rooms of the house Olivia and Gabriel Elsnar had built with their own hands, she marveled at how little Olivia had required of the luxuries most people considered necessities.

In the plain living room with its handmade rugs and chintz-covered sofa, there were four rockers. Olivia must have loved to rock. There were no deep arm chairs and no occasional tables filled with objects. On the mantle of the stone fireplace was a group of animal and bird sculptures Bart had whittled out of wood. Behind them were photographs of the family: Anne and Bart cutting the cake at their twentieth wedding anniversary. Rita in cap and gown and lovely in bridal attire. Bill in a grouping of his own from an infant in his pram to lanky high-school junior in tennis shorts.

The neat little kitchen looked like an old-fashioned print. There was even a black-and-white cat asleep on a cushioned chair. It looked like Thanksgiving with the table and counters filled with delicious-looking food the neighbors had brought in for Olivia Elsnar's mourners. It was an old country custom Anne remembered from her Vermont farm days.

In every room, in every corner, Anne could feel Olivia's presence, hear the echo of her hearty voice.

Bart had taken the children on a walk around the island to his former favorite haunts. Feeling lonely and sad, Anne went out on the wide front porch and sat down in a reed rocker with a high back and wide arms. How many times had Olivia sat here contentedly surveying her five acres? Flowers bloomed wherever they would get the morning sun. The silence was broken only occasionally by birdsong or the grunt of some unseen animal. This was what Olivia had loved—the peace, the quiet, the closeness to nature.

They had to leave the next day so that Anne could return to her duties at the hospital. She had joined Dr. Emmett's staff in late March and was assigned to the children's wing, where she had complete charge. She soon became a favorite. Although she was strict about discipline, the nurses liked her. Even the young male interns respected her. They didn't appear to mind working under her supervision. This surprised her. It was so different from her youth, when orders from female physicians had been resented.

Meanwhile, Bart was realizing his own dream. He had rented a small shop near the beach and moved all the gifts he had made through the years into the new building. The Elsnar gifts were distinctive and individual, no two exactly alike. All of them were of high quality. Most of his time was spent in the back of the shop, replenishing the fast-emptying shelves and showcases.

Anne looked on all this with amazement, almost unbelief. When she stopped to think about it, none of Olivia's advice had fallen on deaf ears. What troubled her was that the relationship between her and Bart had changed so little. He had been sleeping in the guest room since the night of the storm. There had been a few awkward moments at Coquina Key, with only two bedrooms in Olivia's house. She had suggested that Bill and his father take one bedroom, with she and Rita sharing the other. Bart had looked relieved. But this situation could not continue. They had to come to an understanding. she had seen Rita looking at them with questions in her eyes.

One evening, after dinner, she stood at a window admiring a sunset. It filled her heart with hope. Now was the time. The day. The hour.

She stopped Bart on his way out the door. "I think it's time we had a talk, Bart. Do you have a few minutes?"

"I guess so." He seemed reluctant. "I don't have to go down to the shop tonight. What's on your mind?"

She walked out on the breezeway and he followed her.

"This wicker furniture could stand a coat of paint," she said nervously.

"If that's all, we can settle that in three shakes. I'll do it tomorrow."

"Sit down, Bart," she said.

With a patient sigh, he rearranged a cushion on a chair and slumped down in it. She could see he wasn't going to help her.

"It's about the night of the storm," she began.

"You want me to get out. That it?"

"No, it's not. Will you please listen to me?"

He folded his arms and looked patient.

"You know how I am, Bart, how hard it is for me to express my real feelings. You will never know what I went through that day, hour after hour, not knowing what was happening to you, wondering if I would ever see you again." Her voice faltered. She was unable to go on.

"Oh, now, Annie."

"No, please, Bart, let me say it all now. I died a thousand deaths that day. When you came home and I knew you were all right, I fell apart inside. But I couldn't move toward you. I couldn't say what I felt. That night, when I tried to explain, you misunderstood.

That's when you told me you didn't care any more, that you had been resenting me all along, and you were ready to call it quits."

His expression softened. "I didn't realize I was that blunt. I'm sorry, Anne. I didn't mean to hurt you. But you did seem cold that night. We hadn't been getting along for a long time. There was the fiasco over that place down in Miami for one thing. I knew that was a mistake. What I'd been trying to do all along was to get into something permanent, something I could make a go of. I guess what hurt most was when you felt you had to go back to work to get Bill through medical school. It meant I wasn't up to snuff."

"We've been jousting like a couple of medieval duelists, haven't we, Bart? I want you to know I'm proud of your success with the gift shop. It's what you've always wanted. All I did was discourage you. It was your mother brought me to my senses. She said, 'Why don't you use your knowhow to cure the sick instead of sitting around cosseting your own aches and pains?'"

Bart laughed. "Sounds like Mama," he said. "She was blunt. Guess that's where I got it. But she meant well. And so do I. I realize there were times through the years when I strayed from the straight and narrow."

"Probably partly my fault," Anne said. "Things did get rather sticky at times. But that's water over the dam now. I was a regular harridan at times, I guess. But mainly, I think it was because I had to give up the profession I loved. It kept festering inside me until it burst, and I took it out on you and the children."

"I know what you mean. I felt frustrated, but I could go out in my shop and design a piece of furniture

256

and lose myself. First thing I knew, my low spirits flew off into space.''

Anne looked past Bart to where a pair of cardinals were twittering and skimming around an orange tree, hunting for a nesting place. ''I used to envy you that hobby and wished I had something like it to work off my frustrations.''

''Anne,'' he said, ''Do you realize this is the first time in all the years that we've sat down and really talked things over, tried to understand each other?''

''Why, yes, I guess it is. Come to think of it, perhaps that was the secret of Rita's and Ron's happy marriage.''

''Wouldn't wonder,'' he agreed. ''Ron once said they always thrashed things out together. I guess the kids could teach us something.''

''You and I are more mature now. Don't you think we can go on from here and maybe find a little happiness along the way?''

His eyes looked bright and eager. ''Does that mean I'm invited to move back into the room we shared for the past twenty-odd years?''

''Tonight,'' she agreed.

They stood up and moved into each other's arms. There was no doubt now in the mind of either that Anne was able to express the love that was in her heart.

CHAPTER 26

It was June again. On the beach the tourists and winter residents had long since departed, and Oceana Beach belonged to its own once more. The summer heat was tempered by cool breezes from the sea, and the natives were able to take life easy now that the season had ended and business had slackened.

On a Sunday afternoon, the beach blossomed with colorful umbrellas, and there was the clean smell of salt in the air. Wavelets laughed softly as they lapped the shore as the deep, mellow voice of the sea thundered a rhythm to which white gulls swooped and danced. Out beyond the breakers, people bobbed in the surf. Others walked barefoot in the sand or lay under the umbrellas.

Anne Elsnar relaxed in a beach chair under a yellow umbrella, intent on the sprightly scene. Unless she received an emergency call from the hospital, she was free for the day. Far down the beach she could see

Bart and Bill walking barefoot in the wet sand, searching for unusual sheels and bits of driftwood for Bart's gift shop. Anne smiled to herself. Bart's absorbing hobby had become his life work, but he still treated it as a hobby, which was probably why he was making a success of it.

"Hi, Dr. Elsnar," a young voice caroled.

Anne looked up at a pretty girl and a tall boy walking by.

"Hello, Lynn. How are you feeling these days?"

"Just fine," the girl called back. "This is my friend, Paul, Doctor."

"Hello, Paul. Take good care of Lynn," Anne warned. "She shouldn't engage in any active sports for a month or two."

"Yes, Ma'm," Paul agreed. "Our folks are having a picnic, but we won't let Lynn go swimming."

"Slave driver!" Lynn teased.

Anne was fond of Lynn. She had brought the girl through a bout with peritonitis, following an acute appendectomy. Not an earth-shaking event, perhaps, but to Anne Elsnar who, a few short months ago had been a frustrated, unhappy housewife, Lynn's "Just fine" was an accolade. Anne was glad she was a mature Dr. Elsnar, whom everyone respected and trusted, rather than the tough, young, sweeps-everything-before-her Dr. Tallman.

Since she had taken up her duties at the hospital, life had been different for all of them. At last, Bart was working at something he liked, enjoying life in his carefree way, and they were able communicate in a pleasant manner again. Anne had stopped worrying about Bart. She had stopped worrying about Bill, too.

Like his father in many respects, he would have to experiment and experience life in his own way, whether she was near to guide him or not. She wondered what had happened during his spring visit with Olivia. He had said very little about it. Just once, he had remarked, "Grandma is a very special person. I'm so glad I spent that week with her. It meant a lot to both of us."

Now that he had a goal, life was a grand sweet song for Bill. He would come out all right. He had an aptitude for medicine and a sense of dedication. It was not surprising that he had decided to become a plastic surgeon. Bette's misfortune had cut him deeply, and Anne understood.

In the fenced-off area close to shore, where bathers frolicked in the rolling surf with shrieks of laughter, Rita and the children were playing a little game of their own. Rita was wearing the azure swimsuit Ron had given her a few summers ago.

Anne chuckled, remembering Ron's presentation speech: "All the Miss Americas wear full swimsuits, my love. They know that illusion is more alluring than the bare facts of a bikini."

Dear, funny Ron! Memories of his wit and sunny disposition kept cropping up to bring the smile with the tear.

Down near the old abandoned lighthouse, Anne could see Mark Roberts with the Stover girl and her party. Anne knew Mark was in love with her daughter. It would be nice if they . . .

Suddenly, Rita's scream lifted high and clear above all the other noises. "Mark! Mark! Help me!"

Anne jumped up and hurried down the beach. Little

Babs seemed to be in trouble, gasping and thrashing about in the water as Rita swam toward her. Mark Roberts streaked past Anne. In seconds he was in the water, outdistancing Rita. He seized Babs and swam back to the beach, where he placed the child face down.

With fervent prayers tumbling across her lips, Anne knelt beside the child until Babs moved and cried out.

Mark picked her up and carried her to the Wybron cabana. "She's all right, Rita," he said. "Don't make anything of it. She mustn't be frightened by this accident. I'll go watch Bobby to give him a couple of pointers on the crawl. I think the boy was upset about his little sister."

"Mark, I'm so grateful," Rita said.

"Glad I was nearby." He sprinted off toward the sea, and Anne came to sit on the blanket beside Rita, who was holding Babs close. She was still shaking.

To distract her, Anne said, "Mark Roberts is a nice young man, isn't he, honey?"

Rita smiled dreamily. "Yes. He has been kind. Since I've been spending so much time at the lumber office, I've learned to trust him."

Anne was about to say that was a good sign, but she wisely refrained. "Now that Babs is all right, I'll leave you," she said. "Bart and Bill will be heading back to our cabana soon."

Rita watched Mark striding toward her through the sand. Bobby was on his shoulders.

"Not a good idea for a little chap to overdo. That surf is strong today," he said, swining the boy down beside his mother.

She handed him a towel. "How about some orange

juice?'' she asked.

Mark smiled his thanks. "The champagne of the tropics," he said, lifting his cup in a toast.

When Rita looked at him again, Mark was sitting with the towel around his shoulders, squinting at the sea, his hair tumbled into dark curls.

"The ocean is fascinating, isn't it?" he said. "I never tire of watching the waves roll in with that mighty roar. It makes you feel strong and clean and, well, that everything is possible." Leaning across Babs, who was snuggling gainst him, he asked gently, "All right now?"

She looked up at him in surprise and wonder, remembering that night long ago in the dark Carey breezeway when, for just a moment, she had laid her head against the shoulder of a strange man who asked softly, "All right now?"

So it was you, Mark Roberts! she thought. *The same tone, the same inflection, the same words. And you never embarrassed me by alluding to it.*

"Yes, Mark," she said and felt a strange fluttering of silken wings against her heart. "I'm all right now."

"I wish I didn't have to leave you, Rita. Do you realize you called me when you needed help a little while ago?"

"Yes," she said.

"I don't know whether it meant anything, but could you and I have a talk sometime soon?"

It surprised them both when she said unhesitatingly, "Tonight? After the children are in bed?"

"You can count on me," he said. "I'll be there with bells ringing, horns tooting, and Mardi Gras in my heart."

"Oh, Mark!" she laughed. "How could we talk with all that going on.?"

"You have a point," he admitted.

"Don't you think you should go back to your friends?"

He stood up and wafted her a kiss. Her eyes followed him as he walked slowly down the beach to the Stover girl and her party.

"I like him, too, Mom," Bobby said.

Rita looked at her son wonderingly, thinking, *Am I that transparent*?

Halfway down the beach, someone else had become aware of the little group beside the Wybron cabana. Margaret King, leaning against a cushion on a built-up hummock of sand, sat up suddenly and dropped her book.

"Who is that man with Rita?" she said. "They look very cozy."

Tony, prone beside her and intent on the Sunday paper, moved his head. "It's Roberts, the fellow who's running the lumber business for her."

"The children certainly seem to take to him," Margaret said.

Tony reached for her hand. "We'll have kids of our own one of these days."

Margaret smiled tremulously. In spite of the hope in her heart, she wondered if she could ever be entirely sure of Tony. Perhaps, if Rita got married again . . .

At the other end of the beach, where it was quiet except for the sound of the surf, another couple loafed under a blue umbrella. The remnants of a driftwood fire smoldered nearby. The man lay stretched out, half asleep. The woman sat beside him, looking off across the ocean. The sun was dropping toward the horizon. Far out on the sea, a sailboat bobbed like a toy on the waves. As it slipped across the path of the sun, its sails turned scarlet.

Softly, the woman sang the words of a once-popular song, "Red sails in the sunset . . ."

The man opened his eyes and looked at her. "Hi, Beautiful," he said fondly.

It had always been his favorite name for her. Pain flicked across her heart when she heard it, but she gave no sign.

"Have a happy day?" he asked.

"Yes, Dwight. It was lovely."

Bette was watching Rita, too. A lump of sadness thickened in her throat. Beauty is something you never think about much until you lose it, she thought, and then it can become an obsession if you let it. She was trying very hard not to let it, especially now that the plastic surgeon was doing such a good job. Some day, she might even be a good carbon copy of her former self, Dr. Elsnar had told her reassuringly. On the other hand, when she looked in the mirror, Bette still didn't recognize herself. Not her old self. She was a different person, inside and out. Perhaps that was all to the good.

It had been a pleasant, relaxing day, a happy day, Anne thought, while she waited for Bart and Bill to join her. It might be regarded as a culmination of an eventful year, a year of joy, sadness, and change. She hoped she had learned to enjoy the blessings of each day.

The great red ball of the sun sank lower until it dropped out of sight over the rim of the ocean. People all along the beach began to gather up their paraphernalia, their voices muted by the sound of the surf. Night, with its coolness and silences, was closing down. Another day had dropped from the chain of the years.

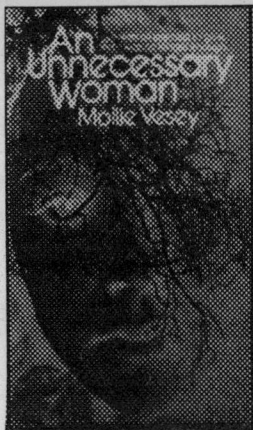

AN UNNECESSARY WOMAN
WOMAN
Mollie Vesey

PRICE: $2.25   BT51503
CATEGORY: Novel

AN UNNECESSARY WOMAN is a journey through
the heart's wilderness. Alice's children were grow-
ing up; her husband's business was prospering.
She had too much time on her hands. Then she
decided to plunge herself into a summer of con-
frontations—the unexplored territory of her own
emotions, her long-suppressed sexuality, her need
for love and, finally, the years of hidden anger
against everyone she loved, an anger that threatened to destroy them all.

THE SEEING
By William P. McGivern
(Author of "Soldiers of '44,"
and "Night of the Juggler"
and Maureen McGivern

PRICE: $2.50 T51493
CATEGORY: Novel (Original)

THE SEEING is a contemporary occult thriller about a child with profound psychic powers—whose gift of prophecy becomes a force for evil!

"McGivern retains his stature as one of the very best writers of suspense novels in the English language."

—The Philadelphia Bulletin

THE PASSAGE
Victor Wartofsky

PRICE: $1.95   T51506
CATEGORY: Occult

After the wife and daughter of science reporter Wayne Farley are killed in an airplane crash, his investigation on life after death takes on personal significance. He decides to submit himself to the ultimate experience—to be killed and then brought back to life. If there is a life after death, he will be in a position to prove it.

"...Wartofsky displays literary skills of characterization and description unmatched by present day novelists."   —UNITED PRESS INTERNATIONAL

A STAR RISING
Jess Carr

PRICE: $3.50   T51575
CATEGORY: Historical Novel

With the crucifixion of Christ, a new era had begun. But it was a time of terror and persecution for the early Christians. Antipas, a wealthy Roman, falls in love with a beautiful young prostitute who tells him of the new faith. More and more Antipas questions the bloodshed and debauchery of Imperial Rome. He gives up his wealth and power to the woman he loves and a belief that could cost him his life. **A Star Rising** is the story of a man caught between Rome's will and Christianity's struggle to survive. A biblical epic of violence, passion, and faith in the tradition of **I, Claudius.**

ASTROLOGY FOR THE WORKING GIRL
By Paige McKenzie

PRICE: $1.95 BT51467
CATEGORY: Non-fiction

In this practical guide, Paige McKenzie combines her extensive business experience, her knowledge of astrology and her good humor to help the career woman understand relationships between recognized Sun Signs and a host of personal and career problems. And she offers specific ways for dealing with conflicts, and such specific problems as: When is the best time to make a job switch?

DESTINY'S DAUGHTER
By Frances Noble

PRICE: $2.25 BT 51462
CATEGORY: Historical Romance (original)

Esmee d'Espey is the illegitimate daughter of
Queen Catherine de Medici. Beautiful, spirited,
and unaware of the royal blood that flows in her
veins, Esmee comes to the court of Queen Catherine to seek her fortune. Both Princess Charlotte
and Esmee fall in love with the rugged Henri de
Conde, leader of the Huguenot forces. Amid the
opulence and intrigue of the French court, Esmee
is plunged into a life of luxury, excitement, disappointment and heartache as she struggles to win
the love of the one man who will never be hers
alone!

SEND TO:

TOWER PUBLICATIONS
P.O. BOX 270
NORWALK, CONN. 06852

PLEASE SEND ME THE FOLLOWING TITLES:

Quantity	Book Number	Price

**IN THE EVENT THAT WE ARE OUT OF STOCK
ON ANY OF YOUR SELECTIONS, PLEASE LIST
ALTERNATE TITLES BELOW:**

Postage/Handling

I enclose...

FOR U.S. ORDERS, add 50c for the first book and 10c for each additional book to cover cost of postage and handling. Buy five or more copies and we will pay for shipping. Sorry, no C.O.D.'s.

FOR ORDERS SENT OUTSIDE THE U.S.A., add $1.00 for the first book and 25c for each additional book. PAY BY foreign draft or money order drawn on a U.S. bank, payable in U.S. ($) dollars.

☐ **PLEASE SEND ME A FREE CATALOG.**

NAME_____
(Please print)

ADDRESS_____

CITY_____**STATE**_____**ZIP**_____
Allow Four Weeks for Delivery